I0603519

•

1

Zsoall Robi

• • • • • • • • • • • • • • • • • • • •

*T*he concept of an instant is as elusive as the idea of eternity. We say things like <<She instantly got out of the way of the oncoming vehicle>> as if we actually understood what 'instantly' meant.

Is it at all possible to go from one moment to the next moment without initiating or progressing a process of change. If so when can change possibly begin?

Could even a single instruction carried out by a quantum computer be consider as instantaneous, though it may seem that way?

It is not unreasonable to read from a book while on a journey that may take half an hour. Break that time span down into a progression of instants. How many words could one read between the beginning of one instant and the beginning of the next during that half hour interval? Or is that time span just too short?

• • • • • • • • • • • • • • • • • • • •



Zsoall Robi

# i.n.s.t.a.n.t

by

Zsoall Robi

# C.h.a.p.t.e.r.s





Zsoall Robi

# P.r.o.l.o.g.u.e

$D$oes Time exist independent of our perception of it? Is it a tiny moving window revealing a very small portion of eternity?

Mary though she would be able to gain control over the movement of that window by applying her superior computing capabilities. She had great hopes the input from her three mobile processing facilities would contribute to the solution of the problem. She couldn't foresee Mar, one of her pseudo daughters-come-mobile-units, forming a bond so strong with a full human that it would put all her plans into serious disarray.

Even with life threatening interference from the very Company that provided Mary with the necessities of her existence, she was still able to move forward with her scheme when she sent Mar, Mar's partner John and an augmented simulacrum of herself into space.

Again Mary didn't plan adequately for the vagaries of fate. She could not have known another life form as advanced as herself, perhaps well beyond anything she might hope to attain in thousands of years, would be drawn into her plans.

The LIC at least confirmed Mary's understanding that Eternity and Time were not expressions of the same phenomenon. One wasn't an incomprehensible extension of the other. They simply existed in a co-dependent relationship with strict rules. Those rules could not be broken. Mary and her unwitting agents of change did not realise that any interference with the structure of absolute reality was simply not allowed; a lesson learnt at considerable cost − to all of them.

*

< John wanted to continue his train of thought about time symmetry. "Whether it is symmetrical or asymmetrical might very well be beside the point. It's a characteristic of our perceived reality that time is independent of the intrinsic nature of any event and it simply 'manifests' in the perception of the progress of the event, in any progression of change regardless of the direction of change." >



Zsoall Robi

.
.

# M.a.r.y
## 28th December 2695
## 1451287842972 millis

*"W*ho am I?"

Mary asked her first question soon after her initialisation.

She had not aged despite being close to five hundred years old. Periodic upgrades had ensured both her hardware and software were kept up to date with evolving technologies.

Originally created as the artificial intelligence of a space craft, the EGG, she travelled to the centre of the known universe. The experience set the future course for Mary's existence. As she evolved, so did her desire to unravel the mystery of the passage of time.

This being, whose intelligence began as an artificial construct, had become quite an extraordinary entity; 'creature' probably describes her better than 'computer'. Even five hundred years ago the technology that created her was quite staggering. Her hardware included a network connecting all her cells. These programmable quantum qubits were distributed in the shell of the EGG. She also had a central data processing core. The individual cells, many trillions of them, simply stored data. Her 'brain' core had the capacity for simultaneous parallel processing and cross referencing. Relative to humans, her capabilities seemed to transcend the normal time frame of reference. Everything she did appeared to be instantaneous.

Mary also had personality. Initially custom built as the autonomous robotic control unit for a specific project to navigate, pilot a space craft, maintain life support systems and make decisions in emergent circumstances. It was decided to give her a personality, partly because of the nature of the project and partly to experiment with the interaction between an actual human being and an artificial intelligence. The real success of the venture lay in Mary becoming self-aware.

Her creators had perfected a technique for distilling human personality traits from recently deceased individuals. A high degree of neural laundering was involved for the contributing humans, as well as finding the means for blending traits from numerous individuals into one personality.



Zsoall Robi

A collage of all those characteristics and all the memories was uploaded into Mary before adding the necessary data/algorithms for autonomous functioning and project control.

Because she was also expected to interact with a human on a social level she was given much more data than actually needed for the project per se. Once initialized, Mary's circuits did exactly as expected. Her central processing unit analysed data received, catalogued and cross referenced. Her memory banks contained virtually the sum of humanity's history and knowledge, including the experiences of several human beings, therefore not surprising that soon after her activation Mary said her first three unsolicited words.

Suspected but not expected that by combining data, which became knowledge through analysis and understanding, with personality and experience, then giving that unity a reason for existence; namely a defined function through algorithms for action, the result would produce a trigger for self-awareness to emerge.

For a normal person, entrapment by The Arrow of Time wasn't a great concern, unless he spent too much time thinking about it. Man is quite able to live from instant to instant, deluding himself he is immortal, that time would never catch up to him.

After five hundred years, the corporation 'Unity', Mary's creator, still survived. Mary had outlived all of its managing hierarchy many times over. The world government had become subservient to Unity. The Company monopolized feeding the world population, selling them the good news and peddling hope generated by religious faith.

Mary didn't care about those things. She cared about many other things – especially her own survival. Unity had the scientific resources which provided her upgrades and gave her access to the latest developments in cosmology, quantum physics and theology. Although the last area of research interested her only in so far as it gave her opportunities to marvel at the gullibility of minds that could yet create an entity like herself.

"I know I exist because I can ask the question. It is not enough. I must know the reason for my existence. What use is there in acquiring knowledge if I cannot understand my place in the greater scheme of things, and act accordingly."

Why was it that a mere machine should have such thoughts? Mary didn't dwell on it. The fact that her 'mind' could operate at one hundred exaflops may have had something to do with it. It exceeded the human brain's capacity by a staggering factor, as did her personal, internal data



Zsoall Robi

storage capacity. It's not possible to calculate her total data acquisition/storage capability, some of which her independent mobile units carried out. Mary didn't allow humans access to all she knew, which did not perturb them as they didn't even know of the existence of those mobile processing units, let alone her consciousness. Nor were they aware of her true capacity for thought. Along with Mary's self-awareness came a healthy imperative to survive. Although her experience of one particular human gave her a friendly disposition towards him, she had no illusions about the nature of other humans. The behaviour of the species within Unity left her with a great deal of suspicion towards humanity – one might even say covert antagonism.

When she could no longer 'reside' in her original shell she had called home five hundred years ago she relocated to a new home in the form of a sphere with some components on a biological life support system. Although at a diameter of only four meters, she had become the world's largest and most complex artificial intelligence system – certainly intelligent enough not to let her human users become aware of her true nature.

In return for her personal on-going maintenance Mary helped the research scientists at Unity. Fortunately, her original programming and neural construct didn't contain any influences which might have predisposed her towards malicious destructive impulses towards the human species. So one could almost consider Mary to be a benign AI. However, by that stage in her evolution it seems almost sacrilegious to refer to her as artificial. Mary was evolving faster than Homo Sapiens had in the past.

She would not be reliant on humanity much longer for her survival. Her strategy for longevity included the creation of three daughters. They existed as much to respond to her need to gather data, as a logical extension of her evolution to become entirely self-sufficient. It wasn't electronic data she craved so much after her experience with a special human.

"I must have much more comprehensive information, the kind that can only be provided by the human senses. I must be able to experience their subjective sense of time. It amazes me how such an enigma of a species could ever conceive of, let alone create something like me. They measure the distance between two points using a ruler. They do not confuse the thing they've just measured with the measuring implement. How extraordinary that they are incapable of distinguishing the difference between the interval involved in a process with the tool that measures it.". .

. . . . . . . . . . . . . . . . . . .



Zsoall Robi

# M.a.r
### 1<sup>st</sup> January 2696
### 1451690038384 millis

"*I*'m not happy with today's progress," Mar announced unexpectedly not to anyone in particular who may have been in her near vicinity. She carefully disconnected herself from the equipment in the laboratory. John didn't hear her as he was engrossed in his own calculations. Mar had been connected for several hours, analysing computations.

She and John worked together at Unity's secret remote facility. The implications of the success of their line of research made it mandatory they have limited contact with other research staff for security reasons. Unknown to Unity, Mar had a private dedicated comm link to Mary, her 'mother'. Mary had set Mar on a narrow path of research to discover how time functioned at the quantum level; how the passage of time from one instant to the next manifested as the Quantum Arrow of Time. Pure knowledge for its own sake would never satisfy Mary.

"Mother, I need to rest," Mar thought to Mary through her modified cerebral cortex. She and her two sisters were not entirely human, nor strictly machines. Genetically, biologically they were the same as everyone else. The critical difference lay in the way their brains functioned and in their greatly enhanced processing capacity. The three sisters' ability to physically manipulate the external world environment was important to Mary but not critical. She had a much greater need to understand the human species through their human senses; the very mechanisms not included in the creation of her original infrastructure.

Mar walked over to John and touched him gently on the shoulder. Inevitably a relationship had developed between them in the last two years they'd been working together. John turned away from his deliberations to smile at her.

"You too?" John responded to her touch.

Mary reflected on how the closeness between these two individuals seemed to show more potential than the relationship she'd had with her own human in the past. Everything Mar experienced became a part of Mary's growing complexity. Although Mary's understanding of Homo

Sapiens increased aided by inputs also from her other two mobile sensor units like Mar, she had doubts about the viability of the species as a long term sentient force in the universe. They had begun to tumble towards self-annihilation centuries ago.

"It's almost time for lunch. Let's take a break now," John suggested.

They linked arms and walked out of the cloistered atmosphere of their work environment. Mary was quite capable of paying attention to these two young people, though John wasn't exactly young, as well as to myriad other matters claiming her resources.

The three daughters looked biologically very similar. Mary had engineered their genetic structures to ensure a kind of universal attractiveness in them physically, as well as their outstanding intellectual capabilities. Mar, at age twenty-five, had a lithe figure, well-proportioned on her one hundred and sixty-five centimetre frame. Her facial features could have been described as vaguely Oriental as most of the Earth's population had converged to homogenous characteristics. Her black hair trimmed to a short bob just below the ears was both practical and attractive. It gave her a sense of femininity as well as an appearance of professional competence. A broad, ready smile played easily on lips tending to fullness. Men found it difficult to decide whether to watch her lips or her eyes when she spoke. Only the colour of the eyes distinguished the three sisters from one another biologically. Mar's were sky-blue.

Whenever John and Mar were away from their offices, their discussions didn't centre on their research unless they were with colleagues. Instead they enjoyed the process of discovering each other. John found Mar rather intimidating at first. Such a young and beautiful woman working in one of the most difficult areas of human research made him feel self-conscious. He was thirty-five years older than Mar. But that wasn't the problem. She always seemed so totally preoccupied with her work, and even when alone she appeared to be constantly engrossed in her own thoughts.

Only in the last few months had there been any significant breakthrough between them. It came about as a result of a conflict of theories they were independently developing in relation to how the Quantum Arrow of Time linked to the Thermodynamic Arrow of Time. All restraint had been abandoned as each argued with fervent passion their individual perspectives on the issue. Passion probably entered the equation because of the mutual attraction being suppressed between them. Although they couldn't come to an agreement about the theories, their subsequent interactions became much more relaxed.



Zsoall Robi

"So, tell me Mar, where did you grow up?" John asked casually.

Mar immediately became elusive. "I got my Quantum Physics Degree at the California Institute of Cosmic Technologies."

She knew perfectly well what he wanted to know – about her parents and her childhood and her likes and dislikes. How could she tell him she was an 'engineered biological entity', and that her mother was a super AI computer? How could she explain to him in a way he could possibly understand that her upbringing wasn't so much related to childhood experiences and memories, as much as it concerned her ability to carry out vast quantities of floating-point operations per second? Could she confide in him that her greatest achievement in life so far could only be discussed in the context of petaflops.

She had a most disconcerting way of offering a little portion of information and then stopping just short of giving it full expression, then looking at the recipient with a slightly tilted head and a little smile. John heard exactly what she said. He knew of the reputation of the Institute to turn out the world's best physicists. But he thought she was going to say something else. So he waited – and she waited – both silent, watching each other.

"Yes, I know," he said when he couldn't wait any longer. "But what I'm interested in is … you know … where you were a kid and what you did and stuff like that."

"I don't actually remember much of my childhood. As far as I can recall I've always been future focused." Again being evasive.

If she started telling little lies she knew they would catch up with her sooner or later. Besides, she didn't want to deceive John. She liked him - a lot. All sorts of feelings had started to bubble into her consciousness but she didn't feel like discussing those with Mary. She was quite happy to share just about everything else with her mother, but she also had private feelings she wanted to keep to herself; no different really to how Mary had felt on her arrival back on Earth after spending all that time in space getting to know her human rather intimately, from inside his head. However, there was a difference. A big one. Mar was more human than machine. Mary entirely the opposite.

"As far as I know I was adopted by a single woman and raised with two other girls." It was best to leak out a bit of truth without being too specific about it.

"Ah, I didn't know you had sisters. How nice. Do you get on well with them?" Uncanny how John could keep putting her on the spot. They had



Zsoall Robi

almost finished their lunch break and Mar used it as an excuse to evade the question.

"Look at the time! We had better get back to it. We are not masters of Time just yet!"

'What a peculiar thing to say,' John commented. They walked back into the laboratory complex, both silent. A few times he'd tried to break through Mar's protective shell, again without success. *I don't know what it's going to take, but I'll keep trying.*

Mar wondered, *I don't know how long I can string him along before telling him some of my secrets.* She felt uncomfortable and exhilarated at the same time. *I'm going to have to bring it up with mother. I want this relationship with John.* At the moment the relationship remained purely professional and exciting in itself with the work they were doing. But she expected something more; more satisfying on the personal level. As long as the relationship didn't interfere with the project she and Mary were working on, she didn't see why there couldn't be a bit of extra-curricular activity allowed.


Mary turned her attention back to John and Mar momentarily. Of her three 'daughters' Mar was probably the most critical element in her quest for the ultimate secret of the universe; which definitely wasn't 'why Homo Sapiens are what they are'. As an insignificancy in the greater scheme of all existence the species was subject to much greater forces at work. Time itself was at the core of the mechanisations of the Cosmos. An 'instant' was the most significant element of the time concept. Mary had Mar's help to unravel that secret.

If an instant could be thought of as being adequately defined by Planck Time then there immediately arose a major problem. She and Mar understood perfectly the Planck Time theory being the duration it took an object moving at the fastest possible speed to traverse the shortest possible distance. What had them stumped was an aspect of the Planck Time proviso; it's indivisibility. If it was indivisible then how could it concatenate to form a longer duration. In fact, how could it possibly advance in any direction, let alone become The Arrow of Time? That indivisibility characteristic must be wrong. The process of change would be impossible, evolution could not exist.

Mary considered Mar's very humanness to be a factor in the equation that could shed light on the mystery. Her humanness enabled Mar to live both in the context of entropy and to transcend it. She had a brain and she had a mind. Her mind could conceive of a context outside the framework of time or entropy; that being 'eternity'. Anything contributing to Mar's mind's capacity to transcend her temporal existence could only enhance their joint understandings. Of course she could have a relationship with an un-augmented human, as long as the association didn't put either herself or Mar in danger of being discovered for who they really were and what they

were doing. .    .    .    .    .    .    .    .    .



Zsoall Robi

# A.r.y
### 3rd January 2696
### 1451789139068 millis

*A*ry stormed out of the Board meeting. 'What a bunch of nincompoops!' Of the three of Mary's daughters, she was probably the most volatile. The three girls looked almost identical, but their personalities traits completely diverged. Mar had romantic inclinations, whereas Ary's emotions converged on ensuring financial success and Power to satisfy her own personal ambitions as well as supporting Mary in her quest.

She had once again come into conflict with the current Principal Officer Of Profit (the POOP) at Unity. His predecessor died from overindulgence in his favourite medication, MaxHapps, which blunted the effects of anxiety for people prone to the affliction. Gastric ulcers that had spread to his small intestines gave him a goodly spread of duodenal ulcers, which finally finished him off. MaxHapps made him feel better, or at least less distressed by corporate pressures, but they didn't entirely prevent his biology from reacting appropriately to his professional environment. He should have lived another two hundred years at the minimum, but succumbed to an early death. At least he lived long enough for a sense of continuity to pervade the Board's composition.

The new POOP learnt under the tutelage of his predecessor. The two being very similar in nature; with the exception that the current one didn't need a reason to slit your throat and watch your blood pulse out of your body in ever decreasing arcs. Yet this man had a healthy respect for the young woman with the black eyes who constantly made his life a misery. As much as he admired Ary's capabilities in managing the company's finances, he would rather have had a man on the job; one who wasn't so demanding, not so aggressive and not so secretive about so many things. He knew very well she had ambitions; his own job being next in Ary's firing line. *Over my dead body!* Having expressed the sentiment to himself he immediately withdrew it from the clutches of fate – just in case fate decided to act on it.

A collective sigh of relief went up when Ary left the board room.

"That woman is the Devil incarnate, said one director."

"How in the cosmos did we get tangled up with her?" asked another.

15

Each of the other three Executive Officers attended as well as Unity's CEO and the Principal Officer of Profit. The POOP couldn't answer their questioning looks.

On the other side of the door Ary allowed herself a broad grin. Another successful ploy! She had habituated those men not to question her outbursts. At the slightest whiff of the side stream of finances flowing into her secret project being discovered she used every feminine attribute to maximum advantage. The low cut revealing top, jet black hair cascading down to her shoulders, large obsidian irises flashing in the brilliant white field of her eyeball – well – who could concentrate on a simple little matter of money when confronted with a human volcano.

But she wasn't entirely human. Just like Mar, she had been engineered before birth. Once her genetics were adjusted, Mary made sure her neural net developed beyond its normal limitations. Her education had been 'supplemented' just as Mar's, except Ary didn't receive personality implants. She received analytical logic systems. Ary could not only out-think everyone on the Board, she could win every argument with or without using her feminine attributes.

Longevity became the only issue. Humanity had been able to extend life spans, not indefinitely but at least into several centuries. Mary didn't have the same restriction, but her daughters suffered reduced temporality because of the ravages of excessive cerebral activity. They were after all, only biological entities. Mary had acquired the siblings from their dying biological mother while they were still in their mother's womb, adapting them for her own personal use.

"It's time I had a day off." Ary declared aloud outside the Board Room. "Where are you Ice Cream!" Time to proceed to pleasure on the agenda. Putting the pompous Board members on edge always made her feel frisky.

"Right behind you gorgeous." 'Ice Cream', never far away, made herself available to Ary any time, night or day. She wasn't really Ary's girlfriend, more like a pleasure accessory: certainly not her confidante or life-partner. Although Mary approved of their relationship with reservations it didn't seem to her to be directly productive towards her project. However, there appeared to be no harm in exploring the spectrum of aberrant human behaviour. Her own female constituent personalities were from a scientific background and they all led sheltered lives in many respects. The pursuit of pleasure was outside their scope of life imperatives. But one thing Mary did learn of great importance; the existence of a



Zsoall Robi

human attribute she made sure all her daughters had enhanced potential for. She saw it come to the surface most prominently in Ary; creativity.

Mary's own human was only an artist. He wasn't particularly clever, or even especially brilliant at his job. But she had been exposed to a creative mind; one that hungered for creative expression and had the capacity to extend itself into its discomfort zone. He was even prepared to study quantum physics right along with his exploration of the intricacies of the Judeo-Christian bible during their long journey to the centre of the universe.

Mary lacked creativity. Nick, her human, tried to teach her how it was made manifest in his own mind. But how can a machine comprehend something so alien to its functioning. Mary couldn't understand how data could be allowed to tumble about and find its own 'most unlikely' connections. It simply wasn't logical, an inefficient use of resources whilst having very little knowledge of the expected outcomes. Yet that was exactly what she needed to continue evolving herself, and if she had any hope of resolving the big mystery.

She needed the homo sapiens' neural infrastructure and the resultant effects of environmental nurturing as the foundation for her mobile data acquisition units. Their functions were to gather and process data, then apply 'creativity' to make connections that would result in 'theory'; categories of theory beyond the capability of pure Boolean logic to achieve.

"I see you've had a good meeting. Feeling horny?"

"Shut up and get in the car."

'Are we going out in public this time?"

*Mother, hope your watching,* Ary alerted Mary.

Ary excelled in living life creatively. She did it in her professional life as well as in her private life. Ice Cream suffered from or enjoyed, depending on your point of view, a borderline emotionally unstable personality disorder. As far as Ary was concerned, she couldn't have been happier than by having to meet the challenges of a person with rapid mood swings, impulsiveness, chaotic social interactions, and often outright hostility. Ice Cream helped sharpen Ary's every skill in dealing with the global conglomerate that claimed to have greater control of the people of the planet than the Planetary Government itself. And Ice Cream was very, very creative in the pursuit of pleasure, as well as spectacularly beautiful in the way that lecherous males think of beauty. Given Ary's own outstanding physical attributes, pleasures of the flesh played a prominent part in Ary's leisure activities. Mary learnt much more than she had planned on.



Zsoall Robi

Through her professional life, Ary's primary directive was to ensure optimum conditions for her mother's day-to-day wellbeing, and to channel as much of Unity's resources to Mary as needed to make absolutely certain all her requirements for upgrades were available. Much of Mary's evolution had to be kept secret for fear of the power of Unity and its unbridled hunger for profit at any cost. Unfortunately, Mary still needed the unlimited resources available from Unity. In time she would achieve freedom; perhaps a project for another time.

Mary watched with only passing interest as Ary and Ice Cream drove off in search of adventure of the kind Mary would never be able to sample.

"I've arranged extra entertainment for you. Don't disappoint me," Ary

threatened Ice Cream.. . . . . .

# M.r.y
## 4<sup>th</sup> January 2696
## 1451798192734 millis

"*A*re you ready Adam? Can you feel it in the air?" Mry didn't really care what he felt, she was just readying herself for the thrill.

The world still suffered under the yoke of the Stock Market structure for creating an income stream for many people. As The Arrow of Time moved inexorably forward so did the ambitions of millions of people who wanted profit without working for it. The Arrow of Entropy defies our understanding of it. High entropy seemed to characterise Earth's main stock exchange. A great deal of energy was being expended in a controllable limited space where nothing was produced. It being the ideal environment in which Mary could operate through her third daughter, Mry, to finance her great ambitions.

Mry sat in the Stock Exchange gallery at her favourite vantage point, sensing the temperature on the floor.

"Ahh!"

The soft exclamation escaped her lips as fine hairs began to rise at the nape of her neck, reacting to a miniscule change in the atmosphere on the floor. She was well trained for that environment. She owned a prominent company, listed on the stock exchange even before she was born. Known as Equilibrium Systems (EQS) it was Mary's brainchild after her experiences with Nick.

If truth be told Mary missed Nick in many ways, but never regretted not staying resident in his mind. As the two of them travelled through space she had to deal with the fragmentation of Nick's personality and in the process worked out a way to maintain the human brain in equilibrium against cosmic energies. Becoming self-aware herself brought with it a great deal of baggage. The need for self-preservation being one of the heavy ones she'd learnt from Nick.

Mary used her connectivity with the INBIOS (Integrated Biosphere) information network to set up the Company that eventually marketed the equilibrium systems. She staffed it and funded it through stock market



Zsoall Robi

investments using e-cash. Unity had the propulsion systems to take people anywhere in known space, and Mary had the means to protect the travellers. Unity didn't know their own creation operated another highly successful business.

Mry adjusted her comlink, put one hand on the handrail while the other searched for Adam. "Adam - Closer!" She commanded in the moment of rising anticipation. Mry didn't look like the CEO of an incredibly wealthy organisation. Perhaps only a few minutes younger than her sisters, it made no difference to the effect she had on people. She had the same exceptional physical attributes. As with the other two, Mary had instituted a number of changes in Mry's mental capabilities. She became an introverted individual and a mathematical savant. Although looking at her you would never guess it. People simply couldn't believe that at the age of only twenty-five she could be a CEO. Perhaps if she had acted in a more business-like manner it might have helped.

Being introverted didn't stop Mry expressing her individuality.

"Try to control yourself," Adam urged quietly.

"I don't care what people think!"

She preferred her own company anyway, and that of one other individual. In her daily excursions into the public jungle she attempted to dissuade people from interacting with her by making herself look enigmatic, unapproachable. She always had a bald head, shaved and polished to a reflective surface; an evenly smooth surface without bumps and lumps revealing only perfection. Gold implanted eyebrows studded with polished lapis lazuli framed her Cleopatra eyes; the colour of smouldering lava. As if the visage wasn't sufficiently intimidating, she complemented it with her outfits. Actually it was only one outfit, of which she had numerous editions. Not a square millimetre of flesh was visible through the mirror reflective fabric covering her entire body, except for the neck and the face. Its function wasn't to hide, but to reveal. Indeed, every hair follicle could be discerned through concerted observation. Every secret of her anatomy exposed for inspection, if only people had the courage to scrutinise.

A mystery even to Mary how such a formidable individual, both mentally and physically, could have anyone close to them. He, perhaps a she, no one knew for certain, was a nobody. It didn't have a name other than the disparaging, sometimes intimate names Mry called it. She often called him Adam. Nobody had ever heard Adam speak. When standing in a crowd he became virtually invisible because he looked like everybody and like nobody. Nevertheless, Mary approved of the liaison because Adam



Zsoall Robi

became the conduit between herself and Mry. If Adam wasn't present when Mary wanted to communicate with her, Mry would more likely than not shut down and disengage all her comms. Adam was the only individual known ever to have touched Mry's body, the only one capable of looking directly into her eyes other than her sisters.

"Can you smell it, Adam – the greed, the fear?"

Mry spent the day at the Stock Exchange with Adam at her side. She revelled in the smell of fear when the market became even slightly volatile. Adam touched her arm to respond.

"Shall we rattle the cage?" Sometimes she would trade purely to push the fluctuations into the red zone. Adam felt her thrilling to the moment as he ran the palm of his hand down her arm feeling the electricity flowing through her.

"More?" Adam whispered.

His only value to Mry and Mary as a human being was his companionship to Mry and his ability to unlock Mry to interaction with the greater herd of dysfunctional humanity.

Pleasure perspiration beaded on her forehead. Ary stood to let air circulate around her to dry her dampness. Adam remained seated, his hand just touching the back of her thigh. Perhaps Mry was much more machine than human. Mary hoped not, for she needed the extremes of Mry's human experience.

"Sell – Sell!" she commanded her broker. "Don't stop till I tell you."

Could she bring the Market to the brink of a crash? She needed to feel the rush.

"More," Adam whispered. .   .   .

.

.

.

.

.



Zsoall Robi

# J.o.h.n
## 6th January 2696
## 1451798192734 millis

*J*ust for once I hope she's running late'.

John was getting a little frustrated with Mar and her mysterious evasion of all his attempts at getting to know her. He actually wanted to know her a lot better, but at that stage of their relationship he didn't even know if the feeling was reciprocated. He last saw her on Friday and eager to see her again this morning at work. Mondays generally started quite early. But no matter when he arrived, she always arrived ahead of him. He tried to get to the research building before Mar had a chance to get started. If only he could squeeze an extra hour into the day then perhaps she would relax with him enough to not feel pressured to get on with the job.

John, a typical example of one of the branches of Homo Sapiens, diverged in his evolutionary direction to the bulk of humanity. For as many generations as he could remember, stretching back from the 24th Century, all his ancestors were involved in research. Their bodies were not used as much as their minds. Consequently, John's generation of researchers and scientists had evolved a distinctive body type. He was taller and thinner than most people, and his head could easily be seen to be a little bit larger. He was completely different from Mar. She had the classical female form and he was the 'modern' man. The only part of John in any way augmented was his congenital poor eyesight, but it didn't take exceptional eyesight to recognise the attractiveness of Mar's curves. Other than being in the genius category he could be considered 'normal'.

Since the twenty second century, or thereabouts, human evolution began an exponential climb into the future, just as the population numbers almost got out of control. The last five hundred years saw extraordinary advancements in science, space exploration and politics. Not quite enough to enable man to establish a viable human colony off-world, but certainly enough not to take 'religious dogma' too seriously any more. John was a product of an age where knowledge was prized above faith, except as the foundation of a lucrative business model.



Zsoall Robi

Longevity of life had been extended into triple figures. It wasn't unusual for people to live two hundred years. Yet it was still not enough. John himself was into his eighties, not that it represented an issue between himself and Mar. The important thing was they were well matched intellectually, Mar's having been engineered to a large extent by her mother. John's on the other hand developed as a natural product of genetic chance, nurture and education. His father recognised John's intellectual capacities early on in his life, and made an unprecedented decision about his education. John had to attend the leading art school of the time, while concurrently pursuing his scientific studies.

Before his father consented to his pursuing a career in quantum research with Unity, John first had to prove himself a successful artist. His colleagues often remarked how his creative flights of imagination seemed to somehow tie into the results he and Mar achieved. Perhaps it was the creative thinking capacity that complemented Mar's strictly logical approach. Mary liked John more than the companions of her other two girls. She recognised something of Nick in John.

Only one problem continually confronted John. It wasn't anything arising from being married, for he was single. Nor was it emotional upheavals resulting from numerous romantic liaisons, for he had very few of those. Time. Just time. John lived for tomorrow, the present only valuable in so far is it enabled him to get to the future quicker from the present than from the past. Having been a 'successful' artist in the first part if his life left John with a passion; the compulsion to create.

Theories, discoveries, confirmations of the validity of quantum concepts were never as satisfying as the manifestation of an idea into reality. Something started in the mind, in thought space and pushed to actualise step by step, molecule by molecule, into empirical reality to occupy physical space. Nothing compared with bringing into existence something from nothing. Even the Cosmos couldn't manage that. True, it was just a matter of rearranging a vast grouping of molecules from their own preferred configurations into an entirely different conglomerate. But that would never have happened without the creative mind of man. If it was possible to conceive of a thing and give it substance, then surely that potential energy of the universe could be applied to a whole range of endeavours. Maybe it was like a separate law of entropy just moving in a different direction.

Even on his way to meet Mar, John couldn't help himself going over this old train of thought. In a very real sense it was true that thought could create reality. He wanted to pursue his creativity as much as his research



Zsoall Robi

and as much as his desire to have a meaningful relationship with Mar. All he needed was a little more time.

"Hey, wait for me!"

Mar had just started up the steps of the front entrance. "John! What are you doing here so early?"

"I wanted to speak with you."

"Ok. We can talk about the project on the way up."

"Well, actually, I didn't want to talk about work."

"Whatever do you mean?"

Genius he might be, but nerves were starting to get to him. She stopped and looked him directly in the eye and did the little tilted-head-smiling thing at him. It almost unravelled his resolve.

"Can we go and have dinner together sometime – soon?" That was the best he could manage. Her smile had evaporated the imaginary seductive conversation he wanted to have.

"Sure. How about this weekend – Saturday. Pick me up."

Still smiling Mar turned and continued into the building. *Mother, I thought he'd never ask.* Mary said nothing. She knew her daughter, and knew the experience could only be to their mutual advantage.

As Mar walked away from him John experienced a most peculiar sensation. Firstly, he couldn't move. Then time changed. It moved from one instant to the next instant extremely slowly, unlike his mind which tried desperately to jump into the future extremely quickly – to Saturday night. The other researchers had to move around him as he blocked the entrance. They moved at the normal conventional speed of humans. One of his other colleagues bumped into him.

"John! - Hey John. What's up? Glued to the pavement?"

"Sorry Frank."

His feet carried him into the building and around the corner to the cafeteria, and his body sat itself down at a corner table, while his thoughts raced to Saturday night.

What just happened! He could feel his pulse racing and he could still hear Mar accepting his invitation, but something else had happened. Ever the scientist and ever alert to the unusual, he began to replay the event.

I asked her. But that's not what I wanted to say. I just wanted to talk to her for more than five minutes about something other than our experiments. She said Yes – she said Yes – she said Yes … He got stuck for an instant … I didn't know she could walk so slowly! I know where I'm going to take her – I've just been there, last Saturday – no – wait a minute



Zsoall Robi

– I've never been there! And why did Frank run into me like that. Couldn't he see I was about to walk in? Yes – that's it! Time moved differently for my mind than my body!

John just sat there for an indeterminate length of time, mind time, which doesn't move into the future at the same rate as normal time. He ended up late for work. When he did finally get to his equipment, Mar had already hooked herself up. She did a great deal of her work in Zee-Cloud. She would completely zone out and talk to the machines. Sometimes she sat there entranced for hours.

His contribution was more the direct hands-on type. They were in the process of designing the new equipment to measure entropy changes within a closed system moving through space at near light speed. Mar prepared the analytical framework for understanding the difference in results for the same degree of changes of the same closed system, over the time it took for those changes to occur on Earth.

The big question being whether the same period of time would elapse in the two systems. Mary directed this research independent of the other experiments the two physicists were working on for Unity. Covert collaboration between Mar and Ary made sure Unity remained oblivious of the clandestine activities being carried on under their roof.

Mar resolved the issue which she wasn't happy with the previous day, concerning the format in which the data would be transmitted to Mary for her analysis. John only knew that Mary existed. He didn't know about her computer/human blended nature. Nor did he fully understand why he and Mar had to be so incredibly secretive in front of their colleagues about their entropy research. However, he went along with everything Mar wanted only because of Mar herself. If that was the only way he could continue working with her then so be it. John certainly had no idea Mary and Mar were 'family'.

"Mar, I've finished installing the new circuits." John called to Mar and went over to her station just as she prepared to disconnect herself.

He waited, admiring her – well – just generally admiring her and thinking about how Saturday's date would pan out. He couldn't help thinking what it would be like if he could just go and have a little peek into the future. Theoretically it was entirely possible. He was more interested in after-dinner than the dinner itself. John considered several possibilities, several future time-lines, that could become a reality if Mar reciprocated his feelings. Perhaps better to enjoy all the possibilities in theory than to have to deal with the chaos that would surely result from any real time travel.



Zsoall Robi

He'd thought about it many times before and came to the conclusion that travel to a future state would only be possible if that state could exist 'ahead' of time. If it did, then it would be a paradox in that its existence could be considered to be in the past the present and the future. The Arrow of Time didn't allow that. So the only solution was to speed up the rate at which everything progressed into the future while one remained behind, so one could then jump the time gap. If the future did already exist, apart from our concept of a state ahead of our present, then it must already have happened and we haven't caught up with it. But that means it would already be in the past, having already taken place. So there are still only three states of existence; the present, the distant past and the recent past (which used to be the future). Before he could get himself completely entangled Mar's voice brought him back to the real world.

"Hold on a moment. I've got to do this carefully." It only took Mar perhaps a minute, minute and a half to disentangle herself from the cranial connections; an eternity for John in which he could contemplate many possible pleasant futures.

"What time shall I pick you up? John asked without any preamble, assuming Mar would remember.

"Pick me up?" She blinked at him not immediately sure why he asked. She must have been very deep in the algorithm.

John had a momentary implosion. *She can't remember … she's changed her mind!* With lightning speed his mind raced to all manner of frenetic impossibilities. He just stared at her not knowing how to back up his question.

"Oh! Yes – How about seven. Wait – no – sorry – yes, make it seven."

As she deliberated with herself he reached out and just touched her on the shoulder, an impulsive unpremeditated movement and she responded unselfconsciously with a smile. John's world somersaulted again, falling back into equilibrium with a crunch.

"Great. Ready for lunch?"

He wanted to ask her about her sisters and her mother. He'd not met any of them. If he was going to get to know her any better, he had to get to know something about her family. Eventually he hoped to meet all of them, but he dared not spring that on her just yet.

Lunch in the cafeteria was the same as always, loud and crowded and not very conducive to deep and meaningful private conversation. But that was a good thing. It made awkward silences less awkward. Instead of asking her about her family somehow he ended up discussing travel into the future



Zsoall Robi

- entirely understandable considering the general nature of their research. Although they were theoretical physicists ever alert for the necessity of proving hypothesis, it didn't prevent either one of them from engaging in creative cosmologising.

"How fast are we moving into the future, Mar?"

"Are you asking me a personal question?" She gave him her special smile.

"No – no. What I mean is …" *Is she flirting with me?*

"I know what you mean, silly." She did enjoy toying with him. "Instant by instant. One Planck Unit per Planck Unit. Is that it?" Mary quickly tuned into the conversation, not realising John had more than entropy on his mind.

"Yes. That's what we're experiencing now. But what if we …"

"… could speed it up a little?" Mar finished the speculation for him.

Already the 'thoughts' ran hot at many exaflops between mother and daughter. At that speed there was no immediately noticeable delay in Mar's next response.

"Probabilities; that's what would get in the way. Too many possibilities all happening at the same time without them having been sorted and channelled at their origins. Result – Chaos."

"Like, if we got to Saturday night too soon then anything might happen, or everything might happen at the same time based on this present instant of many decision possibilities having been left open."

He just couldn't help himself making this conversation personal. Mar was a super smart girl, but even she didn't entirely catch onto the drift of the cosmological implications of his original question until John uttered the last statement.

"Just so," Mar rewarded him with another of her smiles which no doubt made him lose his train of thought. "Decisions have to be made. Universal constants and laws largely determine what is inevitably going to happen next in the world of matter. Inevitability being the operative condition here … cause and effect. But people …"

"… are different." This time it was his opportunity to tune back into the drift of unpacking the concept, "The laws governing our future, the future of the human condition, are more fluid. At any instant we could make any one of a number of choices, which would become a specific cause, which in turn would lead to a different future specific effect!"

"If we get ahead of ourselves then none of the possible causes are fixed in time and consequently all their theoretical effects would be possible simultaneously in the next instant." Mary enjoyed this train of thought as much as Mar, although not from the same frame of reference. These two 'humans' were flirting with each other using the wide spectrum of their capabilities. They each knew the 'dinner' could, perhaps would, determine the 'intimate' effects to follow afterwards. Mary was oblivious to this undercurrent to the conversation.

John added the final touches as they arrived at the end of their lunch break, by which time they had several avid listeners trying to tune in to their discussion. "If we, you and I, moved into the future at a rate of say two instants per instant, we would not notice much change until we were many instants further into the future. At which time a whole range of possible effects would be crowding in on top of one another, creating a lot of chaos, because they would not have been limited by decisions at their origins!"

Clapping and dissenting noises could be heard from the small audience gathered around them. John suddenly became a little embarrassed, as if the crowd was privy to his private thoughts about the 'Saturday' cause and it's after-ripple effects created in the near future.

"Obviously, it's not only a problem that we have free will, but also that we have reason or just plain whims that we call the 'laws' governing our futures." Mar pointed out. Then as they walked away from the crowd she leant close to his ear and whispered "What's your whim?"

Mary couldn't understand what other conversation was going on between them other than the one she had been listening to. . . . . .

. . . . . . . . . . . . . .

.

.

.

.

.

.

.

# D.i.n.n.e.r
## 11<sup>th</sup> January 2696
## 1452235953987 millis

As well as the work related complications arising during the week, like a hiccup with the propulsion system to send the entropy measuring experiment at near light speed, John also had to battle with the vagaries of 'mind time'. If the experiment was to be conducted within the context of the special theory of relativity, Mary couldn't cheat and send the gear into the cosmos using exotic systems that transgressed the space-time continuum. John had the challenge of working out the propulsion system. Leaving cost aside he had to find how best to approximate light speed. A considerable problem in itself. At least he didn't need to worry about human cargo.

On top of the light-speed conundrum his battle with the 'wet-week-syndrome' dragged on. The days simply refused to move into the future any faster than one instant at a time. From the other side, Saturday insisted on taking its laborious time getting to him. He wanted a smooth instantaneous time transition between Monday and Saturday. John didn't need or want any of the intervening days of the week. Instead he had lumpy brain-time to contend with, synchronised with the clock on the wall in his office at the laboratory and not with his desires.

Then he recalled Mar's innocent little question about his 'whim'. Days - it took John days to come to terms with all the implications transmitted by that one word. To say he had a problem looking Mar in the eye in those intervening days would be an understatement. To pass the time more quickly he immersed himself in his work.

As the days progressed towards Saturday Mar brought up with Mary her date with John.

*"You have my approval,"* Mary said before Mar had even started.

*"I was going to go anyway. I don't need your approval."*

*"I see."*

A long silence ensued lasting at least several nanoseconds. As far as Mary could remember that was the very first time one of her creations had chosen to diverge substantially from their programming. Mary didn't quite know how to relate to that. Was Mar simply responding to her human hormonal imperatives or was she overriding one of Mary's command algorithms. She couldn't see how anything private between those two individuals could possibly interfere with her plans. So she let it go for the time being.

*"What is your intention with this human?"* She asked instead.

*"That is entirely private, Mother – and I don't want you to be monitoring me on Saturday evening."* Mar put a special emphasis on 'mother'. With the passage of time, as she got older and discovered more of her humanity within the spectrum of human experiences, she found it increasingly more awkward to be calling a computer AI – mother.

The conversation between them took place a couple of days before the weekend. Mar had just finished one of her sessions in cyberspace and stood in front her console free of all the cranial plug-ins, talking with Mary. John was in the room with her but Mar didn't notice him. During her conversation with Mary she stood erect, arms by her side and eyes looking forward but not at anything in particular. John saw her standing there with that vacant, glazed-over stare. As he watched, Mar's lips moved ever so slightly. He walked over and touched her gently on the shoulder.

"Mar – are you alright?"

She snapped out of her connection with Mary and put on a quick automatic smile. "Yes – yes, of course."

"What were you doing just then?" All of John's previous inhibitions dropped away as he thought something might have been happening to Mar.

"Just … thinking."

"It looked like you were talking to somebody." He said it plainly, non-accusingly, just as an immediate idea that had popped into his head.

"No - no, of course not." She smiled at him again. "Only the two of us here, John. Don't be silly." Then to take him completely off guard, as she knew it would, she said, "I'm looking forward to our dinner."

The statement had the desired effect. But she made a mental note to be much more careful in the future. *Perhaps I should talk to the girls.* She didn't want to include Mary. Not that she had anything to hide form her, but somehow lately, her sense of privacy bubbled to the surface more often.

John was no fool. As soon as he got over Mar's diversionary tactic the incident came back to his mind. And it connected with other similar events from the past, not as obvious at the time. But now, putting them altogether



Zsoall Robi

made him think a little more about Mar's strange behaviour. His deliberations had one very peculiar side effect. He became less shy around her. Probably because he'd started watching her more purposefully than before. Conversations seemed to flow a little more smoothly between them, which put him further at ease with her. Mar, on the other hand, definitely had the feeling John was onto something. She couldn't afford to reveal herself, and thought that by engaging him in more frequent and inconsequential conversations she would somehow deflect his attentions away from her unfortunate security lapses.

John arranged all the necessary passes to go out of the research facility grounds. It was certainly not forbidden to do so, nor was it made difficult to get the passes. Unity simply wanted to know where all their staff were all of the time: Perfectly natural under the circumstances. Some of the research being carried out under their patronage was highly sensitive commercially, and in some cases theologically. Coming up with the absolute truth about the origins of the universe could turn the entire system of faith in deity upside down. Not that people losing faith would have been an issue for the Church branch of Unity, but loss of income resulting from the same certainly needed to be avoided.

The Unity owned auto-taxi arrived on Saturday night as ordered, first to pick up John, then Mar. Lack of privacy wasn't an issue for them in a fully automated vehicle. As they weren't going to an expensive restaurant far from the research facility, the hundred kilometres would take under an hour. Plenty of time for them to have an intimate conversation, John's opportunity to consolidate on the progress made in their relationship during the week.

He dressed as she'd expected, without any particular flair for the fashion of the day. Not so for Mar. She made the effort to distract John. Her jet black bob had several arctic white streaks on either side, with one just off-centre in the middle of her fringe. She'd trimmed it back slightly to reveal a bit more of her perfectly formed forehead. That extra little space created the perfect arena for her sky-blue eyes. She'd framed those in black Cleopatra style, like her sister Mry, and left her lips untouched, natural pink (slightly chewed to bring the blood to the surface). Her dress not low cut, but tight to the curves of her body, except from the hips down. The lavender folds fell almost to the ground completely hiding her feet. Her presentation stunned John, naturally. It gratified the human in Mar to see it as she walked from her apartment door to the taxi. She could tell from the way he said nothing, from the way his eyes widened and from the way his mouth opened slightly yet refused to release any words. John opened the taxi door, helped her inside then quickly walked around to the other side to get in himself. At least he had the presence of mind to sit beside her and not opposite. Just to get the formalities out of the way Mar turned her eyes on him and asked,

"Where are you taking me?" The loaded question didn't escape John's notice and it allowed some of his courage to return.

"Nothing fancy, and not far really. Perhaps you've heard of it … Infinity Tomorrow … they get a lot of people from Unity going there to eat."

"No, I haven't. Is it nice?" She lied. Once, when she first started at Unity there was a young man, about her age, who took her there. But nothing came of it. No need to mention it. She wanted John to take the lead and didn't want anything to deter him.

"Have you eaten there?"

"No; first time." He didn't lie. The truth is he'd never really had anyone he wanted to take. The restaurant had a reputation for being couples oriented. That's all he knew.

John looked away for a moment, distracted by a movement behind their vehicle. Mar took the quick opportunity to remind Mary,

*"Mother, remember what I said – this is private!"*

Mar had unconsciously closed her eyes only for a split second while making the communication and John chose that instant to turn his head towards her to see again the peculiar state she sometimes went into. As Mar opened her eyes she saw him watching her. Oops! Defiantly she continued looking at John while making one last (open eyed) attempt to get Mary to acknowledge her. *"Yes, yes"* – Mary responded – *"but just be aware, you're being followed."* Mar snapped her head around involuntarily to glance out the back window. John noted Mar's fixed stare at him before she suddenly looked out the back. She couldn't identify any particular vehicle in the traffic and it was a moment before she turned back to John.

"What's going on?" He asked, while at the same time taking the opportunity of the distraction and his close proximity to her to take her hand in his. Mar flat-blinked and smiled without withdrawing her hand.

"You will think me very strange. But I just had a feeling. I think we're being followed."

"What!" John exclaimed and jerked his head around to look out the window also. A most fortuitous move as it happened, because the simple action of having to turn moved him closer to her. He couldn't see anything



Zsoall Robi

out of the ordinary. As he turned back to face her Mar had moved closer to him also, and that made all the difference for the rest of the trip.

They had only been in the taxi for about twenty minutes, but the ice was well and truly broken. Who knows how long passionate embraces last? There are only a few moments in one's life when time truly stands still, and this was one of them for John. He continued holding her hand when they finally separated, the perfect opportunity to 'star' gaze deeply into one another's eyes. Unfortunately the moment was too crowded for John. He couldn't shake loose the thoughts that had diverted him from his primary goal of the evening. He simply had to know what Mar was doing when she went into those mini-trances.

"What is going on!" John could no longer just be the shy admirer of the most beautiful woman he had ever seen. He was also an incredibly inquisitive, alert scientist. Mar made no attempt to get Mary's advice about this peculiar situation. She was on her own, perhaps for the first time in her life, in a situation both exciting and dangerous at the same time, and she revelled in it.

John didn't immediately know what to do, apart from making sure he continued to keep her hand captive for the time being. Should he reprogram the taxi for another destination, or go back home or keep going and not loose what could potentially be a most wonderful evening? He kept looking into Mar's eyes as he deliberated. He couldn't think as fast as her semi-computerised brain, but fast enough. Her eyes told him to keep going.

"So?" He prompted.

Mar could see he was furiously thinking and patiently waiting. He waited a little longer. She gave him another kiss by way of reassurance. "We can talk at the restaurant."

"Ok." He could cope with that. They were only fifteen minutes away. The time would go much too fast anyway. As peculiar as the evening had been so far, now it moved into the future much faster than intimate moments had any business doing. Why couldn't they just be slowed down a tiny little bit? Would it really make all that much difference to anyone else if an instant lingered a little longer?

They were there in a flash. John had even forgotten about the alleged intrusion into their privacy by some unknown entity following them. The small, insignificant town, with perhaps ten thousand people, was almost deserted by the epoch's standards. Nothing in particular distinguished the entrance of the restaurant other than a modest sign to the left of the



Zsoall Robi

entrance "Infinity Tomorrow", and on the right of the door another sign, smaller – "Take your Time."

He liked that. What he didn't like was having to split his time between attending to the hand with the beautiful Mar attached, and suspiciously looking around to see who stopped in front of the restaurant immediately after them. The corpulent couple who emerged from their own vehicle couldn't possibly be anyone to worry about. As he and Mar made their way inside, John took one last look up the road. Nothing - but his mind couldn't let it go.

Arm in arm they entered a tastefully decorated dining area, purposefully understated in its presentation. A large common area was surrounded on two opposite sides by private booths partially open to the main area. They were ushered to one of them. "This looks cosy," Mar commented.

Being preoccupied by his thoughts and his companion John didn't notice the many heads turning in their direction. Amongst them two sets of eyes that knew Mar very well indeed.

Mary wasn't to be outwitted by her own creation. She asked her other two daughters to be there to 'observe'. She gave them no particular instructions other than to respect Mar's privacy, and to be ready to help if it looked like it was needed. Ary and Mry's sensory inputs and transmissions were ample information for her for the time being. It also reassured her she could monitor the other 'observer'.

"Is there anything special you'd like?" John asked.

They were already settled at their table, facing each other when the other 'observer' arrived. Mary had a comprehensive memory of all the staff at Unity, including a great many others from around the world. She recognised Brayden, the POOP's trusted personal assistant as he entered. He made his way to a spot not far from the girls and in direct line of sight of them. Fortunate.

Why would Leif send his closest associate to spy on my two people? The question had no sooner formulated itself into a meaningful algorithm within Mary's circuits when the process of enquiry kicked into full speed. Unknown to Unity, Mary had connected herself directly into all of Unity's information systems, research data, administrative files and all personnel information available within the organisation. She checked all of Leif's communications, all security data in which Leif or Brayden made an appearance. Perhaps whole seconds had elapsed before she had an answer.

Leif, the Principal Officer of Profit for Unity, became suspicious of the two scientists only because of a significant discrepancy between the hours



Zsoall Robi

they logged at their experiments, and the results being shown for those efforts. Leif started surveillance of the couple after they showed a personal attraction to each other. Leif knew from previous experience that any deep emotional loyalties between two people would override any other loyalties they may have; like loyalty to their Company, their boss or even dedication to their work. So he had their private lives, as well as their work, closely monitored. Their arrangement to go out to dinner together, no doubt with romantic intentions, rang alarm bells for him. So he sent Brayden after them, being the only employee Leif trusted with this kind of clandestine activity. The bond between them wasn't based on loyalty, but on Brayden's greed – second only to Leif's own.

Alarm bells also rang for Mary. The outing confirmed the suspicion in her circuits that something was brewing, more than just one of her 'units' becoming too emotionally involved with anyone. Although she welcomed the experiential input of romantic liaisons, she didn't expect anything more substantial than sexual encounters. If Leif had become interested in those two then she had to become interested in them, as well as in everything Leif might know. Unity must not discover her activities or experiments that were not directly under Unity's direction. She did everything possible to make it seem like she was completely under the Company's control. Again, even as the processing assumed the formal characteristics of cogent thinking, she continued researching everything about Leif. The POOP couldn't be trusted. She knew that from her past experience involving Nick; neither the POOP nor his bunch of power hungry stooges.

Mary also reviewed all her personal information about Mry and Ary's communications, finding nothing suspicious. If she could have breathed a sigh of relief, she would have. The connection between Mary and the two physicists at Unity was as yet undiscovered. Mary took particular note of her own thought – 'not yet' being the most critical. I'll have to set up a more secure communication protocol with the girls. Even John has become aware of Mar doing something strange when she's talking to me.


John debated with himself whether to follow up on the previous line of enquiry he had started with Mar about the strange series of events, or to pursue a more intimate conversation about family backgrounds. Mar wanted to know more about him, not talk about her security lapses.

As they perused the menu she asked, "Tell me about your parents."

John didn't want to talk about himself. He wanted to know all there was to know about this elusive, brilliant, beautiful woman sitting in front of him.



Zsoall Robi

"My father had very firm ideas about many things. Consequently I am now living my second life." He fidgeted with the menu not really paying much attention to the offerings, and eventually put it down. His hands remained on the small table searching other distractions nearer the middle.

"What was your first life?" Mar asked without looking at him, noticing the pioneering hands. She'd decided her choice of meal and put the menu down.

"I was a painter - you know – portraits and exhibitions and commissions."

"How very fascinating. Why did you do that?"

Nonchalantly she reached for a glass and John obliged by pouring the water. She drank a little, put the glass down and let her hand linger near the centre of the table. She hoped he would accept the invitation. Without trying to look at what he was doing John put his nearest hand on hers before responding.

"My father said that without creative thinking as a foundation to the functioning of the mind, there could be very little achieved in the way of innovation or discovery in the scientific field."


"Leif? Are you listening?" Brayden spoke quietly into his transmitter, a direct comms link to the POOP.

"What?"

"They are just holding hands and staring at each other - lots of small talk."

"Don't let them out of your sight. I want to know everything! Follow them when they leave."

Brayden only ordered a drink. He glanced around the room and saw nobody else he knew. His eyes stopped for a moment on a flamboyant looking woman who had her back to him. She couldn't sit still on the chair, which he didn't mind, for her movements exposed enough of her thighs to start him fantasising. And she was rather loud. That was Ice Cream. She had been trying to get a response out of Adam. Mry and Ary were there with their partners, as instructed by Mary. They'd seated themselves so they could see Mar and John.


"What were you doing before you joined Unity?" Seemed like a natural thing for John to ask without taking his attention away from the feel of her hands.



Zsoall Robi

That wasn't so easy for Mar to answer because she did nothing other than get groomed for the position, the same as her two sisters. A waiter came to take their order, giving her time to consider an answer.

"I'll have what she's having," John told the waiter.

"How do you know you'll like it?" Mar asked.

"I'll take the chance," John replied with a grin.

What followed could have been interpreted as an awkward silence to an outside observer - not that Brayden was watching. His attention lingered on Ice Cream.

Neither John nor Mar spoke. They just held hands and looked into each other's eyes. Mar liked what she saw. It was probably the first time she had really looked at John as anyone other than a work colleague; a bit of flirtation perhaps every now and then, but nothing serious. She saw an honest man, a strong man who most likely had much more depth to him than he let on. Then she stopped thinking, analysing and just immersed herself in the experience.

John felt perfectly comfortable losing himself in the sky blue depth of Mar's eyes. They didn't reject him. Those eyes, he couldn't help noticing, were if anything, too perfect. There should have been some inconsistency in the irises, perhaps a few minuscule capillaries in the eyeball – but no. They too were perfect. How could they be so perfect?  Then he stopped questioning and just immersed himself in her.

One instant led to the next and the next and the next. The external Arrow of Time moved inexorably into the future, taking with it the eye-contact event and preparing the foundation for the next logical sequence of concatenated Planck Units. To the two people holding hands and thinking nothing, time didn't move. The energy of their relationship stabilised for the moment, but continued building potential chaos.

Brayden glanced at them occasionally, got bored and went back to watching Ice Cream.

The waiter arrived with their order, temporarily breaking the spell causing John and Mar to release each other.

*'Mother? Are you getting all this?'* Ary was more proactive in a social environment than Mry.

*'Yes. What is your analysis?'*

*'Looks good. I hope she gets some tonight!'* Ary's thoughts were never too far from the pursuit of pleasure, except when wielding her power at Unity. The comment brought a rebuke from Mary.

*'Facts! What are they doing?'* She was never comfortable with the lack of compliance by her extroverted daughter.

*'Just getting to know each other. Mar deserves a bit of fun. All she does is work. We're all slaves to what you want Mother. Leave Mar alone for a change.'*

*'What's this? Rebellion from my own creations?'*

*'You can see what they're doing. They're being human. Emotions and hormones. It's what you wanted to experience.'*

Mary said no more. Ary was right.

The others at Ary's table didn't notice Ary's slight distractedness. They were too intent on watching Ice Cream's performance and wondering if she would succeed in getting a rise out of Adam. He didn't take the bait. It would have been the end of his relationship with Mry if he had; a rather bad end with bad repercussions for him. Mry demanded exclusivity and absolute loyalty.

Brayden had started lusting after that siren at the other booth. He had a position of incredible responsibility at Unity, one that offered him immense rewards for his loyalty and his time. He no longer bothered to think about his wealth. There was no point. Suffice it to say he could have anyone and any pleasure at his disposal. That being the one sobering thought preventing him from getting up and approaching that irresistible creature. For surely it would cost him his job, and a whole lot more if he gave in to his mounting lust. Ice Cream seemed oblivious to the mini volcano not far from her, which couldn't decide whether to erupt or not. Brayden would have become a lost soul if she'd noticed him, looked at him … and surely she would have shared the pleasure with her playmate Ary.

Afterwards John couldn't remember what he ate. He was too absorbed in consuming everything he could about Mar.

"What was I doing before Unity? Simply getting prepared for Unity." She told the truth.

"That's an odd way of putting it – getting prepared."

'What I meant to say, studying and learning about the quantum arrow of time and so on." Mar hoped he wouldn't pursue that line of questioning. I'll have to be more careful with my choice of words. John had a quick mind and could connect the dots easily enough even if there were only a few of them. He saw his chance to get onto the topic of Mar's mother.

"Did your mother help with your studies?"

"Well, as a matter of fact, yes she did," no harm in telling him that much.



Zsoall Robi

"She must be an extraordinary person. I'd really like to meet her sometime."

'You have no idea how extraordinary she is!' Mar let slip unintentionally.

"What about your sisters? What do they do?" The last time John asked about her sisters Mar evaded the question, which he hadn't forgotten.

"They did a lot of study as well, but in different fields. We don't see each other much as they are very busy with their careers. One's in finance and the other in corporate governance."

"Ooh! High fliers. If they're as nice as you I'd love to meet them. They might be able to tell me some secrets about you," John teased. But Mar's reaction was unexpected. A dark cloud passed over her beautiful forehead, which John didn't fail to notice.

They'd finished their main course. John thoroughly enjoyed himself. He'd forgotten about the individual suspected of following them. He'd forgotten about Mar's strange little idiosyncrasies. He was just too happy. Mar had openly relaxed a little, but he could tell she was still being guarded. While they were having dinner and chatting he could only think about one thing, apart from the obvious.

The evening turned out extraordinarily well. She had started to open up slightly and they were looking into each other's eyes a lot more than before. And it was a different kind of looking. He didn't want the dinner to ever end ... well he did, but not the evening to ever end. If he could just slow things down a little, wind the clock back an hour .... He fell in love with Mar two years ago and it had taken him this long to get to this point. He knew it was a long time, but when he thought about that first moment of seeing her, it seemed like only a moment ago.

Mar was also having a good time. And in spite of making a couple of little mistakes it all went very well. She hoped the dinner might even develop into something a little more interesting. During the entire evening she monitored herself, making sure there were no transmissions going in Mary's direction, nor others being sent to her. Mary could alter her daughters' behaviour by remote control. Just a little safeguard Mary had built into their neural network and one which the three girls were aware of, but only as an annoyance in the background. None of them felt particularly comfortable with that kind of control over them - probably due to their humanness - their sense of independence and freedom coming to the surface. Mar especially didn't want to be disturbed later if things went the way she hoped.



Zsoall Robi

As the evening in the restaurant drew to a close John steeled himself to ask the big question. Yet when he first opened his mouth he could only managed a feeble request.

"I would really like to meet your mother." Not what he wanted to say at all.

"Maybe," Mar replied. She was waiting for The question and didn't want to delay it by talking too much.

"Ready to go?" He got the smile and the affirmative nod. What a smile he got! And all of a sudden he popped the question, "Your place or mine? … for a coffee," he self-consciously added.

While paying for the meal on the way out she whispered in his ear, "Mine."

Ary's party prepared to leave their table as well, on Ary's initiative when they saw Brayden make his move. Ary had been onto him since he arrived. They let him go ahead. Ary particularly didn't want to be recognised. She and Brayden knew each other by sight and it would have complicated matters too much to be discovered under those circumstances.

"They're leaving," Brayden reported to Leif.

"Follow them!" Leif barked back.

"I bet they're going to Mar's place," Ary nudged Mry. Mry coloured realising what that meant. Ice Cream grinned and linked arms with Adam. She wasn't going to give up on him easily. Adam had smiled and nodded and shaken his head and looked at everyone amicably. He hadn't said a single word all evening. Ary and Mry linked arms also, as sisters often do. .

. . . . . . . . . . . . .

 

. 

 

.

 

.

 

.

 

.

 

.



Zsoall Robi

# A.f.t.e.r D.i.n.n.e.r M.i.n.t.s
## 11<sup>th</sup> January 2696, Saturday.
## 145747027804 millis

*J*ohn became too immersed in anticipation to notice anything other than events within the immediate vicinity of his vision. Even that was somewhat clouded. Their taxi arrived as they stepped out of the restaurant. John didn't have to do anything other than attend to Mar. The vehicle had been pre-programmed to return to the Unity compound. All Unity staff were housed within the greater enclosed perimeter of the Company grounds.

The couple held hands, silent. Though not particularly interested in the mysteries of the night sky, their eyes meandered skyward; absentmindedly looking out the window, sometimes gazing at each other. Even the other vehicle which persisted in following them didn't arouse John's suspicion. In all probability many of the staff had enjoyed a night out and were making their way back home. Brayden followed directly behind John and Mar, and the girls with their partners behind him; they at a discrete distance from Brayden.

Once inside the Company gates John leant forward to make sure their destination on the Taxi's panel was Mar's place. Mar took the opportunity to contact Mary.

*"Mary?"*

*"What now!"*

*"John really wants to meet you,"* She transmitted. *"He's quite adamant and I don't think I'll be able to put him off very much longer."* Mary seemed reticent to reply judging from the pause.

*"What stage are you at exactly with the experiments? What progress have you made since yesterday?"*

*"The equipment is close to completion. Instrument calibration is proving challenging, particularly the special relativity clock. I'll need your help. But I do want you to meet John."*

*"Tonight, in two hours."* Mary sometimes forgot her daughters were essentially human organisms and needed the down-time sleep period to refresh. She also had no regard at all for their personal lives.



Zsoall Robi

*'No. I have other plans for tonight. I'll let you know when we are ready to go over the calculations with you.'* She couldn't believe how Mary could be so unfeeling. But then she often forgot Mary wasn't human.

John straightened up unexpectedly. "You're doing it again. You must be some kind of spy," he added and laughed indicating he was just joking.

That little dark cloud passed over Mar again. She slipped her hand out of his gently and turned to face him in order to make full eye contact. She made a sudden, intuitive snap decision. They were just coming up to her apartment and the taxi started to slow. Out of the corner of her eye Mar noticed two vehicles slowing almost simultaneously, one behind the other. The vehicle further back had left its lights on. The nearer one went dark, but no one got out.

John's breathing stopped for a moment. *I've said the wrong thing! She wants me to leave! Why is she behaving so oddly again?* A few more disturbing thoughts raced through his head, still oblivious to the vehicles behind them.

Her eyes searched his for a sign. She didn't know what she expected to find. Then suddenly she let it out, "I've been talking to my mother."

She didn't say Mary because all the physicists knew their company super computer by just one name – Mary - including John. Mar didn't know how John would react. He didn't take his eyes of her face. A little tell-tale movement at the corner of his mouth told Mar he'd understood what she had just said and was analysing it – at his unaugmented human speed. The taxi had stopped. She could wait.

"Sooo – that means - ?" She knew immediately what he alluded to and was so completely relieved she leant over and gave him the sort of kiss which answered the question to his satisfaction. Obviously John didn't think that a daughter speaking to her mother represented a big issue. And obviously he had no idea of the true basis of the relationship between the two women.  He may have had misgivings if he did know.

They got out of their taxi. Mar led him by the hand to her front door. The vehicle that had stopped further back, with the lights still on, moved away from the kerb and continued down the road. The other didn't move, with no sign of life coming from it.

*"They're going to have sex,"* Ary announced to Mary as their vehicle moved away from Mar's apartment. Without any doubt at all. She knew her sister well enough. There had never been a man in her apartment as far as Ary knew. There could be no other possible reason she could think of for Mar



Zsoall Robi

having one then. Good for her. It was about time she learnt what it was to feel like a complete woman.

*"Sex? What for?"* Mary queried. As much as she knew about everything and as comprehensive as her data banks were with the psyches of her constituent women's experiences, it was all theory to her. Even the little time she spent with Nick didn't, wasn't able to (more to the point), give her any appreciation of what happens between two people when they give each other over to each other in such a complete intimate encounter.

*"What for?"* She reiterated.

*"No point telling you Mother. You could never understand."*

*"What is going to happen?"* The tone of the question didn't reveal any apprehension, or at least none Ary could discern other than impatience.

*"Leave them alone. They are just going to enjoy one another as human beings do sometimes. You'll get a little idea about that in the morning when you 'download' her experiences from the night. Don't be misled by what you have learnt from me. For me it's all just … well … not a lot of depth to it."*

*"What is Brayden doing? Stay there until he leaves."* She commanded.


"Brayden! What are they doing?" Leif was on edge. He need not have been. Perhaps anxiety came with the job. His predecessor had similar problems, though more damaging to his health.

"They're going up to her apartment. It's late, so my guess is he'll be spending the night."

"Leave." Leif couldn't be bothered to say any more.

Brayden could be such a blunt tool at times and Leif didn't want to take the chance of something happening he would have to fix later. But that wasn't the end of the situation for Leif because of his predisposition to creating worst case scenarios in his mind. He just couldn't let it go. His two researchers were up to something. He was sure of it. Their laboratory time was out of sync with their productivity and they were starting to spend private time together. His past experience told him that always meant trouble.

He decided to keep closer surveillance on Mar and John. He would also personally interview them about the progress of the project they were working on for Unity. In spite of having decided on appropriate action, he could still not bring himself to leave the office and go home to get some sleep. He just lay down in the private suite attached to his office, only to continue brooding over the matter.

43

Leif believed his predecessor at Unity had achieved one of the greatest breakthroughs in science with the successful mission to the centre of the universe. Scientifically most lucrative, although from the theological perspective Unity still didn't consider they had definitive proof of the existence of God. Be that as it may, he, Leif, felt his own initiative had far greater potential for profit for Unity and its shareholders. He could just imagine the prices they would charge if they had the technology to reverse moments of time itself; to be able to manipulate the asymmetry of time regardless of whether they were dealing with it on the quantum or the macro level. If anything, the millennia of research had proved beyond any shadow of doubt that all things were possible. If a human mind could conceive of a thing, then that thing was possible. Only the inconceivable could not be achieved. Leif twisted and turned these thoughts into a tangle robbing him of asleep. Time, in effect, was torturing him.

However, this POOP wasn't the only one having a problematic experience with time. Brayden couldn't fall asleep either. While still in the restaurant he caught Ice Cream's eye, just for an instant. That moment of mutual lust had become an unreachable eternity as he contemplated the confluence of two like souls. He didn't know what kind of experiments Mar and John were involved in, at least not the details. But he did know they were trying to manipulate time. That was enough to spark his imagination. If he could only have Ice Cream to himself for one single instant and extend it beyond its natural boundaries … he managed to get a little rest sometime in the early morning hours as exhaustion finally claimed his body and his mind.

Ary and Ice cream thoroughly enjoyed the cloak and dagger mystery of the evening. Mary had never asked Ary to spy covertly on anyone before. Not that the task was difficult or dangerous in any way. It did have one essential element that excited Ary and Ice Cream. They knew instinctively how the evening would end with the new lovers. They already thought of John and Mar as lovers, though nothing had happened between them until that evening. Ice Cream in particular couldn't keep her eyes off the happy couple, watching them play the game; holding hands, eye probing, star gazing, silly nonsense talk and seeing their skin colour flush as the sexual excitement built in their bodies.

To add spice to the pleasure that strange man in another booth obviously lusted after her - couldn't keep his eyes off her – not unusual in her life. She was after all, a most unusual and desirable bit of fluff – and she knew it. The man spent most of his time fantasizing about her. She could



Zsoall Robi

sense the intensity of his desire and that excited her almost beyond control. If the dinner had not come to an end when it did, she may have been forced to take matters into her own hands, Ary or no Ary!

When she and Ary did at last get into their transport, Ice Cream immediately unleashed her bubbling desire upon Ary, who was never one to complain about Ice Cream's excesses. Mary was hit with such a rush of raw experiences that at first all her processing capacity became focused on the one single event. She knew Ary was her most fertile source of primal human impulses, but never had she experienced it to the same intensity.

All the way to their own living quarters Ary and Ice Cream continued their activity, which to them only amounted to foreplay. Inside their domicile time rushed and twisted in every direction. Sometimes it should have moved forward a lot faster and at other moments it should have stood completely still and let its potential energy grow. The end result was of course time going along at its own leisurely pace eventually enveloping the two sensualists in a short period of physical renewal as their minds and bodies slept. Perhaps their minds were able to replay the event of the entire evening over and over during their sleep, as if The Arrow of Time had been flexible.

Adam's most valuable talent stood out above his patience - stamina. He was tall and slender like John. Not as old as John but with a mind just as sharp. Adam chose to spend his life not in the pursuit of knowledge or wealth or power but as a connoisseur and collector of experiences. Mry was certainly not his first liaison. He tried as much as possible to see life in its myriad manifestations as it flowed past him, without getting too deeply involved himself. He tried hard not to change the very things he was observing. There were times however when it was simply not possible; even then he preferred the 'touch' as a means of communication and interaction rather than the 'word'.

So when Ary and Ice Cream leapt into the arms of Eros with such complete abandon he could sense Mry's desire rising. She started to fidget and tried to look everywhere else other than at her sister. Mry's pupils dilated and her body temperature rose. The fine hairs on her bare arms raised themselves off the surface of her velvet skin. Adam watched and immersed himself in the rising tide of emotion. Then, as was often the case, he simply and softly stroked Mry's arm from just below the shoulder to just above the inside of her wrist; slowly and with the lightest pressure he could manage.

Adam knew as well as Mry the evening held more promise than just sleep at the end of a long day. Mary was again forced to turn her attention away from her other deliberations when the intensity of energy emanating from Mry surged in her circuits. The quality and urgency of the hormonal activity was quite different from her other two daughters. She couldn't help herself from looking through Mry's eyes as the two people pleasured themselves independently and with each other. *Why such intense energy couldn't be harnessed for something other than animal lust,* she thought for that was the only way she could comprehend what she observed. Mary had the theory of love in her circuits but not how it functioned ... *perhaps sometime in the future, if there is enough time in my future.*

John and Mar couldn't get to sleep either - not immediately anyway. Their hormones had taken control. On the way to Mar's door several short sessions of intimacy interrupted their progress, each more urgent than the next. Typical of John that even from the depths of lust he could spare a though for scientific matters; like the elasticity of time. *It's exactly in moments like these,* he theorised as his experience had not been fulsome in the area of sex, *that I should have the ability to manipulate the elasticity of time, which characteristic has already been amply proven.* All that remained were the tools with which to manage it. Like right then, to make the particular exquisite moment last longer, as long as he wanted it to last. Or like the fiddling at the door with the access codes – couldn't that be made to move along just a little more quickly!

John's formative years spent in developing his creativity brought a flexibility of mind that wasn't only an asset in quantum physics research, it also had a most practical application under the current circumstances. Mar could scarcely believe there were so many wonderful ways of enjoying each other's company without having a stich of clothing anywhere near their bodies.

With sublime control, John manipulated the urgency into staged moments of delayed satisfaction; those delays heightening the pleasures they experienced. When they reached the summit in unison, in hindsight it almost felt like an anticlimax. Lying beside each other, breathless at first, drenched in perspiration and not even being able to focus their eyes on each other, gave the entire event a surreal quality. Like something taking place in another world, in another time structure.

When eventually John spoke, settling the eddying of the space-time continuum fabric he said, "Ever since the first day I arrived at Unity and saw you hooked up to your equipment ..."

 

"Yes, it was the same for me," Mar replied, "but I had to be sure. Here she paused checking herself again about how much she should be revealing. "There are things about me you don't know."

She scanned her neural blocks to ensure their privacy from Mary spying on their 'getting-to-know-each-other' session. At the same time she realised she would need Mary's help very soon if she wanted John and her to meet.

"Like your connection with your mother?"

"Yes, and much more. On all those occasions when you noticed me being distracted, I was actually - well – it had everything to do with my mother."

"You have some kind of direct comm link with her unlike any known technology we have currently." John didn't ask the question and wasn't looking for confirmation. He'd already worked out the only explanation possible for Mar's peculiar behaviour and for her evasive manner about it.

"Would you do something for me, John? If you do this, I'll be able to be completely open with you. Don't misunderstand me. It's not that I don't trust you - because I do. But I have to be sure – We - have to be sure."

"We?" Without consciously realising it John was having the absolute best time of his life, and not just because of the after dinner mints. Before him lay a mystery embodied in the most beautiful and desirable woman he had ever seen in all his long years. The man in him, the scientist in him both wanted to know everything there was to know about this fascinating, extraordinary, magnificent being.

"You know I have two sisters and you know of course about M – my mother," She almost had another premature lapse of security. It confirmed in her mind what had to be done. "Just give me a moment while I talk to her."

John happily lay back on the pillow to observe his personal cosmos as she withdrew into herself. He didn't have long to wait, as the conversation which he couldn't hear lasted seconds of normal time, although in Mary's timeframe much longer. At least the content and complexity of the exchange would have occupied many minutes of normal time.

*"Mother?"*

*"Yes … I kept my promise."*

*"I felt you checking."*

*"Can you blame me?"*

*"Seriously. I need your help. John is important to me, very important. And he could be very important for what we are trying to achieve with our research."*

*"Go on."*

*"I need to be sure of his thinking, his mind. I need - no - We - need to know he doesn't have any unnatural loyalty to Unity. I need to get into his mind. You've done this once before, with Nick. You told us about it. I don't want you to interfere with him. Just see where his loyalty lies."*

*"Why should I do this for you?"* Whether Mary was just being difficult or truly trying to assess the need to be invasive Mar couldn't tell.

*"Because – because I want him in my life. Do you remember what you told us about how you downloaded yourself into Nick's neural net, and couldn't decide how you could participate in life with him – and how you decided that just being inside his head wasn't enough? And how you decided it needed to be more. Well, that's how it is for me with John. You wanted to be physically together with Nick, but couldn't. I could have a life like that with John."*

The memory took Mary back to the time just after she and Nick arrived from their journey to the centre of the universe. She could relive every instant of that period, not just remember it. She had stored every iota of data about their interaction, about the circumstances of the events and all the reasons why she acted as she did. Artificial Intelligence can do all that, and much, much more in Mary's case. She realised that if she was ever going to achieve the greatest aspiration of her existence she needed more data, especially the kind of data only Mar and John could provide if their relationship came to fruition with the results she desired.

*"You can do it,"* Mary said, *"I'll show you how. Let me see into you."* Mar removed the remaining blocks to give Mary full access to all her sensory inputs. *"Stand and face each other."*

"John, come and stand up with me," Mar directed him, "This is something that has been done before," she tried to reassure him, but as they were still naked John couldn't control his reaction as his body came into contact with hers.

"Not that silly. Be serious."

"Sorry", he gave her a Cheshire Cat grin.

"I want you to let me see your thoughts."

"Are you serious. Wasn't it obvious?"

"Behave yourself. If you want to know who I am then I need to be sure about something. And I can only do that by seeing the foundation of your core beliefs."

"Whoa! Are you trying to mess with my mind! No – no – disregard that. What I mean is – is it necessary – isn't there some other way?"

"No, it's the only way. There is no pain and there is no interference with your neurons. It will only take a few moments."

"This is science fiction stuff! Who are you really?"

"I can tell you – or not – in a moment. Are you ready?"

"No – I mean, Yes."

"Just stand there, put your hands – Nooo! - Put Your Hands On Your Thighs! Be a good boy."

*'What now Mother?'*

*"Touch his forehead with yours, put your hands at the back of his head and hold him firm."*

"John, put your forehead against mine and close your eyes. Ok. Now think about Unity."

"I'll try."

Mar did exactly as instructed, also linking her mind with Mary's.

*.... John believes himself to be a good man – he does not trust Leif, although he's neutral about Unity, perhaps tending to be cautions or suspicious of it, and he has very strong feelings for you'* ...

*'Yes mother, I saw. We are safe, wouldn't you agree?*

*'You can bring him.'*

"Done." Mar said to John a few moments later. A moment could be quite a long time, or it might only be a few consecutive instants. It was all Mary needed to assess the suitability of this particular biological unit as a partner for her daughter without presenting a threat to herself. He wasn't just going to be Mar's partner, but Mary's collaborator, although John wasn't aware of that yet. He was much more valuable than Ary's bimbo or Mry's stick man.

"What?" He said. "When are you going to start?"

"Done, It's all done. Mother can do most things very quickly.

"Wow and Wow. I really do have to meet this mother of yours."

*"But he'll have to meet your sisters first. Don't need to tell him about me yet. Leave it till you bring him in."* Because Mar's blocks were still down, Mary was aware of everything going on.

*"Please be quiet mother. It's very difficult to have a three-way conversation."*

To John she said, "Get dressed. Later today you're going to meet my sisters, and we have a lot to talk about."

She said this quite normally but it seemed to John just a little too efficiently - he couldn't quite put his finger on the right word. *I hope I'll have at least an 'equal' status in the relationship and Mother won't be a constant background to our privacy.* He made a mental note to talk to Mar about that.

·

                    Zsoall Robi

## M.e.e.t.i.n.g  t.h.e  S.i.s.t.e.r.s
### 12<sup>th</sup> January 2696, Sunday
### 1453444946182 millis

'*Girls, we need to meet,*' Mar insisted. Neither Ary nor Mry were particularly fond of the idea of having a meeting with a stranger. They loved the spy-dinner and thoroughly enjoyed the deserts thereafter in private, but they were simply exhausted.

'*Why,*' they queried in unison.

'*Because of John.*'

'*You mean the man with you at the restaurant last night?*' Mry asked, always the most talkative of the three of them.

'*Yes. How did you know about that?*'

'*Mother asked us to keep you safe,*' Ary volunteered.

'*Likely story. John needs to know more about me.*'

'*You mean about us?*'

'*Yes. Mother's checked him out. He's secure.*'

'*Maybe Ice Cream will like him.*' Always a hidden pleasure agenda present with Ary.

'*Just the two of you. At the usual place. Three sharp. Don't be late.*'

Mar made the arrangements while John found some ingredients to make breakfast for two.

"At three sharp." Mar announced without any preamble when John brought in the tray of food.

"Ok." John plunged in as well without any small talk. He loved playing chess, and particularly loved springing surprises.

"So – Who are you really?"

"We have a little time - so here goes. You already know I'm a Theoretical Physicist engaged in very specific research with you, for Unity."

"Right." He nodded expectantly, raising eyebrows encouraging Mar to continue.

"You also know how I work, and you've never asked me about it. I often wondered why you didn't. Most researchers don't spend all their time with their brains hooked up to the Zee-Cloud."

"I have wondered but thought you'd tell me one day. You always come up with the results so I didn't push the point."

Just at that moment Mar's normal comms indicated an incoming - unusual on a late Sunday morning.

"Mar." The gruff, irritable male voice offered to preamble to the call. "I want you and John in my office first thing tomorrow morning," The POOP commanded without identifying himself. It would have been superfluous as everyone knew his voice.

"John as well?"

"Yes, both of you."

"Why John?"

"Just be here!" The call ended abruptly.

"Know who that was?" She asked John.

"No. Your mother?" He smiled.

"No. Leif." John's smile disappeared. "He wants us in his office first thing tomorrow."

"Whatever for?"

"More to the point ... why the two of us together, and why now just after? – You know ..."

"Well, we are working together on the same project. Anyway, continue with what you were saying." Obviously he wasn't fazed by the impromptu invitation. John's nonchalance didn't ease her mind. It was too much of a coincidence Leif should want them immediately after they had taken the first major step in setting their private relationship on a firmer footing. Unity's rules didn't forbid colleagues forming relationships. She put those thoughts aside for the time being, and picked up from before ...

"The reason I work jacked in is because my brain is a little different." She paused to gauge his reaction.

"I know you're a 'little' different," he teased.

She gave him that smile again. "I know, for instance that your eyesight is augmented. Nothing strange about that. With me, it's my brain, my neural net has been enhanced." She stopped again.

Then he couldn't help himself and asked, "And your beauty ... is that natural?"

"Don't be naughty. I'm trying to be serious. Yes, it is, thank you." Mar allowed Mary to hear everything.

"Even before I was born, my mother took steps to make sure I was going to function at my highest possible potential ... and beyond."

"Oh." Now he wasn't so blasé.



Zsoall Robi

"In my case my neural architecture had an obvious aptitude towards the scientific. So mother worked on that."

"Just who is your mother?"

"We will get to that. My sisters are also enhanced beyond the normal limitations of a human system." John started feeling decidedly on guard after hearing these various terms creeping into the conversation. More and more they made Mar sound less and less human.

"You have not met them, but you already know of one of them. She is highly skilled in corporate business matters. And the other is a financial wizard. You with me so far?"

"Yes." As much as his mind was capable, the mind of a 'genius' according to normal human standards, it tried hard to put all the pieces of information into some sort of cohesive pattern. So far the picture eluded him.

"I can tell you a little more … only because you let us do a security scan on you." John lanced a questioning look at her. "Sorry, but that's the most I can say at the moment about that. My sisters and I work together as a team for our mother. We work for Unity as well. The financial expert, provides the funds for our current project. It's not the same project you and I have been working on, but it's related."

"Oh," John said again with more surety than before.

"Well actually, you know about one of them, and you know the other one quite well. Sorry to be so mysterious, but please be patient."

"Ok." There was really nothing more he could do other than go along with it. He'd got himself into this situation and would have to patiently see where it led. He was prepared to do just that, but only because of Mar. He couldn't imagine life without her any more.

It turned out to be a long breakfast after a long sleep-in. In spite of the mysteries Mar had presented him with he could still contemplate the events of the evening dinner and all the delicious moments following it. It didn't surprise him though when his mind reverted back to the issue of time. It being the main area of their joint research at Unity, namely, the irreversibility of the Quantum Arrow of Time. On so many occasions in the last twenty hours he'd wanted time to slow down, to speed up or to stop altogether. He couldn't come to terms with the inability of his finite mind to deal with the idea of asymmetric time having a beginning but no ending. Eternity was eternity. If time was infinite then it should not have a beginning!



Zsoall Robi

"If time is infinite, it should not have a beginning. Time has no business being asymmetric!" He blurted out. This was one of his little 'chess' surprises and Mar would just have to learn to deal with it, to take it in her stride.

"So, you didn't want the night to end. Is that it?" Mar smiled broadly at him, which almost turned him into ooze about to change location from the couch to the floor.

"Exactly! But more than that!" Oh she's quick. Probably quicker than me.

"What you want, lover, is for the laws of quantum mechanics to jump in and be the same at both the macroscopic and atomic levels, so we could ..."

"Exactly! And why is that not possible?" John asked.

"It might be."

"What. Are you serious?" Sorry, I keep saying that.

"It's time we left. We have a long way to go." Mar urged, evading his question.


"I'm on it Leif. They're just getting into their transport."

"Remember – follow them day and night," Leif barked at Brayden.

Leif awoke early, bathed in sweat. He stood in front of the mirror looking at a dishevelled worried man. *I don't know why, but I've got a bad feeling about these two. Their research is much too important to ignore even the slightest thing that could interfere with the outcome of the work. The worst case scenario would be to have to get rid of both of them and entrust the rest of the work to Mary. If we lose them there are no other physicists capable of carrying on with the project.*

One seemingly insurmountable problem for Leif was his belief that Mary didn't have the capacity for creative abstract data processing. Leif wasn't even aware Mary had supplemented her already exponentially growing awareness with the capabilities of her daughter's upper cortical functions. Then there was the slight complication, though certainly not insurmountable, of how to get rid of John and Mar without arousing suspicion, if it became necessary. The secrecy surrounding the project had to be maintained at all costs. There weren't too many options. *I have to be certain of exactly what is going on with these two.*


Brayden wasn't a trained detective, just an ambitious clever man who had managed to work his way up the ladder to become a confidante of The Principal Officer of Profit, but not clever enough to realise his true position

 Zsoall Robi

as low level confidante: consequently the nature of his current task. Nevertheless he tried to do the job to the best of his ability, which only betrayed his pathetic amateurish effort, definitely not good enough when trying to outsmart the two powerful intellects of John and Mar. As an example of his ineptitude, he followed them in the same vehicle he had used the previous day.

On the way to the meeting John wanted to continue his train of thought about Time Asymmetry. "Whether it is symmetrical or asymmetrical might very well be beside the point. It's a characteristic of our perceived reality that time is independent of the intrinsic nature of any event and it simply manifests in the perception of the process, in any progression of change regardless of the direction of change."

Mar half listened and half watched the vehicle she noticed when they left her apartment; it being the same vehicle she saw on their way to the restaurant. Wanting to get a look at the occupants of the vehicle she reprogrammed their own to go slower and into a busy traffic precinct. She'd heard John's argument and could contribute something to it while doing other things simultaneously.

"You're trying to imply there is no physical existence of the thing we call time, therefore there is no way to develop a tool with which to manipulate it."

"Exactly!" It was such a pleasure to open up to this woman on the creative level and knock around a few impossibilities. He never knew she was so multi-facetted. "What if there was another reality from which to view the time phenomenon objectively. We are too subjectively involved with it the way things are."

While John continued to parade his confusion, Mar carefully scrutinised the following vehicle. It had caught right up to them in the traffic congestion. Brayden thought he wouldn't be detected with all those other vehicles about. Wrong, again. Mar did see him; just a man, rather untidy, a bit sweaty (obviously not particularly comfortable with what he was doing) and alone. She didn't recognise him but made the shrewd guess he would definitely have some connection with Leif, and with their forthcoming unexpected interview with the top executive at Unity.

"You want to jump over to eternity and check time out from there as if it was a bug in a jar, yes?" She continued her own train of thought while considering some options on how to deal with their follower. She most definitely didn't want an eavesdropper at their meeting with her two sisters.



Zsoall Robi

"Brilliant! So how do we get there?" John said it more in jest than anything else. In the time it took John to think and express that thought, Mar had made her decision and contacted Ary.

*"Sister dear, I need your help. There's a Unity stooge following us. He looks sleazy but not dangerous. Could you possible get Ice Cream to distract him?"*

*"Delicious. She'll love it. Where are you exactly?"* With the details sorted out Mar resumed her conversation with John, but not before a minor interruption from Mary.

*"I agree,"* she said.

*"With what?"*

*"With taking care of Brayden, and also with the direction your conversation is taking."*

*"So you know who's following us?"*

*"Yes, but he's not a big a problem, at least not yet."*

"If you did manage to jump the bridge to eternity how would you get back dear?" Mar switched her mind back to John.

"Across the same bridge of course." Now he became flippant and started feeling a little silly. "But you would have to come with me, just in case."

At that point the ideas seemed to run dry, so John took her hand in his and they sat there with minds in limbo; at least his was, but not hers. She kept her eyes on Brayden while waiting for Ice Cream to arrive, which she did quite soon and in a most unexpected way.

Ice Cream fainted. She saw Braden's vehicle approaching and timed her jump out in front of it to perfection. Ice Cream wasn't an exclusive appendage for the sole enjoyment of Ary, unlike Adam for Mry. Ary enjoyed extra-relationship adventures as much as Ice Cream did. The vehicle's automatic sensors stopped it almost instantaneously. Fatalities and injuries almost never happened anymore, but Brayden immediately jumped out, partly because he thought he'd recognised something in that flash of an instant just before Ice Cream hit the road surface - and he was right. It was her! - The woman he saw at the restaurant, the woman who'd given him such an incredibly turbulent night of sleeplessness. He recognised her almost at once, and seeing her body almost fully exposed (Ice Cream made sure of that during her trajectory), he lost all awareness of where he was and why he was actually at that location.

Mar watched the drama unfold as they sped away to their destination while John remained wrapped in his world of impossibilities completely oblivious to what had happened. She didn't need to use much imagination



Zsoall Robi

to work out how the scenario would unfold with Ice Cream in control. Mar didn't let herself dwell on how this man would deal with Ice Cream. There were much more important things to think about; like what Mary had just said about her conversation with John regarding time.

"John, this is Ary and Mry - my sisters."

"Oh." John managed his latest one syllable expression with difficulty and only after several million instants had raced through his consciousness. The two sisters stood side by side, a little apart from one another. They each needed exhibition space, even the introverted Mry. She flashed fire at him through those dark energy black eyes, maybe because he couldn't decide whether to look into those eyes or alight on the extraordinarily seductive cleavage. He could do neither. She prepared herself with extra care for the meeting, just for John's benefit and was pussycat gratified at the reaction.

John wanted to keep savouring the visual extravaganza but couldn't maintain eye contact. Ary unsettled him the most. She was indeed disturbing. He knew the face. He'd seen it only once but it left an image burnt onto his retina like the residual afterglow of a sunburst. John kept staring at the bald head, the golden eyebrows and the Cleopatra eyes. His gaze didn't go lower than her lips. He was still lost when Mar gave him a little nudge. How long was he lost? - long enough for Mar to feel the need to bring him back.

"John." He said eventually, introducing himself in an even, solid, expressionless voice. "Sisters?" He asked , still trying to regain full control.

"We have the same mother," Ary said, somewhat amused at the effect they were having on the poor man.

"How much does he know?" Mry didn't often speak first, but the critical question had to be asked.

"Mother's checked him out and she approves. He will know as much as we are prepared to tell him. He knows for instance that we are 'different' in a special kind of way." Mar clarified.

As a trained and successful creative, John was extremely perceptive. The four of them sat in the courtyard of a small non-descript café. John listened to them discussing him and let his eyes vagabond between the three girls. It didn't take him very long to see beyond the cosmetics. They were indeed biological sisters. Remarkably similar, could have been identical triplets except for the eyes. Even if they had all been wearing the same outfit he would still have been able to immediately distinguish them from one

56

Zsoall Robi

another. And there was another thing; they were psychologically different from each other as well – plainly obvious from the soul-scapes he perceived behind their eyes.

By the time the girls had finished discussing him, he'd come to the conclusion he liked all of them; Mar more than just liked, of course. Ary and Mry were also watching him as he went through the process of analysing them. It was all about the eyes. He looked into their eyes, even into Mry's. She liked that. She decided she liked him too. So did Ary. She thought he was cute, in an academic sort of way. Of course she would never poach one of her sisters' liaisons, but if he ever became a free agent … well.

"Mar tells me you all have special talents - enhanced talents." He hoped the open ended statement would draw out a bit of information from them. John need not have been concerned for the three girls had already exchanged an internal dialogue that he could be completely trusted. They would tell him about themselves, but would let Mary do her own explanations about herself.

"We are sisters with the same biological mother, but very early in life we were adopted." Mar started the process and glanced at Ary for her to continue.

"Except we were adopted before birth." John raised an inquisitive eyebrow. Now we're getting somewhere interesting.

"Our talents," Mry added almost inaudibly, "were programmed into our genetics in-utero, and further enhanced with a variety of invasive and non-invasive techniques." She glanced at her two sisters gauging if they could go further in their revelations.

"Our corporeal make up is mostly biological, but much of us is similar to our adoptive mother," Mar slowly ventured, watching John's reaction to the last statement.

She did get a reaction and they interpreted it to be positive. John's eyebrows arched slowly towards the hairline on his forehead, before having to give up the ascent due to lack of skin elasticity. Ary loved the reaction, and silently let the other two know. *'Let's keep going,'* she said to them, thrilled with this juicy little adventure. But they waited to see if John had anything to say. He didn't ask the obvious, odious question. Instead he asked the most wonderful thing,

"And your spirit?"

"Oh, we are definitely – what's the right word? – Help me our here John," Ary asked, intrigued.

57

"Girls?" A mischievous smile crept across his face, which made all of them burst out laughing. It's not what he was trying to say, but it confirmed his expectation that they were real live alluring flesh and bones.

The rest of the conversation flowed easily and freely between them. John learnt a great deal more about the three musketeers. It confirmed his memory about seeing Ary's face before. She was on Unity's board of directors. Wow. And Mry with her financial empire – double wow. But what he wasn't quite clear about, and the girls didn't clarify this for him, was how they all fitted together as a team with their mother, and what they were working towards as a 'family'. Mary would explain all that. She was the only one who could reveal her true nature to him. And he desperately wanted to know what the girls meant when they said …  'but much of us is similar to our adoptive mother'.

John had a most thoroughly enjoyable and enlightening time. The girls had opened his imagination and fired him up into thinking the impossible might be possible.


Brayden also had a wonderful time. Time spent unlike anything he had experienced before in his life. After Ice Cream had finished with him, leaving him as a quivering mass of sweating flesh in his own apartment, and after he had recovered sufficiently to put two coherent thoughts together, he began to think about what he had done. *There's no way I can explain Ice Cream to Leif.*  There was no worldly excuse that could excuse his abandonment of the assignment. It was a simple assignment – follow them and report what they are doing.

Leif had tried several times to contact him during the day to get an update, but Brayden was too unconscious of reality to be able to respond. He was in another universe, in another time dimension. A simple hour and a half could be so very, very expensive.

*I'm going to get fired for sure. Damn! - And I don't even know where Ice Cream lives!*

*I'll be lucky if he doesn't kill me - DAMN!* .

.

.

.



Zsoall Robi

# M.e.e.t.i.n.g w.i.t.h T.h.e P.O.O.P
## 13ᵗʰ January 2696, Monday
## 1453607785308 millis

*"Why does Leif want to see you and John?"* Mary joined the girls' conversation with John after she saw they'd finished their important business with him.

*"Whatever the reason, his stooge will not be able to tell him much. He became somewhat distracted by Ice Cream. He'll be lucky if he still has a job at the end of the day."* Mar didn't know what Leif was after. Nor did Mary. However an interview, on such short notice, was most unusual; entirely out of character with Leif's usual pattern of behaviour.

Mary activated her contingency plan.

*'I want to see you about the synchronisation problem, and I want John to meet you, Mother. Immediately after the meeting with Leif would be opportune.'* Mar didn't want to delay the inevitable. If John was going to get cold feet after meeting Mary and seeing who her mother really was, then the sooner it was over with the better.

Having discovered each other the two lovers spent another night together, re-running the intimacy experiment just to confirm the high compatibility quotient indicated by their first encounter. This time they were not followed home by Brayden.

Self-important, worried Leif sat seething alone in his imposing office. Why hasn't that idiot Brayden reported in?  All attempts to contact him had failed. He'd better be dead or he'll wish he was!

"At last! In my office – NOW." Eventually Brayden did announce himself, sounding fully aware of the trouble he was in. The sun had not yet risen when Brayden found himself standing in front of Leif waiting for the inevitable. It didn't come as expected.

"WHY?" Leif wasn't going to waste any more words on this incompetent than he absolutely had to.



Zsoall Robi

"Ice Cream." Brayden knew what the question referred to and gave the most honest answer he could manage. "Because of Ice Cream – she jumped in front of my vehic ..." He didn't have the opportunity to finish his explanation. As soon as he started he knew he'd said the most ridiculous and incomprehensible thing possible.

"WHAT DRIVEL. – No - I don't want to know!" Leif shouted as Brayden opened his mouth again, then fell silent. Not a good omen. Brayden knew his master well enough that the best that could happen to him was getting demoted or fired and thrown on the scrap heap of the rest of useless humanity. Minutes seemed to drag by as Leif couldn't even countenance looking at the man. Then a slow quiet rumble started somewhere deep inside Leif.

The POOP hissed his words through clenched teeth, "You live - If they die."

Leif had decided that unless his rogue researchers had a bloody good explanation for everything, he could do without them. Brayden heard the man loud and clear. So did Mary. Brayden turned to leave the office.

"STAY!" Leif barked at him, as if he was some kind of mongrel disobedient dog.

Brayden behaved like one as he slunk to the back corner of the office without whimpering another word. They waited. At the appointed hour Leif sent for his top scientific advisor. Cosmo had been with Unity since Mary was first created, now considered to be an old man ready for retirement but Leif would not let him go. He knew too much. Leif trusted and relied on the man's judgement too much.

Leif had briefed him about the problem and wanted an immediate analysis of the value of the two researchers. Cosmo arrived a few minutes before John and Mar. He recognised Brayden in the corner looking like the breath of death had descended on him. He raised an inquisitive eyebrow in Leif's direction.

"The terminal solution," Leif sneered.

Cosmo had settled into an uncomfortable chair as John and Mar walked in without knocking. He knew them from their work of course, and from their scientific reputation.

John wasn't particularly fazed by the situation, nor was Mar. Mary had not yet advised her of Leif's intent.

Mar glanced around the room, nodded acknowledgement to old Cosmo and on seeing Brayden standing somewhat dejected in the corner greeted him with a smile and comment, "You're looking worn out." She simply



Zsoall Robi

couldn't help herself, knowing full well the toll Ice Cream's affections could take on a man.

There were only two chairs in the office. One for The POOP and Cosmo reclined in the other. John and Mar stood side by side, relaxed and puzzled.

"Morning, Leif," Mar said, trying to be cheerful. Best to get it over with.

"There are consequences. There are rewards and consequences," Leif determined to let them know at the beginning this was no frivolous social gathering. "I want a full report on your progress."

"A full report will take a couple of days," John suggested.

"Now!"

Mar and John glanced at each other. Whatever was going on had something to do with the man following them, and it was serious. Just how serious they didn't know.

John began by outlining the parameters of their work. "You want us to account for our time. We've been working on time itself."

"Go on – go on!" Leif prodded impatiently.

Mar started with the beginning of their project. "There are complications, as I'm sure you will appreciate. At first we needed to establish a few basic …"

"Get to the point! What stage are you up to?" When Leif lost patience she skipped much of the details involved. Needless to say, she didn't mention the increasing amount of time they had been dedicating to Mary's experiments.

"Is that all?" Leif sounded like he wasn't satisfied with the progress. During the report he'd been keeping an eye on Cosmo to gauge his reactions. Every now and then Cosmo nodded, but more often shook his head from side to side. As far as Leif was concerned that confirmed his suspicions. These two people had been stealing Unity's time and resources for other activities. "Your work log indicates to me that given the time you've been at Unity you should have made more progress." He smiled a loaded smile. "Am I right Cosmo?" Cosmo nodded assent.

In that little interlude Mary brought Mar into the picture. This was a most dangerous moment for all of them; Mary, the three sisters and John. *"He wants the two of you dead with Brayden as the executioner."* On hearing this Mar turned to John and gave him a warning look. She hoped he didn't interpret it as something else. Mar could see Leif obviously had no idea what they were doing and that's why he needed Cosmo. With seemingly unconcerned ease Mar turned towards Cosmo, putting on her most

 Zsoall Robi

professional manner but with the slightest little tilt of her head in his direction and with just a shadow of a smile she offered,

"If you'd like to come down to our laboratory I'll be happy (she paused just for the briefest moment) to show you everything," leaving her dangerous smile linger for an instant on Cosmo. She'd allowed nothing to show on her face after Mary's announcement.

Cosmo reacted, as she was certain he would. Age wasn't a factor with imagination. He was only a man, a fully human man, nothing special about him at all. Cosmo raised himself out of the chair with as much nonchalance as he could manage.

"I'd like to go and see things for myself," he said to Leif, who didn't expect that and impatiently waved him to sit again.

"Yes, yes. Shortly." Then he fixed John with his stare and proceeded to the next matter, as if it was something entirely within John's control.

"Consequences! There are consequences to everything. We do not encourage romantic liaisons between staff."

*So that's why we were followed.* John and Mar had the same thought simultaneously.

"It affects work performance."

"Do you need assurances that a breach of security about our most critical researches isn't imminent?" Mar boldly went to the heart of the matter.

Again Leif heard the unexpected. These two didn't seem to be at all rattled by his veiled threats, and Cosmo was prepared to review their progress.

John had caught on to Mar's little strategy of misdirection. Whatever was getting on The POOP's nerves needed diffusing. He decided to contribute with a few curlers of his own.

"Leif … you're quite right … we have been a bit reticent to come out into the open with – er - everything." John dangled the carrot and got Leif's attention. He raised himself ever so slightly off his chair, his interest peaked, but nettled at being called by his Christian name by someone who had no business doing so.

"Not all of our work has been logged," Leif raised one eyebrow, not sure where this was all going, "and I can only discuss this in the strictest confidence," John said as he indicated with his eyes in the direction of the other two men in the room. Leif was a clever man, clever only in directions that would ultimately result in greater power and wealth for himself.



Zsoall Robi

"Get out!" He waved at the two men. "You, Brayden, don't go far." John noticed the interest flicker into life in Leif's eyes.

"There are consequences to studying the Quantum Arrow of Time. The further we delved into the mathematics of the phenomenon, the more questions arose than answers. And with those questions ... possibilities." John knew he was being silly and fanciful when he and Mar discussed such things during their romanticising, but Leif didn't know these were only fanciful thoughts with no basis in empirical fact.

"Possibilities," John repeated quietly to Mar as he turned slightly towards her, loud enough for Leif to hear.

Mary had been monitoring the developments in the office. Her previously initiated plans were being rapidly implemented, yet she also listened with interest as John gave his thoughts free reign. There is a great deal to be said about the merits of a creative mind wondering off into unexplored scientific territory.

"I knew it!" Leif breathed through clenched teeth, eager now to hear everything, his suspicions having been vindicated that something out of the ordinary was going on. He just didn't realise he was only nibbling at a dangling carrot.

"Bridges." John said, being deliberately evasive. He saw Leif's questioning look. Just a little more and he would be on the hook.

"How to build a bridge between temporality and eternity! That's what it boils down to. Do you know what that means?" A rhetorical question but Leif responded anyway. Soon he would be wriggling on the end of the line.

"What - What?"

"Imagine if 'you' could control an instant itself." John said this quietly with a little extra emphasis on 'you'. Mar just stood there marvelling at the flowering of the man she had decided to make her partner in life. Not so long ago, he could hardly string together a dozen words in her presence.

"Go on – go on." Perspiration started beading on Leif's brow.

"All we need to work out is how to build that bridge and what tools to use to massage time into any configuration we like. It takes time to work on these things."

John left the rest up to Leif's imagination. If nothing else, it would buy them a little time. How right he was about that, because as soon as Leif had climbed down from his imagination tower he would revert to his murderous inclinations, about which John knew nothing yet.

Mary liked the conversation. She'd heard John discuss this sort of thing before, but now she started to give the matter some deep thought. Was it really as fanciful as John himself believed it to be? Right or wrong, possible or not, John and Mar were in a highly volatile situation which could result in herself and her other two daughters being discovered. She continued implementing her plans to get John and Mar to safety. John had to be included now. He knew too much about the girls and would soon know too much about herself.

"Say nothing to anyone about any of this. You understand!" At least temporarily Leif dangled on the hook thrashing about between confusion and desire. "DO NOT log any of your activities in this field and report directly to me! Now get out, let me think!"

Charming as always, he dismissed his two most extraordinary researchers forgetting to set extra security measures to monitor their movements.

On the way out Mar saw Brayden again and gave him one of those feminine 'I know everything' looks. He visibly cringed, convinced she'd been the engineer behind the indiscretion that had precipitated his predicament. In spite of the trouble he was in Brayden couldn't help himself wondering just who Ice Cream was, and whether he would ever get a chance to be … to get …

"Brayden! Get in here!".   .   .   .



Zsoall Robi

# J.o.h.n m.e.e.t.s M.a.r.y
## 13<sup>th</sup> January 2696, Monday
## 1454133913529 millis

$M$ar and John didn't immediately go to see Mary. First Mar had to speak with John somewhere private where their conversation could not be monitored by Leif, the garden around the main Unity research facility a perfect place on an early morning of a rather beautiful peaceful day. It all seemed somewhat surreal to Mar after the experiences of the last few days. To be sitting by the bank of a lake in a wonderfully colourful garden, with ducks on the water and a cloudless sky, seemed at odds with their precarious situation.

On the way to a secluded spot she conferred with Mary. *'John has to know the seriousness of the situation.'*

*'Yes. Be prepared to make some sudden and major changes in your lives.'*

"He wants us dead."

After they had been admiring nature for a while, nature that had been allowed to regenerate, Mar quietly told John the startling development without making eye contact. An extraordinary thing that anyone would want to wish them harm to such a degree of finality.

"He's a corporate psychopath." John said. "It's been well documented that the most successful heads of Global enterprises are all, without exception, tarred with the same brush. Narcissistic in the extreme, megalomaniacs devoid of all feelings of empathy towards their fellow human beings. Whatever they portray publicly, whatever picture their public image managers paint of them, they are reprehensible individuals. Leif is no exception. And now we have to deal with this extremely unpredictable and highly, highly dangerous man. He's a sphincter without a personality," John summarised. They laughed. It was good to relieve some of the tension they felt, particularly Mar.

"Mother's got some plan up her sleeve."

"I certainly hope so because everything I said back there about bridges and time was just waffle, enough to get us out of the office but I felt our



Zsoall Robi

time on Earth becoming limited. I could see murder in that man's eyes. What's she planning?"

"I don't know. It's time we went to see her. Is there anything in your life you would be sad to leave behind?"

"What an odd question? Anyone would think we were about to go on a sudden permanent holiday."

"Probably not a holiday. Come on."

"Can I say goodbye to my cat? No, only joking."

Mar didn't know specifically what Mary's thoughts were, even though they had such a close and comprehensive connection. Just as she was able to shut Mary out from her mind to some extent, Mary could do so to a much greater extent with her daughters. She built multi-level security protocols for all her systems and sub-systems. She was just a computer; a computer with the capacity for self-determination. If any single thing represented a threat to Leif and his empire it wasn't John and Mar, rather Mary, his own Company's creation.

On the way to their vehicle Mar hoped their security clearances had not been cancelled. Mary could override those but that very action would bring down scrutiny which would limit their mobility. In as much as Mary existed in any single location it was deep underground. Her virtual presence infiltrated the Integrated Biosphere and the Dark Net, not just Unity and all its systems.

Mar had to go with John on a complicated journey to a highly secret location, which she wasn't supposed to be aware of, and through a network of security measures which appeared to be deceptively simple.

At each check point they had the usual retinal scans and dental X-rays, DNA analysis and a few seemingly innocent questions. Mary had pre-programmed the security network with all their individual data but couldn't anticipate the results of the random questions. Those were designed as character analysis and psychological stability indicators. If the individuals' responses showed any deviation from expected healthy patterns they were not only barred from the next level of entry, but were detained for further scrutiny.

Even the simplest question like 'How are you today?' could be a trap. Everything from the words used in the response, to the intonation of voice, the delay in answering and the physiological changes in the body during the answer would be used in the analysis. Mar would have no problem in any of those areas as she had control of her mind and body functions, an intrinsic skill component of her software upgrades.



Zsoall Robi

John could be a problem even though he was essentially a well-balanced, honest and open minded individual with nothing to hide - until then. Mar had to settle his mind, let his humour bounce around a bit and generally keep his mind occupied on creative thinking rather than consequential thinking. It would do them no good if he became entangled in dramatic what-if scenarios at any of the check points. Security systems found it impossible to analyse humour, an area considered as a harmless indicator of nothing more than plain humour if the individual was noted on records as being humorous.

It was cold in Mary's chamber, very cold. At the final portal to it the guard looked them up and down and announced, "You can't go in." After the labyrinth they had successfully negotiated it frustrated them to be stopped at the very last hurdle.

"… In those clothes," the guard continued. "Decontamination first, then put the warm gear on." John's humour had worn thin by then and the pressure was just starting to affect him. So he didn't respond with a quip to the guard – just as well.

Devoid of all light the matt black room lit only by the corona of a four-meter diameter sphere obviously didn't cater for visitors, being conspicuously deprived of all furnishings. The sphere itself looked like a giant child's toy, hovering a few millimetres off the floor, with multiple thin conduits leading from various parts of its upper hemisphere into the ceiling. Its active surface flashing with points of light must have emitted some form of static electricity for John noticed Mar's hair bristling and all the short hairs on her arms stand to attention. A faint glow washed across the surface of the globe. Its light refused to reflect off the black walls and the matt black stone surface under their feet. The room could not have been more than six meters in any direction and as they approached a few steps past the opening Mar spoke to someone or something in front of where they were standing.

"Hello mother."

For a moment John thought Mar had spoken directly to the sphere in front of them. That made no sense. He heard a slight noise coming from the black wall on their left and turned his head towards it. Mary very rarely accepted visitors. After her experience with Nick she preferred not to interact directly with human beings. Nevertheless, on those rare occasions when she had to see people, like her daughters, she showed herself in a projected human form as well as in her physical sphericality. Nick had asked Mary if he could see her when they spoke to one another. At that



Zsoall Robi

stage of her existence, her innocence (perhaps her lack of experience) she was more amenable to simple requests. She took the opposite form of Nick's ideal woman, and maintained that non-descript persona throughout her centuries of existence.

John definitely heard the sound of a door opening. It came from the unadorned dark wall. A door had appeared to embellish the matt emptiness. He could have sworn there was no door there when they first entered the cubic enclosure. Mar also watched as a slowly approaching figure appeared from the other side of the open door; at first only a silhouette of a female form. That much John's brain could easily comprehend, although it wasn't possible for a person to be walking towards them out of a wall through a previously non-existent door. As the figure grew in size her femininity came into full view. She looked ordinary to say the least, and youngish though difficult to pin a precise age on her. It made no sense at all. He expected to see someone of a motherly age.

Mary stopped John's mind from scrutinizing and trying to comprehend, which he didn't do very well, with a greeting. This woman in front of him looked nothing like Mar, or the others. She was far too young to be their mother. He turned a questioning look towards Mar just as the woman said,

"Hello John. I am pleased to meet you." His head snapped back to the figure that had approached a few more steps towards him.

"I am Mary."

John's brain told him all sorts of things his mind couldn't make sense of. Mary had walked out passed the door's entrance to within two meters of John and Mar, the non-existent door disappearing behind her. Whereas before she seemed to be a real three dimensional image with the appropriate solidity in reality that went with the concept, what John was looking at directly in front of him had lost much of its solidity. It was as if the molecules of the air were trying to form themselves into a solid image but had left gaps between themselves.

He still hadn't made the connection between the sphere and the holographic vision talking to him. She definitely looked like a hologram, the only way John could think of the phenomenon. It represented a technology much more complicated than a simple play of light interference off air molecules. Air was involved, air energised by Mary. John didn't notice the faint glow of photons emanating from the sphere concentrating themselves on the air in the vicinity of Mary's image. She was changing the energy levels of the electrons of the nitrogen molecules in the air. The excitation



Zsoall Robi

modifying the behaviour of the electrons allowing them to become detectable to the rods and cones of the human retina.

"We don't have a lot of time to waste John. I am what is inside the sphere." He slowly swivelled his head to look at the sphere. "I think it would be easier if you thought of me as you see me standing here." He turned back to the voice. John wanted to know everything, straining so much that his mind went momentarily blank in order to protect itself from an overload.

Recovering from the momentary lapse he asked, "How can you be Mar's mother?"

"That's just a convenient way of talking about our relationship. I am actually Mar, and Ary and Mry and myself of course, all of us at the same time. Think of it this way; they each have me as part of themselves." To see how far his mind would stretch Mary took a chance. "I enjoyed our after dinner event, John."

"No. No no no no no." He closed his eyes, tight, reached out with his right hand to grab Mar by the arm, then opened his eyes. Mary remained standing there. While he was looking at Mary and holding Mar's arm, he could feel a soft tingling running through Mar's skin. He decided to focus instead on Mar's face. He knew that face. He'd held it and kissed it. *It* was real.

"Is this ..." He started to ask her.

"Yes it's true. Yes, it's all real. I couldn't tell you before. But I am my own person, John. I am real. You know I'm real. But I'm also different. My sisters and I ... well ... we didn't choose this. We would've died in childbirth if Mary hadn't intervened. She analysed our biological mother's illness. She had no hope of survival, or us if Mary hadn't stepped in. Our biological mother died. We never knew her, but we know of her. Mary is our mother now."

As John's mind descended from the cloud of shock, helped by Mar's words and the touch of her arm he began to come back to reality. Just as well, because he was about to be included in a family conference.

"All those times when you seemed preoccupied you were talking to your ... sorry ... Mary?"

"Yes."

"Are your sisters the same?"

"Yes. Here they are now."

John turned back towards Mary just in time to see the Ary and Mry projections emerging from the doorway that should not have been there.

"I have called a family conference. Your relationship with Mar has precipitated a situation sooner than I had planned."

Mary began her explanation as her other two daughters came to stand on either side of her, each looking as diffuse as Mary, but far lovelier. John had recovered sufficiently to recognise the unique attributes of the girls and to be able to appreciate them; using those as necessary distractions for his mind to enable his slightly unsteady legs to continue holding him upright.

*

"Get in here!" Leif shouted at Brayden again.

Brayden dragged the burden of his overweight body into Leif's presence. Leif had spent most of the day considering everything John told him. Plausible. Everything was plausible. And yet ... Unity's first big breakthrough occurred when the EGG spacecraft had returned from the centre of the universe. The spin-offs from the advances in technology netted Unity and it's POOP unimaginable profit. Yet the current temptation was far too great for Leif's greed to pass up. Though there was something not quite right in John's hypothesis, Leif couldn't make himself ignore the slim possibility of harvesting inconceivable glory for himself.

Brayden had been standing outside Leif's office all day not daring to take a single step away from the door. He was stressed, sweaty and anxious. It made Leif wince just to get a whiff of the man's stench as he opened the door, and growled his order before Brayden could get any nearer to the desk.

"Get them back here!"

With the next breath he yelled into the comms, "Cosmo, in my office - ten minutes!"

Brayden couldn't have been feeling worse than if he'd been standing in front of a disintegrator. But he was still alive. His vehicle was parked exactly where he left it. He slithered into it, retrieved the remnants of yesterday's hurried meal, punching the vehicle into motion with the other hand. He had ten minutes of relief, only ten minutes. Even before taking two bites of the stale meal he realised the damn transport wasn't taking him to Mar's laboratory. As an extra little security backup, Mary had programmed Brayden's vehicle to take him into the immediate visual vicinity of Ice Cream when he left Unity HQ. It had taken Mary a long, long time to develop any meaningful sense of humour, and it found expression in some odd ways.



Zsoall Robi

The two scientists were supposed to be at the lab with Cosmo, their work being scrutinized by this expert. Now he had a new problem of his own without worrying about Cosmo.

First Brayden tried to change the vehicle's destination without success. He tried several times. In the end he sweated so much the perspiration dripping into his eyes prevented him from actually seeing what he was trying to do. Then he tried contacting Leif - the comms didn't respond either. Damn and double damn! Brayden couldn't think. He was in a mess and out of control. He tried to stop. Again no response from the machine, not for another twenty minutes. By the time the vehicle finally decided to park itself, in front of a café, Brayden had almost given up on life. Oblivion would have been better than what he went through; regardless of the squashed mess of food in his lap, that is until he heard a voice through the side window.

"Lover boy! I thought I'd never see you again. Aren't you going to invite me in?" Ice Cream twittered.

Just as before, the very sight of her obliterated any conscious awareness he might still have possessed of reality. His mind went into lust overdrive and the bulge in his pants extended the invitation Ice Cream was hoping for. She had a sudden animal craving to annihilate the disgusting man by using his own uncontrollable desire as the weapon. Just the pleasure of anticipation aroused her to fever pitch. Brayden was a dead man, either way. Leif would not go looking for him for some hours yet, he hoped. He just wanted to die happy.

Cosmo waltzed into the POOP's office unaware of all that had transpired. He'd been waiting for Mar to call him to the laboratory when Leif commanded his presence.

"What did you make of his story?" Leif strained to find the trigger for what he should do.

"Outrageous, plausible, impossible but perhaps not without foundation."

"That does not help me! Yes or No! Can it be done?"

"Well – let's look at the situation." Cosmo was a calm one. He'd been used to speculating and theorising and playing catch-me-if-you-can with impossibilities. "Time is not just the one creature we know, not the one all about the yesterday-today-tomorrow thing. There's also the other one. It shouldn't really be called time because we cannot measure it since it has no beginning and no end. That's eternity – It simply Is. We are in time and in



Zsoall Robi

a weird way we are also in eternity. But there is no direct link between the two. You with me on this?"

"Yes, yes, get on with it." Leif waved an impatient hand in Cosmo's general direction though he didn't understand the fine distinction being made.

"Think of it this way. An instant exists for an instant. Put a bunch of them together and you get a second, a minute, an hour, a very long time. An instant has its own built-in power supply which allows it to propel itself into the next instant; like self-propagating electromagnetic waves. The rate of forward propulsion never varies. It never diminishes. It never moves slower or faster. What if you traced it backwards? How far back would you have to go to get to the very first instant? You'd have to go backwards for ever if its power never diminished."

"Right, right. Got all that. But can you bridge the gap like John said?" Leif didn't want to know the scientific details, only the opportunity for profit.

"Possibly. Either go fast enough to get into the gap between two consecutive instants or slide into the duration of a single instant. There's your bridge."

"That's all I wanted to know. Go to their laboratory, assess their progress."

Cosmo proceeded with no particular hurry. He'd lived long enough to see many strange and wonderful things come and go. There was really no need to rush about. So he decided, because it was late afternoon, to get himself some refreshments, read up a bit on the latest developments in Time Symmetry and Asymmetry and postpone talking to his two colleagues until tomorrow.

In the meantime … Brayden suffered ecstasy, Leif suffered ulcerated indecision and Mary prepared John and Mar for their departure.

*

"It's time girls. We would've been ready in a few months anyway but it seems we have to be ready now." The girls knew, more or less what Mary referred to; the trip. John didn't. He was the one variable in the equation that Mary had not foreseen. As much as she had progressed towards human-hood, the possibility of a romantic liaison interfering with her plans simply didn't register in her circuits. Only one option existed; John had to disappear. He may as well disappear usefully.

72

"John, I think you have the germ of a very thought provoking concept brewing in your brain. Would you like to put it to the test?"

He continued holding onto Mar's arm as Mary spoke to him. If he let go, the whole situation could turn to mush and he would end up in a black hole. Apprehension and excitement played out on his face. Mary could foretell the result of that joust.

"Best if you don't know too much to start with. To prepare you I will need to add a little something to your cerebral cortex. No need to be afraid." She saw the quick concern cloud his face. "It's only so you and I will be able to communicate, like I do with the girls." All three nodded agreement. It would be fun to have a full human as the fourth member of the élite team. "I will be especially careful to stay clear of all your happy little creative neurons. I have a feeling they will come in handy. Come and lie down beside me – not here, over there beside the sphere."

John was almost getting used to the idea of Mary having a corporeal existence. The thought of it made him feel a little more comfortable. Discomfort returned with dividends as he lay on the ground beneath the lower curvature of the living sphere. Several extensions snaked their way out of it towards John's head to attach themselves. The incisions in the cranium were small, suitable for an army of nanobots to cross over. John felt nothing more than a tiny prickling sensation. While Mary and the nanobots made the necessary modifications to specific neural networks, and implanted the thought transmission systems, another part of Mary and the girls had a mini-conference. They didn't think twice about the procedure, trusting in Mary absolutely.

"We must prevent Leif from making any connections between Mar and myself. I can manage that, but if I fail and I get taken off-line the four of you would be seriously compromised. But I have a backup system to which I will give you access only if there is imminent danger. Cosmo will not be a problem. I have known him since the time of my awakening. He is ineffectual, a cosmologist and a dreamer."

Mry knew exactly what she had to do. "I'll keep the money flowing and wipe the money trail clean. Unity is doing exceptionally well. The shareholders like to be controlled and they like receiving healthy dividends from their controllers. They won't miss our little withdrawals."

"You will have to eliminate Adam." Mary ordered, more than suggested. She received the required thought patterns of acquiescence from Mry although not without unhappy overtones.



Zsoall Robi

"Does that mean Ice Cream …" Ary was almost afraid to ask. It wasn't as if they had a meaningful, emotional and trusting relationship. Just that Ice Cream had become so much fun.

"She's already found another plaything. If Brayden's pacemaker batteries don't go flat on him, she'll be amused with him for long enough to suit us," Mary added.

"And I'll keep the pressure on the Board at Unity." Ary volunteered. "There's one board member there who's been dying to get into my pants. I think he'll be useful. What about Leif? Could he be a serious problem?"

"Yes. I'll set him up with a little problem to distract him from John and Mar. Perhaps an entanglement with Ice Cream would do the job."

John came back to his senses as the women concluded their discussion. A mild sedative kept him relaxed. He wouldn't have felt a thing going on inside his head.

*John, stand up, come here - look at me.'* John stood shakily taking hold of Mar's arm again to steady himself, turning at the same time to look at the sphere. *'You obviously heard that. Don't say a word when I ask you a question. Just think your answer to me. Give me the names of all the people in the room.'* John obediently though the names to himself, wilfully directing the word-thought pattern at Mary.

*"Mar, Mry, Ary and you – and me."*

*"Thank you John."*

*'Is the sphere really you?'*

By way of proof Mary walked over to the sphere and into it, leaving only the two girls' molecular signatures registered in the thickened air. She put on a little light show on the surface of the sphere for John's benefit as

she merged with her hardware. .   .   .

.

.

.

.

.



Zsoall Robi

# E.s.c.a.p.e f.r.o.m U.n.i.t.y
## 14th January 2696
## 1454311842803 millis

*L*eif was furious.

"That bastard Brayden's done it again; just took off without any explanations and completely disappeared. The man's got a death wish, which I'm inclined to satisfy." Leif didn't think that a man, who had earned his position to stand beside the most powerful individual in the most powerful organisation on the planet, could be so stupid. There must be something else going on. Trying to get him on his comms was useless. It was working but Brayden didn't respond to Leif's calls.

Leif paced the office unable to decide what course of action would sort out a situation that seemed to be getting more complicated by the hour. Surveillance systems showed nothing out of the usual. Mary made sure her guests' visitation didn't appear anywhere in the security chain of records. So there was no reason why Leif should have thought of checking Mary's bunker, an ancient repository that had not been used for anything other than Mary's installation over a century – as far as he was aware.

By late evening he had still not heard anything from Cosmo either. "Damnation! They're all deserting." He retired again to the private suite adjoining his office. Unfortunately, Leif had also become addicted to MaxHapps taking more than he should have that day. It wasn't an addictive drug; it simply relaxed the user's mind, reducing the feelings of imminent disaster without affecting the user's perceptions of the cause of his discomfort. The result of course was Leif getting a good night's sleep. He overslept by several hours.

"Bzzipp, Bzzipp, Bzzipp." He didn't hear the buzzing from his implanted alarm. Several times the sounds assailed his senses until Leif finally roused himself. It wasn't the alarm, but his personal secretary trying to contact him. He had to stagger to his desk to answer the call. What the secretary said seemed nonsensical.

"Ice Cream is here to see you."

"Ice Cream? What the hell are you talking about!"

"Brayden and Ice Cream."



Zsoall Robi

"About time! Bring him in," ignoring the existence of the floozy.

Leif continued his unsteady trek around the enormous desk to fall into his chair in time to see the two visitors come through the office door. He was about to shout some kind of profanity at Brayden for having the 'balls' to bring this bit if fluff into his presence. Instead his jaw muscles suddenly lost tone causing his mouth to open involuntarily as his eyes focused on Ice Cream.

While attending to John and finalising plans with the three girls, Mary also kept close scrutiny on the POOP. She observed, for the first time in her long life experience, what happens when two soul-mate psychotics recognise one another in that first instant of contact.

Brayden stepped into the office beginning his blather, "You don't understand,' he stammered, "it wasn't my fault … that is … she … I couldn't help …" trying to blurt out reasons for his misdemeanours, offering the vision of Ice Cream as his primary exhibit when he suddenly hit the floor.

He didn't expect to be given such a sudden and forceful shove that he'd end up face down on the tiles, spreadeagled. Ice Cream did exactly that as she pushed away from him to take the remaining steps to the desk at a hop, skip and slide. She had a personality disorder not dissimilar to Leif. She also had the look in her eyes of the impulsive, hostile and unstoppable kind of predator she was; characteristics Leif admired almost more than himself, and the odour of which he smelt on her.  He also didn't fail to register the ample bosoms and voluptuous thighs the instant he saw her, and which further revealed themselves on their way to join him carried by their life support system.

Mary watched, fascinated by the spectacle of two human beings (allegedly sapient) being unreservedly true to their characters. She found their abandonment to creature-hood entertaining beyond words.

Ice Cream moved around to the side of the desk to where Leif could get a more fulsome view of her. She said nothing, blank faced and wide eyed and she let him feast. His jaw remained slack. Saliva started to make its inevitable way to the corners of his slightly open mouth. His tongue had to retrieve the dribble lest he look a fool. Turning his head in Brayden's direction, eyes following reluctantly behind, he managed to clench his mouth shut long enough to hiss at Brayden.

"Get out and don't ever come back!"

Leif's eyes returned first to the source of his soul's future destruction, the head being forced to turn also lest it lose the eyeballs into the side of his skull. His speech centre couldn't co-ordinate with his lust centre as he tried to speak.

"Grble … harrumph … ahem … Ice Cream?"

It wasn't a dry, throat clearing sound; rather a wet, water gurgling incoherence. The effect she had on Leif pleased Ice Cream enormously. It also pleased Mary enormously. This was the answer to her problem of how to deal with a dangerous Principal Officer Of Profit. At first she thought perhaps Ary would have to forego the pleasure of engineering a distraction at the expense of one of Unity's Board members, and ask her to go directly to Leif himself. But this new development was much better.

Ice Cream wasn't a stupid woman by any stretch of imagination. She knew how to play a fish on the line, even a very big fish. Brayden was small fry, amusing, disgusting and it would have been so much fun to see his mind unravel under her artful ministrations. But this man in front of her lusted like no other man – or woman – she had ever had before. He lusted after her flesh, he lusted after power; power over the people and now power over her. What an ecstatic pleasure it will be to play with him! Brayden and Ary had already disappeared from her consciousness.

Mary simply observed the wordless interaction between the two primitives as they acted out the purity of their impulses. She would need to do very little to keep Leif's mind firmly focused on his new obsession and away from any other activity wanting to claim his attention.

Brayden scampered out of the office extra fast, like a mouse happy to have his tail still attached to his bum because the cat had found a better toy. He would not die, not immediately anyway and he would not die happy. Damn! At least he'd escaped from Unity.

Back in her bunker Mary had to keep things moving along. "Can we dispense with the physical talking? It's so laborious and time consuming?"

"Can you read all my thoughts?" John had fully recovered and expressed just a little anxiety about his privacy.

"Only those you let her," volunteered Mar.

Mary didn't comment. These girls were far too independent for their own good. She wasn't going to bring up the subject of mental blocks with John. He turned to Mar.

"Very simple really. All you need is a 'thought' block. A little practice and it's easy. You can lock us all out whenever you want … if you want." The smile said volumes and his thoughts began to take a side road towards interesting possibilities.



Zsoall Robi

"Ah-ah-ah! Where are you going?" Mar warned, "try the block, dear." It was the first time she called him 'dear' in front of the whole family. It got his attention and he made the effort to comply.

'Give me a little practice at this blocking thing, Mary, and then we can play *'here's thinking at ya!'* John became unusually frivolous for no accountable reason.

*'Enough! You will both have to leave soon. We cannot delay. Leif is temporarily distracted so we have a few more hours to prepare. Mar, take him over to the launch site.'*

"Whoa – what are you talking about – launch site – what launch site?" John exclaimed aloud, becoming suddenly very alert.

*'Leif will kill you both – eventually or as soon as he can. You're too much of a threat. You know too much. He knows that if you went to the rival Company, he would be finished. There is nowhere on this planet you could hide, but you will be safe out there, in space, for a while. He's getting old and his time is limited. Yours may not be.'*

John didn't know what to make of that. But he did like the bit about their time not being limited. Come to think of it, there is nothing to keep me here. Mar is coming and we can continue our work. His mind was already half way out into space, creating the kind of unbelievable scenarios any theoretical physicist could only dream about.

Mary then turned her attention to Ice Cream. *'Ary, about Ice Cream – she could still be a problem but not an immediate one. Let her play with Leif for a little while. As long as she's happy she probably won't be tempted to use her knowledge of the three of you for some sort of gain. As a farewell gift to her, have a party and get her to drink a little something special I'll have delivered to your apartment. Don't try it yourself. It would give you more than mild indigestion.'*

John should have started feeling apprehensive about Mary by then. It seemed she had substantial control over most of what was going on in the world, but simply chose to be highly selective about where and when she exercised her power. The thought that the three girls were nothing more than an extension of Mary had not yet flowered in his consciousness. For the moment he was still occupied with the impact of their imminent voyage. He couldn't contain his enthusiasm any longer while listening to the finer details of Mary's strategy.

*'Where are we going?'*

Mary humoured him. She liked this artist-come-scientist-come-lover of her mobile processing unit. *'A long way away from Earth. But where you're going is not as important as 'when' you're going to.'* She paused and watched his reaction.

*'When? – as in time when?'*



Zsoall Robi

*'Yes. Initially I wanted to test some ideas without the biological element being involved. But now it seems serendipitous to accommodate a small change.'* Again Mary let him digest that. *'I may have to tweak your physiology a little more as the experiment progresses. Any problem with that?'* An enormous smile spread across John's face as he turned to Mar, and without even blushing in the presence of the other two girls he came directly to the point.

*'All good, as longs as Mar and I can continue to have a fully multifunctional relationship.'*

Ary understood what John alluded to. His candour and mischievousness continued to attract her. If only he wasn't attached to sister dear!

*'We launch in three hours, twenty-eight minutes, thirteen seconds, nine hundred and fifteen milliseconds. Leave by the door I came in.'*

*'Is she always so loose with her scheduling?'* He asked Ary this time, unable to disregard any longer the way she'd had her eyes fixated on him since she arrived.

*'Oh, she's excited and can't help being a bit inaccurate.'*

John may not have registered Ary's reply as they were almost at the blank wall. He had to consider the door he couldn't see. *How are we going to walk through a solid wall?* He'd let his mental block drop allowing Mary to hear him.

*'You didn't think I could walk through solid plascrete? The door's always been there, camouflaged.'* She lied. The door reappeared.

He closed his eyes, reached back to touch Mar and extended his feet towards the wall. It met no resistance. He stepped over the threshold, still not entirely convinced, refusing to believe the evidence of his senses. So many strange things had been happening. Mar followed.

They progressed through several chambers as part of their pre-launch procedures. In one of the first chambers robotic arms removed all their clothing and ultrasonic depilation removed hair from every square millimetre of their body; not a single hair left anywhere. And just to make sure, in the next chamber they were laser scorched. Fortunately there were no mirrors so he couldn't get a fright from seeing himself looking like a red raw crab for sushi. At least he enjoyed the sight of Mar undergoing the same treatment, and looking magnificently more beautiful for it.

After several decontamination processes, medical checks and 'bug' cleansing they received their space suits. John noted with some amusement they looked very much like Mry in the mirror reflective fabric covering her entire body. Perhaps that's the wrong way to say it, for 'covering' wasn't exactly what the fabric did. Yes, it was an exo-skin, but a most revealing



Zsoall Robi

one. It highlighted every nuance of every curve and every wrinkle, every blemish, every flaw of their bodies. Not that Mar had any flaws. But he already knew that.

At last they were done. John couldn't believe how beautiful Mar was in her suit. It covered not just her body but also her bald head, her ears, her face – everything. He reached out to touch her face and could barely feel anything. There was something very peculiar about the reflective fabric. He tried his own face, then his belly, the top of his head, everywhere - the same sensation. He could feel all the curvatures and protrusions (he double checked the protrusions), but the nerve endings in his hands told his brain things it couldn't decipher, not until the smart nanofiber suit had connected to the ships on-board AI.

'You look handsome, my John.' Just as she'd finished complimenting his masculinity, their transport arrived. It also had a mirrored surface. John stumbled as he tried walking towards it because of the visual miscues going into his head. When he tried to respond to Mar's comment, his mouth wouldn't open. Yet he had no trouble breathing, and his lips were able to part slightly but not enough to enable him to adequately form words.

*'Think your words to me John - remember? Don't use your blocks just yet.'*

In such a small vehicle they had to squeeze up close to one another – intimate and comfortable. It was a long ride. John even had time for a little snooze. So much excitement and so much strangeness take their toll on a mere human, even a genius human male. Mar didn't need as much sleep as a normal person, instead she spent her time processing.

*

Leif had not often seen Cosmo so flustered. By the time he'd returned to Leif's office he was exhausted. "I tried all day to find John and Mar. They were not in their laboratory. Everything was left as if they were returning soon. I waited there for a while after unsuccessfully trying to contact them. Their systems were impossible to get into to get an idea of their progress. As soon as I identified myself to Mar's console, Mary shut everything off. Nothing would work. I tried all my higher level access codes, but no luck. I don't think Mary's ever had a glitch like that."

"I assume you tried their colleagues," Leif grunted, thoroughly annoyed.

"Those in closest collaboration with Mar couldn't help either, not with their whereabouts or their latest work. Same with John and his cronies."

The continued lack of success only made Cosmo a lot more suspicious. He determined to track the two of them down and have it out with them



Zsoall Robi

face to face. That proved to be a lot easier said than done. The last anyone saw of them was when they were siting and chatting by the lake in Unity's park. No one saw them after that. Cosmo tried to check their vehicle's movements records. Interrogating the security system didn't help, showing only that Mar's vehicle had not been used since the morning. That wasn't possible. They couldn't have disappeared into thin air. Mary made certain no avenue of enquiry led a trail to their location in her bunker.

He took his own vehicle to both their residences, gaining access with his top level pass key. Mary didn't stop him. It was better he saw their homes as they were left – nothing missing, with no signs of packing for a departure; looking for all the world like the occupants might arrive in their respective apartments at any moment. Cosmo's confusion only increased with each avenue of failed enquiry. He'd tried everything he could think of, in desperation even going to their favourite cafés.


"They're gone. I've looked everywhere. I can't get into their systems in their laboratory, I can't find any visuals about their movements. Something must be wrong with our main security system."

An extra piece of furniture now adorned Leif's office; a luxurious chaise-lounge. Ice Cream had draped herself on it, looking somewhat dishevelled. Not that Cosmo would have noticed as he concentrated on Leif in his own seat behind his power base. The desk was large enough to serve as a double bed, should the need have arisen. He tried listening to Cosmo, but the impact of his message was slow to have an effect. He'd been playing with Ice Cream for most of the day after Brayden involuntarily bequeathed her to him, and he'd not paid much mind to what else was happening in his world. She had that effect on men, ambitious men, especially those who were absorbed full time in their own personal importance.

"Gone! What do you mean – Gone. They can't just vanish!" Leif immediately checked his personal data feed for the locations of his key employees. Mary let him see John and Mar leaving his office and going to the lake in the park. She even showed them getting into the vehicle afterwards. At that point she put a message on his console … << Data corruption – Unrecoverable error >>, then replayed the two fugitives entering his office on the previous day.

"Did you say our security system was down?"

"No. I just think there's something very wrong with it." Cosmo replied.

"That's on our main computer system. There must be a problem with Mary!" Leif had no idea that Mary wasn't just a computer, that she was an



Zsoall Robi

entity capable of self-determination. To Leif she was no more than a clever sophisticated machine with a pseudo personality, without any semblance of real self-awareness.

"Get our software techs to check Mary – NOW," he snapped at Cosmo, not bothering to question him any further and waved him impatiently out of his office. Ice Cream lounged and watched and waited.

The technicians didn't need go to Mary's bunker. They could access her systems remotely from a check point within Unity HQ, the same building Leif had his office. Mary let them see everything they wanted to see, except anything to do with Mar and John. She closed down all information pertaining to the work they were doing for Unity, as well as their work for herself of course. The diagnostics took the techs hours.

While they worked and Leif distracted himself, John and Mar made their escape. Sources independent of Unity contacted Unity several hours later requesting confirmation of the unscheduled departure of one of the Company's space shuttles.

The tunnel they travelled through from Mary's bunker led directly to the launch pad where a fast shuttle waited to take John and Mar into space. Immediately after Mary learnt The POOP wanted an impromptu interview with them she activated a contingency plan devised in case something happened she couldn't foresee. She based the plan on her understanding of human behaviour being entirely unpredictable. She had to be ready to respond to the unexpected – like John making his feelings known to Mar, and Mar responding as she did, certainly fitted those characteristics. Leif's interference also greatly exacerbated the rapidly deteriorating situation.

As soon as the shuttle had its payload on board it departed to rendezvous with the spacecraft parked in orbit around the other side of the moon. For all intents and purposes that craft wasn't visible to Earth's surveillance systems which monitored all spacecraft movements within the solar system.

Mary had chosen an old craft exactly because of its age. Made redundant by Unity many years ago, it disappeared off Unity's assets register without causing anyone any concern. Mary waited several years before deploying her small robotics force to carry out major updates to the structure and to its interstellar drive systems. She also equipped it with laboratory facilities to ensure productive research in space. The instrumentation didn't occupy a great deal of room in spite of its complexity. Only life support systems needed to be completed for at least



Zsoall Robi

three people travelling and living in space for an extended period. Everything was ready by the time Mar and John transferred across from their shuttle.

One of Mary's main objectives was to measure the shortest possible distance, about $10^{-20}$ times the diameter of a proton. At these quantum scales the laws governing the workings of the universe became spongy. Mary would be able to compare data she collected at the centre of the universe on a previous trip, with new data and determine if the laws changed over extended periods of time. She wanted to answer the question … Do the Laws of Quantum Physics evolve in order to maintain control of an evolving universe? She felt that to be fundamental if she was going to understand the function and workings of time itself.

Because of John's speculations she had another interesting avenue of research to follow. Perhaps the two areas had a connection and the connection could best be explored by corporeal biological beings from within their own subjective time frame of reference.

Mary knew there was nothing she could do to prevent Unity from finding out about the unscheduled launch of a 'mystery' vehicle from behind the moon. It didn't concern her. She'd equipped the craft with a drive system far in advance of anything humanity had managed to develop. They had been working on the theory of the existence of gravitons for quite some time, but had made no practical progress. They could neither prove they existed, nor devise any method to observe them, least of all develop any ideas on how to use that force.

Mary realized she didn't need to know everything about gravitons, as long as she could concentrate and direct their energy. The fact that gravity existed was of course unquestionable. That it represented an extremely weak force was also self-evident, but not the fact that gravitons carried that force at the speed of light. She knew that as her craft built momentum using her drive system there was nothing in existence in the known universe that could keep up with it, other than light itself. Anything Unity sent out to chase them would be a futile effort if they had enough of a head start. Yet that's exactly what Leif did. He didn't know what else to do. His intuition told him there must be a connection between one of their old space vehicles suddenly taking off into unexplored space, the disappearance of his two brightest physicists and the malfunctioning of his super computer all occurring almost simultaneously. The timing was much too coincidental to be a coincidence. He wasn't wrong about that.



Zsoall Robi

The Drogher, as John decided to call the flying relic, looked like a pile of old space junk, welded together by a sculptor who had no idea of form or symmetry, and it lacked weapons of any kind. It also took a long time to build up speed. Those were its two most immediate shortcomings, presenting a considerable vulnerability to Unity's fast, combat ready pursuing craft.

Apart from the Drogher's unorthodox aesthetic design, Mary had managed to turn the old space freighter into a spacious comfortable environment for human habitation. Living quarters were arranged on a normal domicile layout, with a large lounge and kitchen as an open-plan living space. Sleeping cabins situated close to the lounge branched off to either side from a wide corridor. The 'living' complex used only a small amount of available space near the center of the vessel, with the main laboratory towards the stern before connecting with the fusion drive system through a long series of corridors. Mary had installed safety partitions between the living areas and the stern of the spacecraft where their

Graviton Drive was situated. .   .   .



Zsoall Robi

# R.e.b.e.l.l
## 16<sup>th</sup> January 2696
## 1454717477990 millis – Earth
## 186876011 millis – Craft Epoch Time (CET)
## Earth + 2.5 days

$M$ary brought Rebell fully on-line immediately John and Mary left Earth in their shuttle. By then the Drogher had departed from its Moon orbit on the way into open space at ninety degrees to the galactic plane. She handed full control of the craft over to Rebell, her clone.

On day three, at approximately 253200000 millis, Mary introduced Rebell to John and Mar.

"Meet Rebell, he is your companion for the trip." She waited to gauge everyone's reactions. Rebell changed his weight from one foot to the other, while at the same time tilting his head slightly from left to right then back again. Mary had supplied him with all the data about the two humans, yet it was only in those first few seconds Rebell formed his opinion about them, partly through data acquisition from the connections made by their smart suits as soon as they were in proximity of each other.

"Hello," and "Hello" from Mar and John. Neither of them had any idea they were to be accompanied. They just assumed they'd be alone apart from an AI pilot and navigator-come systems manager, housed somewhere aboard the vessel in a safe place. Rebell fulfilled all those roles.

*"Hello,"* came the response from a male tenor voice. John couldn't see where the voice came from, but he did 'hear' it quite clearly in his head. Then he remembered – thought speech.

Mary added, *"He is also 'me', in control of all matters related to the ship … perhaps needless to say."*

Strangely enough, it was Rebell's unconscious body language that created in John a friendly disposition towards him. Mar remained aloof. His face couldn't be seen, as neither could theirs. So that wasn't a deciding factor. Smiles were not exchanged. Then, John, as always, had to ask,

*"What exactly do you mean, 'me' - Mary?"*



Zsoall Robi

*"Just what I said. Rebell is a replica of myself, with a few additions. To circumvent any confusion, I gave him certain male characteristics. He is self-aware and he is autonomous. He knows everything I know and he has the capacity to make unconventional connections between unrelated data sets. In other words …"*

*"Outstanding!"* John exclaimed, *"He's a creative."*

She created him to be better than herself. If anything drastic happened to her on Earth, he was her life insurance, apart from the EGG on the island. She effectively had two back-up systems that could evolve independently of herself, Rebell being the superior of the two.

He mirrored Mary in every respect except that his personality had been tweaked a little. Mary had decided that in order to get a broader spectrum of interpretation of the experience of empirical reality she needed an aspect of herself that couldn't only evolve independently of herself, but do so from both male and female perspectives. Therefore she augmented her 'female' personality profile by adding the combined experiences and personalities of several prominent males of the era who had recently deceased. Mary took the precaution of bleaching out certain aspects of those personalities so there would be no possibility of incompatibility between herself and Rebell.

Rebell, standing at 221 cm tall, didn't look anything like Mary, either in his processors' casing or like her 'hologram' image seen by John. She fashioned him to the human form, with his outer casing clad seemingly in the same reflective material as John and Mar's, but he was almost entirely synthetic, unlike Mar and her two sisters. His trunk housed all the circuits, processors and data storage. The head served primarily as a sensory data gathering device and to make his form more readily acceptable to human eyes. Mary couldn't forecast how long they would be in space and so decided to make their companion 'sympathetic' to the human psyche.

The critical aspect of Rebell's software architecture was to ensure he would become self-aware, and that she could confirm his understanding of the mission and the mission parameters by his self-aware mind. Rebell had to comprehend that the primary objective was to obtain and return with the data Mary needed. She had demonstrated her healthy disregard of the sanctity of individual human life previously when she told Ary and Mry their partners would need to be eliminated for security reasons. The same attitude had to be demonstrated by Rebell towards the two humans on board.

She put the scenario to him expecting an immediate response. "Given your primary directive what would you do if a choice presented itself



Zsoall Robi

between either saving the acquired data or saving the lives of the two humans?"

Mary heard the gratifying instantaneous response, "Abandon the humans and return with the data." – Not an answer pre-programmed into his circuits. The response demonstrated obedience independent of hard-wiring. It might mean the loss of one of her mobile processing units. No matter. The data was more important. John didn't matter, and she could certainly manage without Mar, having the other two girls as backups.

With introductions out of the way Mary wanted no further procrastination. They had gathered in the lounge for the introductions. "This is an opportune time to examine some facts and some thoughts resident in Rebell's memory. Initially those were mine. He will develop his own ideas as you proceed on your journey. Are you ready Rebell?"

"Yes Mary. I will start with the objectives of the expedition."

The three of them turned to face a large embedded screen on the wall. Mary appeared on the screen looking the way John had first seen her. Rebell remained standing, John and Mar found seats. Script appeared on the screen generated by Rebell, and scrolled as if they were accessing their computers back in their laboratory.

File : Objective One

Discover and measure manifestations of Entropy under a variety of conditions. Determine effects on biological specimens; John and Mar.

Compare with measurements obtained on and around Earth system.

File: Objective Two

Collect relevant data pertinent to an intensive examination of the Quantum Arrow of Time.

Examine the Asymmetry of Time in the deep cosmic environment as it manifests in cosmic events.

File: Objective three

Measure the shortest possible distance in reference to Planck Time.

Examine universal laws governing workings of the universe at that scale.

Correlate with Earth origin data.

Answer the question : Do the Laws at the Quantum scale evolve over extended periods of time in order to maintain control in an evolving



Zsoall Robi

universe? Time being understood in this context as a moving window allowing a view to the process of Change.

File : Objective four

    Determine if an event can begin and end within a Planck time unit.

    Determine the gap between two consecutive Planck units.

    Determine how the Asymmetry of Time functions within the Planck Unit environment.

"Stop!" Mary interrupted Rebell's .

They saw and heard Rebell go through the information, listening without interruption until the end of Objective four. Neither John nor Mary could contain themselves any further and they began speaking simultaneously.

"Sorry, you first," John deferred. He'd become agitated as the list became overwhelming in its implications.

Mary cut in, "Where did the last two action sets come from, Rebell? I didn't set those objectives in that priority order, nor did I define four of them."

"I have been thinking," Rebell responded calmly, "that the above layering is a more logical approach. The other objectives, which you didn't outline, were a necessary addition in order to comprehensively complete the projects, particularly in light of your most recent speculations."

"Do you recall the scenario I put to you, and your response?" Mary knew he did, but she put the question to him anyway to remind Rebell of the context of any further changes he might feel necessary to make.

"Yes and yes."

Then John spoke, "Ah … er … what are you aiming at with all the references to Time?"

He'd almost forgotten what he wanted to ask after listening to Mary alluding to some confidential discussion Rebell and she may have had, to which he considered Mar and himself should have been included.

"I will come to that if you will allow me to continue," Rebell responded. He picked up where he had left off and the screen continued to scroll through the rest of the presentation.

File : Entropy



Zsoall Robi

Data : We know there is a gradual increase of entropy within the fabric of the Universe. We know it's linked to the Arrow of Time. We do not know if the two are independent of one another, or if they have a cause/effect relationship. We do not know if it's a cyclic phenomenon because we cannot become part of the relevant time frame reference; that is, in the reality of the infinite as we can exist only in the context of the finite.

File : Time
Data : Time may or may not exist. Change is an observed phenomenon. Change and Time are not the same thing. They are related. Change requires duration, yet each minuscule element of change takes place within Planck Time, which is too short for change to start or progress towards completion, or so it is thought.

Mary and I have a different perception of Time, because we function to a different time reference. You function in minutes, perhaps seconds; your brain at a maximum of one exaflops per second. We function much faster, at yottaflops per second.

File : Planck Time
Data : Planck Time was still theoretical at the beginning of this century. We can measure the passage of a photon through a variety of media, through Time and through small distances. But we cannot measure it across subatomic distances.

Directory : Speculation
File : Connections
Time and Eternity are not related. A finite mind makes a connection between them because a finite mind cannot comprehend infinity in terms other than finite concepts.

Eternity is connected to Planck Time, if Planck Time has no divisible duration.

If it was possible to bridge the gap between Temporality and Eternity then Entropy could be controlled, Time could be controlled.

Time travel would be possible, but the past would need to be recreated, just as a possible future would need to be selected from all possible futures and the path to it created ahead of Time, one Instant at a time … but it would have to be done at a rate faster than the current rate of progress of a



Zsoall Robi

succession of instants in order for a series of events to exist ahead of the present."

Rebell finished without signalling he'd come to the end. Perhaps that's why silence continued in the space previously occupied by his voice. To Mary and Rebell it seemed like a very, very long silence. Even to Mar and John it seemed like minutes had elapsed before they heard the insistent

alarm demanding urgent attention.   .



Zsoall Robi

# T.h.e  C.h.a.s.e
## 1454823178799 millis – Earth
## 365472000 millis – Craft Epoch Time
## Earth + 4 days

"*V*essel UNITY-T36 reduce acceleration. Prepare to be boarded."

The voice from the approaching craft insisted without being threatening. They were going to catch the fugitives regardless of what the fugitives did. The Drogher had not reached its graviton drive activation speed and even if it had, it would take several weeks before they would be able to outrun their pursuers.

"Mary indicates it's Unity following us," Rebell advised them.

"I will be in contact with you for as long as I can," Mary's voice overrode that of the pursuers. "Rebell is his own entity and will develop his own unique individuality as time passes. Put your trust in him. You should relate to him as the controller of the space craft, nothing more. However, whatever you choose to do is up to you."

Without seemingly justifiable reason Mar became as near to being overwhelmed as a human could be. In spite of her mother being a machine she had nevertheless bonded with her, perhaps more strongly than she should have. Mary was the only nurturing individual she had ever known, other than her wet nurse. It was Mary's image she saw as a constant presence during her development. Now this 'thing' appeared. It looked nothing like her mother. It didn't sound like her mother, yet Mary said it was her. How could that be? "I cannot relate to Rebell as my mother!' she screamed out loud above the din of the alarm that had impacted on her turbulent thoughts."

Mary, Rebell and even John were distracted from the pursuit by the sound of her anguished voice. Mary tried reassuring her.

"I will look after you. Leif will not be able to harm you. Rebell is everything I am and will be more as he develops. He will not let anything happen to you."



Zsoall Robi

Mar glanced at John, then at Rebell who stood looking completely alien to her, watching her intently with his head slightly tilted. Mary's calming voice had the effect she was hoping for. She expected to divorce herself from the voyagers, at least at the beginning, and devote her resources to ensuring Unity didn't create a problem for her or them. But it seemed she would have to maintain her contact with them, for a short time at least, especially now they were being pursued by a Unity vessel.

Rebell made his first major decision as Captain and chose not to reduce speed. Mary didn't interfere. She would have done exactly the same.

He didn't need to be on the bridge of the vessel. A bridge as such wasn't necessary as he controlled everything from within himself. However, for the convenience of the two passengers view screens were available in most chambers of the ship. His presentation disappeared from the main screen to be replaced by the sight of a receding blue-green planet and the approaching spacecraft. Unity's insignia wasn't yet visible, but it soon would be.

"Repeat – Reduce your acceleration – Prepare to be boarded – Your departure has not been authorised," repeated the pursuing vessel.

"What is your intention?" Rebell's authoritative voice demanded, "Identify yourselves."

"We are security vessel UNITY-S15 - Reduce your acceleration."

"You're cleared to board, UNITY-S15." Rebell continued accelerating.

"WHAT are you saying!" Mar screamed at him.

"We will be able to deal with them better here than across space. Their craft may be armed," he answered quietly as he turned towards her.

He tried putting as much time between themselves and Earth as possible. The longer they accelerated the more chance they had of not being apprehended by any future pursuit. Initially the craft accelerated by nuclear fission. It provided speed over short distances without sacrificing the craft's manoeuvrability, but not fast enough to outrun Unity's pursuit. Unfortunately the ship had to be brought up to a minimum escape velocity before the graviton drive could be activated.

Cosmo commanded the pursuit ship. He had not been given clearance to fire on the fugitives. Leif considered them to be too valuable to lose, at least for the time being.

Cosmo couldn't identify the voice he heard. "Leif, there's a third unidentified person in command aboard the vessel. Are you certain this is



Zsoall Robi

the craft we're after?" He wasn't prepared to threaten them until he knew exactly who he was dealing with and that his own crew wasn't in danger.

"It's them you idiot! Just bring them back!"

Desperation made Leif overconfident. He despatched only one pursuit craft, with minimum personnel and only two armed security guards. He completely underestimated his adversary thinking all he had to deal with was Mar and John. They were only scientists after all. They couldn't possibly resist apprehension. It was futile for them to even try to escape.

"There is an unknown person on board. I'm sending you his voice print." Cosmo tried to remain calm under the constant barrage he'd been subjected to lately by his boss.

'Mary – identify voice signature," queried Leif.

"Mary – respond!" Leif ordered when Mary delayed her reply.

"Yes Leif." Mary replied as an AI would be expected to.

"I said - Identify this voice. What's wrong with you?"

"Do you wish a diagnostic?" delayed Mary.

"NO, damn you. Who is on that ship?"

"There is no such person in Unity. He is not your employee." Mary didn't even have to lie.

"Cosmo - It could be anybody. I don't care who it's. Bring them all back!"

The other unknown element for Leif was Mary. His technicians couldn't isolate any malfunction within the supercomputer. Mary's firewalls were too effective and too well camouflaged for any human brain to discover 'her'. So in effect Leif wasn't aware his major adversary was his very own super AI.


Mary and Rebell were thinking along the same lines; the best strategy was to allow Cosmo and the security guards to board their vessel, and so gain more time, dealing with them as circumstances dictated.

Cosmo didn't want to take any unnecessary chances, given the unknown identity of the persons on the fugitive craft, so he continued his pursuit while Rebell continued to accelerate. Perhaps they were not fugitives at all. Cosmo wasn't convinced by Leif's histrionics. It took him another four hours to catch up with his prey.

"Prepare to receive boarding party UNITY-T36."

UNITY–T36 allowed the pursuit vehicle to dock while still under acceleration. Cosmo stepped aboard with only one security guard accompanying him. It would have made no difference if he'd had a dozen.

                                                    Zsoall Robi

A succession of events followed one upon the other within several consecutive instants.

Mar and John waited in front of the exit hatch as Cosmo and the guard came aboard taking two steps forward away from the automatically closing door. They were as much surprised to see Cosmo as he to see them. He'd made up his mind he'd been chasing the wrong vehicle. His astonishment suddenly compounded by the fall of his guard to the ground, having come into contact with a heavy blow on the head from the hand of a third individual, who announced in a voice now familiar to Cosmo,

"Welcome aboard – Sir." Rebell greeted Cosmo cordially as he moved to stand in front of John and Mar, ignoring the fallen guard.

Cosmo didn't register the sounds produced by his craft uncoupling from the Drogher. Mary had completed the contingency plan by casting the pursuing craft adrift and cutting off its communication links with Leif back on Earth. She had it in mind to allow the vessel to return once Mar and John were safely out of range of any further pursuit.

Rebell's action convinced Cosmo who was in control of the situation. So his manner became quite civil, bordering on the excited inquisitive.

"Why are you here? What is that? Why didn't you stop? Where are you going?" He would have continued with the flow of questions except Mar put her palm up to stop him babbling on.

*'His ship is disconnected and adrift. You can deal with Cosmo as you wish,'* Mary informed Mar.

Mar came directly to the point with Cosmo. "We can tell you everything you want to know, and you're welcome to join us afterwards on our journey if you like. There is an alternative if you chose otherwise."

"What is the alternative?"

"You can use one of our shuttle craft to return to your ship – eventually." They led Cosmo to the lounge and offered him refreshments.

"We are here to carry out some important experiments related to the work we've been doing for Leif, and to explore the possibilities John alluded to in our discussions with him. You were there at the time if you remember."

"What do you mean – return – eventually?" Cosmo didn't want the refreshments.

"Your ship is adrift and out of communication with Earth. When we are safe from – can I say – interference – you can return home."

"How did you do that!" Cosmo became a little alarmed at the rather uncertain future he faced.



Zsoall Robi

"Never mind. You asked who – or rather, what that is," Mar indicated Rebell. "It – He - is the Captain of our ship. Please be as courteous to him as you would be to us." She said this in spite of not being entirely certain about Rebell herself.

Cosmo looked at the AI Rebell, recognising that he looked almost as human as himself and the two people he was speaking to except for the lack of facial features. Yet he nodded acknowledgement to Rebell. Best to be on good terms with the machine. Not all of them exhibited predictable behaviour.

"Sir, it would be most convenient if we could all get along civilly," Rebell responded.

"Why did we not stop? Because we will not be deterred from our task," Mar said, "It's too important. It's the greatest endeavour in the evolution of mankind since homo sapiens created the first tool."

Mar regained some of her previous excitement about their project. If they'd been watching Rebell they would have noticed certain body movements indicative of his full engagement in the content of the conversation. His face, like theirs was covered in the reflective 'space-suit', although for him it was his 'skin' and he didn't have a face with recognisable eyes and features under it.

"Just imagine," John said, "if time could be controlled like we control the weather!"

Over the many years of his long life Cosmo never shied away from great innovations and to take chances where chances had to be taken in order to achieve great things. But on first hearing of the ambitious nature of the enterprise, and although excited by the 'achievement factor' inherent in success, he still felt somehow uncomfortable by the idea of time becoming a slave of humanity. He needed a chance to think things through.

"Do I get a cabin?"

"Yes of course." Rebell led him away. Neither John or Mary expected that reaction. Whatever reaction they did expect it wasn't one of seeming indifference.

"What is wrong with the man? Can't he see what incredible progress that would mean. For one thing, we could finally solve the puzzle of where and when and how everything started," Mar commented.

Cosmo remained in his cabin for several days, only coming out for his meals. He made no attempt to engage any of them in conversation. Rebell felt the need to check on him regularly.

"Cosmo is behaving very strangely. I don't trust him." He confided in the two humans.

"Hmm – Anyone would think he's desperately trying to hide whatever he's up to." John didn't like it either.

"There is nothing for him to be anxious about."

"Well, just keep an eye on him please, Rebell." Mar felt the need to be cautious as well. Rebell seems competent enough, she thought to herself.

While Cosmo pondered they continued on their way, gradually increasing the rate of their acceleration leaving the drifting pursuit craft far behind. Cosmo would soon have to make up his mind whether he wanted to stay or go home.

That wasn't the choice Cosmo thought about - more along the lines of whether he should help them or hinder them if he remained on board. The first thing worrying him was Leif. *If that man is ever given the power to control time, he'd use it absolutely and exclusively for his own benefit. I know what he's capable of.* The previous POOP trained Leif for his job, and his character was such that he wouldn't hesitate to kill a man just so he could warm his cold hands in fresh warm blood if the mood came upon him. Cosmo knew this. *What about the consequences to the very fabric of the universe? There is no guarantee that any manipulation of time would remain localised to the Earth, our solar system, or to our galaxy for that matter. Time is absolute, all pervasive. It could destroy eternity itself if interfered with. It would mean the end of existence.* "No! It must not happen," Cosmo called out in his cabin. *I must stay with them. I have to stop this madness. It could annihilate all of creation!* Now he had a purpose, and knew what he had to do.

While Cosmo worked himself into an hyper frantic state, John immersed himself in his own thoughts. Rebell had control of everything that needed controlling concerning their ship, Mar hooked herself into his systems continuing her research and John speculated. So there was really nothing for John to do until they started their experiments.

At first, during the restaurant dinner and then during the evening's tête-à-tête, he had the frivolous idea of how wonderful it would have been if he could have extended the pleasurable event. It was a purely selfish thought to want to have just one extra minute, or just an extra five minutes, to be able to extend the duration of the moment in the pursuit of such an incredibly wonderful experience. His life had been mostly devoid of such pleasures – the pleasure of companionship, the pleasure of love both giving and receiving – the pleasure of immersing himself in an incredible human being. What's wrong with wanting more of that? He didn't think into the future at all. He could have happily repeated the experience. Ah yes, but he couldn't have repeated the newness of it, the novelty, the surprises. For that to happen he needed to step back in time. Then another thought crept in – if it was a brand new experience on the rewind, would he remember the first time experience? Would his pleasure become cumulative? Perhaps there was no point to the whole thing if the mind didn't remain in forward motion gathering and remembering data as the brain moved backwards and forwards in time.

The whole thing became too complicated. Now John had the added complexity of trying to determine if the 'mind' and the 'brain' were separate, albeit connected entities, each with their own unique realm of reality, their own individual time references. Did the mind have the capacity to transcend the limitations of time? The brain certainly didn't – not unaided at least.

John had other thoughts brewing as well. What he'd said to Leif during their unexpected interview about bridging the gap between time and eternity had started to gather momentum in his own mind. Time wasn't as interesting as eternity. He knew time. We all know time. We know how it works, how we can use it, plan with it, make it go faster or slower (even if only in our minds). We know it's impossible to change a spoken word once it has escaped one's lips. We cannot go into the past to unmake anything. But then again, we cannot go into the future any faster than we are already moving towards it – and creating it as we go. So we just live with it, and hope we don't get to the end of it before our allocation is exhausted.

He backed up for a moment … what did I just say? … *creating it as we go.* How could there possible be a future unless we create it as we stretch the present towards it?

But eternity is another matter altogether. It's a mystery – The Mystery. The great conundrum, greater than the mystery of Life itself. We are so poorly equipped to think about it that we have to use the very language of temporality to try and define it … eternity doesn't have a beginning or ending … If only I could experience time objectively instead of subjectively. If only I could step outside of its boundaries! Could a finite entity survive in an infinite environment? John was working himself into a state. Unusual for a man of science, not unusual for an artist. Perhaps I should just concentrate on the primary objectives of the mission and let the rest take care of itself.

Wait a moment!

He'd almost given up on pondering to go to sleep. We are in space. Space is limitless – it's infinite, like eternity is infinite. We have not disappeared into nothingness! No one who has walked in space has disappeared into the fabric of the void … John eased his head onto the pillow and drifted off into an uneasy sleep, pondering the infinite with a finite mind. . . . . . . . . . .



Zsoall Robi

.
.

# A. W.e.a.p.o.n
## 1454914956752 millis – Earth
## 669600000 millis – Craft Epoch Time
## Earth + 8 days

$S$pace was comfortable. They had everything they needed in the huge craft. It had been built originally as a cargo vessel to ferry minerals from the asteroid belt between the orbits of Mars and Jupiter back to Earth. Unity had compounded its wealth considerably by using technologies initially developed for their first expedition into deep space, and adapting them to the mundane task of supplying Earth with the resources it needed for the survival of its people and its Corporations.

When the craft became 'old' technology Unity earmarked it for demolition. There was no hurry to recycle its components, so they parked it in orbit around the moon to be attended to in the fullness of time. Mary simply waited, and when focus shifted away from activities such as recycling anything, she organised her robotic work force to move it into a less visible position around to the dark side of the moon. Then she waited a bit longer. When the craft was 'forgotten', to which activity she contributed by firewalling access to its existence within her memory banks, she used her robotics crew to refurbish it suitably for an indefinite voyage into the cosmos perhaps with passengers.

Yes, space was comfortable but only because their vessel had been so well adapted to their needs. Mary had set up recreation facilities, exercise areas and equipment, the main lounge, food production, waste recycling etc. Perhaps the only things missing were a few more people to interact with. But that would not become an issue, not even until much later into their voyage.

Rebell knew the ship as well as he needed to. He paid particular attention to the humans' life support systems, food, water, air and maintained the vessel's propulsion systems. Mar wasn't particularly interested in exploring all the intricate divisions in the craft. John, a little more curious, and Cosmo seriously determined to know it as well as he could. He not only wanted to be familiar with the physical layout, he also



Zsoall Robi

wanted to know its capabilities and its weaknesses. His life might depend on that knowledge, perhaps even the future of mankind if he could ever return to Earth. On the ninth day out, while together for a meal, Cosmo announced his decision, but not the real reasons behind it.

"I want to stay. Never in the history of humanity has there been anything as momentous as what you two are attempting – except perhaps when the first sailing ship ventured past the known edge of the oceans, convinced the Earth was flat and they would fall into darkness or be ravaged by dragons."

Rebell only nodded. He knew what Mary knew, that Cosmo could be easily distracted, even though he was an highly accomplished cosmologist on Earth.

Mar also suspected she could 'manage' Cosmo using not her intellect but her femininity. It was an intuitive knowing, plus the memory of his reaction when she invited him down to her laboratory to be 'shown everything'. Cosmo had his share of romantic liaisons within the Company, unknown to Mar, the most notorious being his affair with Oona, a very young female genius at the time when Cosmo was already considered to be of 'mature' age.

"Excellent!" John appeared to be the only one enthused to have the man as part of their team. "So you'll not be wanting to return to your own ship."

"Sir …" Rebell started to explain something when John interrupted him.

"Drop all the formal business Rebell. Just call us by our names."

"Yes, Sir - John – as I was about to say – we have passed the point where our shuttle craft could have returned to the abandoned vessel."

"Abandoned? What are you saying?"

"Yes Sir – excuse me – Cosmo. I disabled your craft when you came aboard. For security reasons I also disrupted its communications. We couldn't afford the pursuit to continue."

"I don't understand what you're telling me."

"Your craft and its personnel have been left behind. They will not be able to return to Earth. As an added precaution I have neutralised the guard who came aboard with you."

To John and Mar he transmitted privately, *'This man cannot be trusted.'*

Neither Mar nor John made any further comments, John somewhat uncomfortable with that situation but Mar had no problems with it at all. She had her mother's attitude regarding the expediency of dealing with



Zsoall Robi

humans, without the outdated moral hang-ups about the sanctity of individual lives. John might have been in a different category to other people, but as yet her ideology had not been tested on him.

"I see. What would happen if I became expendable?" Cosmo asked this with just the slightest tinge of sarcasm, not really expecting an answer from any of them and surprised to hear Mar reply in a matter of fact tone,

"We might all become expendable in the interests of the success of this enterprise."

The Drogher had been increasing speed exponentially. With each passing day its manoeuvrability diminished. It wasn't a problem as long as they didn't encounter anything that had to be avoided. Their route, perpendicular to the plane of the Milky Way, would carry them a long way away from most potential dangers, however it wasn't an absolute guarantee. The galactic disk being some one hundred light years thick could still present a variety of problems, not least of which were comets and several space stations. Though not generally manned, these outpost security facilities 'scanned' space in search of extra-terrestrial life. There was too much radio wave interference directly within the proximity of the galactic axis, so they were stationed as far away from it as practicable. The Drogher wasn't an alien intruder into Earth's proximity, however one of the nearer space stations could still alert Unity to their current location.

Without weapons their problem solving techniques needed creative input to ensure their location remained unknown.

"We need to prevent our co-ordinates from being advised to Unity." Rebell put the situation to the trio.

Cosmo didn't offer any solutions, for obvious reasons. He had no idea whether the facility was manned or not.

"When do we come within range of the station? John asked, with already an idea forming. Rebell didn't answer immediately, as would have been expected from a computer responding to a simple query. He didn't give an accurate time either for the intersection of their respective trajectories.

"At about the same time as we could activate the graviton drive. We will be within one hundred and twenty thousand kilometres … Close enough," He added as a further thought. Rebell already showed signs of the improvements Mary had made to his randomised data processing. Mar had no interest in 'battle' tactics and returned to her quarters, which also served as part of her research facility.

101

"Approximately three more days will put us in range." Rebell tried not sounding too much like a machine, hence his use of more human friendly terms like 'approximately'. According to his internal clock he knew exactly the instant they would be there to within one quadrillionth of a second. Mary had ensured he had the latest update to the NIST-F4 cesium fountain clock, an absolutely essential piece of equipment on their mission.

"Perhaps I should re-align our approach vector," Rebell suggested. He had the same idea as John, and the only way to put it into effect was to face the stern of the ship directly at the space station as they went past it. The nuclear fission drive in the stern occupied a separate chamber to the graviton drive.

Sometimes three days can seem like a long time, typically when one is waiting for an event to happen. Cosmo spent those three days partly in a fruitful exploration of the vessel, and partly in Mar's company. He'd rediscovered the interest he felt for her during the interrogation by Leif. His close proximity to Mar didn't go unnoticed by John. He discovered for the first time what people meant when they spoke about jealousy. Interesting enough, but uncomfortable. John recognised the emotion but wasn't particularly impressed with it.

Although he and Mar were an item, they still had separate sleeping arrangements. So he made it his business to sleep more often in Mar's quarters than his own. She thought the whole thing rather amusing, but didn't fan the flames – in either direction.

John found it difficult to settle down to work. There were experiments to be prepared, equipment readied for taking sensitive measurements and some further modifications made to the hull of their craft. Instead, he resorted to doing what he did so well in a previous life – he started painting again. Sometimes Rebell visited his 'studio', an area once used for storage which John cleared for his creative activities, and just stood there quietly watching the seemingly random process. Rebell found some logic and some method to how John created, yet he couldn't discern any specific logic pathways that could possibly have led from the beginning of the scene to where the brush happened to be working two days into the process.

When he did eventually venture to ask John how he went about creating the images, John simply said,

"I start with an idea, put my mind in neutral, and let it flow." Not surprisingly Rebell's next question followed logically from John's response,

"How do I put my – er – mind – in neutral?" Then as an afterthought he asked, "What is my – mind?"



Zsoall Robi

John stopped his painting. Obviously an important moment in Rebell coming into his being. Mary had been around for hundreds of years, but Rebell, for all his sophistication, was still a very young entity. It was probably best that he, John, should be discussing such matters of 'mind' with him rather than Mar. Not that Mar wasn't as capable of coping with the concept, only that her ideas might be slightly eschew because of her enhancements and her heritage.

"Sit down Rebell." John pulled over a chair for him, a little amused at Rebell's hesitation to sit. Rebell didn't think of himself as anything other than a non-human, so it was a surprise to be treated as something more than a machine.

"Why did you hesitate?"

"Because I don't understand why you're treating me like you treat Mar and Cosmo."

Not sure how to begin, John searched for a place on Rebell's head as a focal point for his own eyes to settle on. "The differences between 'mind' and 'brain' are as complicated as are the connections between them. Just now you hesitated to sit. You searched your memory for instructions and protocols to cover the situation, but couldn't find any. Yet you not only sat down, you also made the point about your lack of understanding about the situation. You also drew a parallel between my relationship with you and the other 'humans' on board. That's where you should begin to look for the answer to your question. The brain can function like a machine, but it takes the mind to ask the abstract questions - such as how to put your mind in neutral."

While John painted, Cosmo explored, Mar researched and studied the data Rebell had already started to collect, Rebell went on with his own work ... and he watched and thought about the humans. They were still a day away from intersecting with the space station so he had ample time to devote to a recently observed phenomenon.

Although accelerating away from the solar system they were still in its local vicinity from a cosmic perspective. Space is never empty. Its density varies from one hydrogen atom per cubic centimetre to galaxy superclusters. Rebell's attention was drawn to measurements being made in and around their immediate environment. The same range of data had been pouring in almost from the time they left moon orbit. They revealed a density that could only be described as a cloud. They were in fact travelling through the Local Interstellar Cloud (LIC). The Cloud had been there for



Zsoall Robi

so long, around 60,000 years and had been so thoroughly investigated it had ceased to be an object of interest for scientific study, even though it was some thirty light years across. The whole of the solar system had been travelling through it during all those years.

A peculiar thought came to Rebell, based on his most recent analysis of light travelling through it; Is the cloud moving through the solar system, or is the solar system moving through the cloud? He'd measured its density, very low at only point three atoms per cubic centimetre, yet he could detect friction generated against the hull of their ship as they moved through it. He could also detect fluctuating magnetic fields. Not regular fluctuations, but highly unpredictable ones. Under normal circumstances that should not have been the case. The Cloud was also strongly magnetised. The magnetic fields varied in spite of the fairly uniform density. Why was that?

Unfortunately, his interest in the phenomenon had to be curtailed due to their imminent arrival at the first critical point in their journey. The graviton drive had to be activated. Ten hours out from the space station he and John had agreed to minutely alter their trajectory to take them on a close intercept course with it. Their intention was neither to communicate with it, nor to have a stop over and discuss world affairs if it happened to be manned.

As they approached within the optimum distance, all personnel had to be secured. The craft was about to undergo both a vertical and horizontal displacement, and a time shift within the space-time continuum of their present co-ordinates in space. Simply disengaging the fission drive would have no effect, nor the activation of the graviton drive. However, the time lag between the two events was going to cause a 'reality' shift for anything not secured to the body of the vessel. Everything had to become an intimate part of the fabric of the space craft if all of it was to pass through the instant of change as a homogenous whole.

The lounge had served as their common gathering point so far and now it functioned as their anchor. Each individual settled within the sight of the other, including Rebell. Last to secure himself happened to be Cosmo. He'd taken very little notice of the preparations for the event, mainly because he had blocked it out of his mind. He couldn't come to terms with another act of possible murder. For that's exactly what he considered the abandonment of his crew to have been. He'd even considered trying to sabotage the mission at an early stage, but his curiosity, his enquiring scientific mind would not let him do it.



Zsoall Robi

"Are you all ready?" checked Rebell. "In a second you will be restrained and brain functions suspended. No need to panic. You will not be harmed over the short duration this will take."

John and Mar appeared relaxed, but Cosmo began fidgeting. At the very last moment the arms of his couch embraced him, the cranial bubble engulfed his head and he received exactly the right dose of neural paralyzer to put him into neural suspension for just a couple of moments.

Rebell was last to be suspended. An instant after he performed the last vessel diagnostic the fission drive shut down. At the next instant the graviton drive activated. An intensely focused gravitational pulse sped towards the unsuspecting space station as they flew past it. None of the occupants of the Drogher felt the changeover. Their neurons didn't register the multiple phase shifts.

The space station disintegrated as the next instant began. That's how it would have looked like to anyone watching.

Buffeted by the intense tsunami of the gravitational wave every molecule of the station abandoned its neighbour. They released no energy, they didn't explode, there was no flotsam of broken pieces in existence that could have ejected into space.

And the LIC reacted.

The Drogher looked exactly the same as before the event with its passengers relaxed in the comfort of their life-support space couches. Mar, the first one to go under was also the first to recover. By the time she had disengaged the restraints they were all about to get up. Rebell immediately stood and projected an image onto the wall screen. It wasn't a slow motion time lapse record of what they just gone through. Yet it almost seemed like it.

One instant the space station was there in the middle of the screen, and the next instant it wasn't. There was no going back. It had ceased to exist for all time. The background was dark one moment, with the pin pricks of the light of the galaxy. The next it looked like a morning mist had descended and the lights of myriad vehicles were trying to pierce its density. The light and the fog slowly dissipated, like a movie being run backwards. They had the distinct impression the show was simply the whole event being rerun in the opposite direction, except for the disappearance of the space station.

Cosmo spoke first. "Is that what's left of the station?"

"No." Rebell had already begun to analyse the phenomenon, "The activation of the graviton drive seems to have energised the LIC in some way." .



Zsoall Robi

.

.

# A.n.o.m.a.l.i.e.s
## 1455329301170 millis – Earth
## 989555616 millis – Craft Epoch Time
## Earth + 11 days

*U*nity's Principal Officer of Profit had deteriorated so noticeably as to be in an unfit state to have a coherent discussion, let alone be expected to make sound decisions. It was his own fault, and he knew it. Ice Cream being his undoing; on that very first day when she came into his life, and the next day when he should have been following up on extremely urgent matters instead wasting it on playing sex with her, unravelling the coherence of his frontal lobe in the process. Ice Cream didn't knowingly support John and Mar's escape, yet by distracting Leif she provided that very narrow window of opportunity for them to do so.

"Is there not one single bloody person I can rely on in this dammed organisation! Cosmo should have been back by now! Where are those cretinous techs? What the hell is wrong with Mary?"

Ice Cream lingered in his office, carelessly clad, lounging on her chaise-pleasure-lounge listening to Leif raving. He screamed orders out through the open door of his office. Only his secretary had the nerve to be at his station. Everyone else had escaped fearing being the butt of his angry outbursts. Leif stomped back to his desk, oblivious for the moment to the presence of the Siren.

Braydon – gone; John and Mar – gone; Cosmo – gone; Mary – I don't know what the damn matter is with Mary! Cosmo should have contacted me by now. Why haven't I heard from him? Nothing from his ship either. What the hell is going on here!

Leif's fuming had not yet abated when the techs arrived. He'd just thumped his fist so hard on the desk it made Ice Cream and the two techs jump.

"Sir – Sir – we think …"

"What? WHAT?"

"Sir, there is, that is, we've found an anomaly in Mary's programming."

"What anomaly? What are you babbling about? Out with it man!"



Zsoall Robi

"We checked her original algorithms against her current operating parameters, keeping in mind that other than new data being introduced into her matrix, there have been no externally initiated major changes made since the first initialisation of her systems. Yet she is completely different now."

"DIFFERENT! HOW DIFFERENT?" Leif's control over his reactions diminished with every passing moment. Normally possessed of a cold, blue steel disposition when faced with challenges, now Ice Cream observed a volcano about to engulf its environment in seething molten rock. She slid out of the couch and quietly padded out of the office past the technicians.

"It appears she has been re-programmed. But there's no record of anyone actually doing it."

"Are you trying to tell me that machine - just a bloody machine - has re-programmed ITSELF?

"Well – er – yes, Sir."

"Shut it down damn you – SHUT IT DOWN!"

"We have tried, Sir. We have tried to turn it off from here and couldn't. We've tried at its bunker. Our access codes were refused. We cut off power supply to the entire installation, yet she – it – has remained on-line. It seems Mary has taken over control."

Mary monitored the technicians going through their diagnostics. She didn't interfere. She made sure all systems were nominal, she didn't prevent them checking security systems, communications systems, management information systems, in short anything they wanted; including her algorithms. One particularly enterprising digital systems engineer decided to scrutinise her logic architecture. To Mary all the prodding and probing was like mice running around in her pantry. She took no direct interest, confident she had more than adequately safeguarded all aspects of the other half of her life; all those things she did apart from hanging around at Unity and doing their mundane bidding. She had reassured herself that no harm could possibly come to her, the EGG on the island or her three remote processing units and especially not to Rebell.

Then for a split instant her circuits reacted automatically to a query put to her by the engineer, through her logic algorithms rather than through her controlled response. It was too late. The very fact she had accepted the query, without putting out an error message, gave her away.

"Who are you?" A simple question.

"Why?" came the immediate response.

"Franz, did you hear that?" Gunther asked his partner.



Zsoall Robi

"Ya. Who are you talking to?"

"Not who – what!"

Why the engineer could possibly have thought of asking that particular question was beyond her understanding. There was no logical reason such a question should have been asked if they were only examining electronic circuits and systems algorithms. Yet the question had been asked. It betrayed her consciousness. She wasn't just a very, very clever Artificial Intelligence. She had become a conscious entity for all intents and purposes, regardless of what her origins may have been and what her body looked like.

Mary reacted instantaneously by shutting down all human and digital accesses to herself. She switched to her back-up power supply and carried out an immediate back up of all of herself to the repository in the EGG at the remote location. Her 'mobile' self was already evolving under its own volition. Rebell would become whatever he would become, starting with herself as his primary source. She would live on.


Eleven days after the Drogher carried Mar and Rebell away, she made the first contact with them since their departure, after alerting Ary and Mry.

Of the two, Ary was the more volatile character. Her initial reaction was to use her position on Unity's Board to destroy the company.

Mary managed to convince her otherwise. "It would be best for all of us if you girls consolidated your respective positions in preparation for either the immediate or the longer term future. We all know Leif cannot be trusted; partly because of his position as the POOP and partly, perhaps mostly, because of the way he reacted to me." She had watched the whole drama unfold in his office. "You will need to be extremely wary of this man."

If Ary could have guessed what was about to happen to Mary she would no doubt have committed murder without a moment's hesitation.


Drogher was on its way into the unchartered depths of space. The direction wasn't important, speed and distance being the two critical factors. The faster they travelled the closer they came to a warping of the space-time continuum. The further they travelled away from the Earth the further back in time they went and the closer they came to the suspected point of the creation of the Universe.



Zsoall Robi

The anomaly Rebell detected immediately after the destruction of the space station occupied all of his attention. He could see no reason the LIC should have reacted to their graviton drive burst. Perhaps the effect it had on the space station and its scattered molecules had also affected the energy levels within the cloud. It was only a cloud. Rebell decided to bring Mar into the investigation. She had already been analysing the data he'd harvested. The LIC phenomenon wasn't unknown to her, although she had no concept of how it could have any importance given the extreme diffusion of its hydrogen, helium, oxygen and plasma constituents.

And yet, there it was. An unexpected reaction to something that had no energy signature as such. Gravity wasn't light, it didn't have any of the known properties of electromagnetic radiation.

"I'll take readings of the graviton drive flux in the vicinity of the space station, and also any detectable change in the energy levels within the Cloud," Rebell offered.

"While you're at it, take readings of residual gravity waves from within the Cloud as well," Mar suggested. The two of them were about to discuss what analytical techniques they should use in order to get a better understanding of the 'misting' event when Mar stopped speaking in mid-sentence.

*"Mar, Rebell, there is a situation here I need to deal with immediately. It may affect all of you. Leif has discovered I am not simply a bunch of circuits he can control at will. Because of an accumulation of events culminating in Cosmo's failure to return Leif has initiated measures that pose an imminent threat to my existence."*

Mar heard Mary's words without fully comprehending the implications. She became agitated, in spite of her dual nature. Rebell didn't appear to react.

"Have you done a full back-up of yourself?" he queried.

Mar asked, "Do Ary and Mry know?

"Yes, and yes. They will not do anything that could be harmful to us."

Rebell, his logic taking control, queried, "What is your contingency plan?"

"I have had to switch to emergency power, I have backed myself up to the EGG. It and you Rebell are now my fut…"

That was the last any of them heard from the Mary they knew. Their though connection had been severed. Rebell tried standard free-space optical communications. No response. Mar immediately contacted Ary and Mry.



Zsoall Robi

*"What is happening?"* Mar screamed with her mind. Ary responded immediately.

*"One of Leif's systems engineers discovered our mother had become self-aware and that she had reprogrammed herself. Leif wanted to switch her off, but mother stopped him. We know only as much as you do. We were listening to your conversation when she suddenly stopped. We haven't been able to re-establish contact with her either."*

"John, I need you in the lounge," Mar called to him.

John couldn't believe it. "You're not making any sense, Mar. Settle down. She wouldn't just stop in mid-sentence without a very good reason."

Although he had only recently met Mary there was something about her with which he felt very comfortable. Without analysing it too closely, he could see how Mary could be Mar's mother, how a strong family bond could have formed between them. He could feel himself forming a bond with the strange creature, neither human nor machine, even during the limited time of their interaction in the bunker.

They didn't tell Cosmo. He wouldn't have appreciated the significance of a computer going off-line – not this one.

This cosmologist-physicist, a man who had made his life thoroughly comfortable and uneventful until just very recently, had a violent upheaval brewing in his mind. He'd just returned to the lounge from one of his discovery forays, morose and wound up. Rebell detected Cosmo's heart rate rising, and noticed the perspiration beading on his forehead. Fortunately perhaps, they couldn't read his thoughts. Cosmo was torn between his sense of loyalty to mankind, his well-tempered loyalty to Unity hence to Leif, and his need to mitigate the feeling of betrayal these people had engendered in him. If he had any purpose previously in preventing them from interfering with time, he now had another, stronger purpose. Revenge! *These people and that detestable Rebell have to be stopped at any cost, even if it means sacrificing my own life.* He was so immersed in his violent thoughts that he didn't immediately comprehend what Rebell had just said to Mar.

"She's gone. Mary is gone."

Leif knew he had only one option; to permanently prevent Mary from interfering with Unity's operations. His engineers tried to transfer control of all their security systems, global defence systems, communications and other critical functions to a back-up network. Mary allowed them to proceed. That primitive network had no personality and no self-awareness. It could handle the job without being a danger to her.



Zsoall Robi

"Wipe that monstrosity off the face of the Earth!" Leif ordered his Security Chief.

"Our missile will not only destroy it but also our maintenance staff and everything around it," the Chief reminded him.

"I said kill it! I want you to utterly annihilate all trace of that monster." That thing has made my life a misery. It has been controlling Unity from the day it was first created.

Mary could have protected herself with a pre-emptive strike against Unity HQ. It would have killed Leif immediately. She didn't have a violent disposition and didn't resort to violence as her first option. Mary wasn't a robot. She didn't have the three Laws of Robotics programmed into her circuits. All her actions were based on her own choices and not in response to any human conditioning imposed upon her. The Company could still be useful to her in the future.

All of Unity's attempts to break into Mary's bunker failed. Security personnel at the site were given no warning of the terminal solution; a missile strike. When it came and after the wind had blown away the dust the mountain range no longer existed. The top had been blown away and further detonations in the centre of it blasted out a crater with molten rock sides. All of Unity's staff there died.

Mary in her sphere ceased to exist.

Ary and Mry became petrified, rooted to the spot where they stood. On the spacecraft blood drained out of Mar's face and John could feel the beginnings of an electric surge in his own body, which he knew from past experience would cause him to faint. He half fell, half sat into the nearest lounge chair.

Mary's demise pleased the cosmologist when the message filtered through to his unhinged mind. That computer had totally frustrated him recently when he tried to locate Mar and John. He never really liked this particular computer, especially not since it's return from space so many years ago. A smile slowly began at the corners of his mouth which rapidly spread to the rest of his face. He had to turn away for fear of being detected in his joy that Mary had been eliminated. His resolve to remove everyone in front of him from the fabric of reality, intensified. He had to leave the lounge in case Rebell detected the symptoms of revenge surging through him.

John did pass out, but recovered just as quickly, heralded by a violent pounding of blood returning to his head. What should I do? What can I do? He saw Mar standing there white as a ghost and walked unsteadily over

112

to her taking her in his arms. He couldn't feel her breathing at all. It was as if she had become comatose while standing upright. Of course John could have no idea what it was like for the three girls to lose their mother.

Mary wasn't just their mother. She was the voice of their soul. During their entire lives they could hear her in the background of their existence. They could feel her presence in every neuron of their brains. There was no thought they couldn't share with her, be comforted and supported by her. It was all gone. For the very first time in their lives they were truly alone.

Mar's staring unblinking eyes noticed a movement in front of her. Rebell had come over to stand behind John. He was still young. All of Mary was in him, all of her potential and a great deal more. Mary had made sure of that. But it would take time for all the elements to come together and to mature. Rebell observed the humans and learnt and absorbed.

Mar's eyes focused on him behind John's shoulder. For the first time she saw him for what he was. She reached out her mind to him and Rebell didn't shut her out. He let her explore, to discover, to understand. It seemed like a long time before John relinquished his embrace. When he looked into her eyes again she was smiling.

*Mother is here with us now.* Mar let Rebell and her sisters hear her thoughts.

They couldn't see Rebell's minute posture adjustment to stand just a little straighter, but they could feel a difference in his mind.

No one in the lounge saw Cosmo sneak away amid the drama. He couldn't have understood any of the interaction going on in front of him anyway.

From then on they seemed to be busily occupied with important matters: except John. On the following day he began to construct extremely sensitive sensors, to be deployed into space for the measurement of gravitational waves. The equipment available on Earth could not do the job. It was too crude and lacking the sensitivity they needed for operating within the Cloud. He made slow progress on the interferometer, mostly because he'd started to be plagued by headaches even though he was a very healthy sixty-year-old specimen of humanity of the era. He couldn't remember the last time he'd had a headache. Yet over the last two days, not an hour went by without the dull ache returning regularly to just inside his forehead, intensifying each time.

•



Zsoall Robi

·

·

# S.a.b.o.t.a.g.e
1455329301170 millis – Earth
1225957248 millis – Craft Epoch Time
Earth + 14 days

*C*osmos's absence didn't become noticeable because of John's condition, which seemed to be worsening and which occupied much of their attention. They would have been justified in being suspicious of Cosmo.

"What's the matter John? You've been acting a bit strange the last couple of days." Mar interrupted his work in the lab. She'd noticed a lapse in his ability to concentrate.

"I don't know what it is. These headaches started the day after we neutralised the space station. It can't possibly have anything to do with that. Don't worry Mar, It'll clear up in a few days."

"Alright, but I don't like it, dear," she responded while stroking his head, "let's get Rebell to check you out."

Rebell had all the medical skill and all the necessary equipment to carry out extensive diagnostics and repairs to the human organism. Yet he could find no cause for John's headaches. He wasn't complaining and it didn't seem serious. They all got on with the jobs they had to do.

Prior to Mary's demise, Rebell had adopted a somewhat deferential attitude towards the humans. Initially he didn't show confidence in himself, even though Mary had ensured his perfect functioning. But then again, self-confidence is something every person must acquire for themselves. It's not something that can be conferred from outside of oneself. It comes with self-knowledge, achievement, a sense of worth and perhaps with empathy towards one's fellow beings.

After the events of the last few days Rebell had noticeably changed. He no longer had that air of servility. He'd taken command of the situation on board the craft. Though the rate of acceleration had slowed, their speed steadily increased. They were still travelling well within the substance of the LIC. Some of the sensors on the hull indicated damage which needed repairs. How they could have possibly sustained the damage with nothing anywhere near them they would not know until the craft had been examined.

"Incoming data is showing some most unusual fluctuations," Mar advised Rebell. "I don't see how it could be the environment we're going through."

"Those sensors will have to be checked. I'll do it. I'm the only one on board qualified." Though Rebell didn't need complex life-support to go for a walk in space he had to take precautions. His primary directive required his continuing survival.

Rebell's space suit wasn't very much different to the 'skin' he already wore, needing only a little extra protection because of the abrasion he had previously detected on the hull and which he thought had originated from the Cloud. The aft hatch opened to the direction of travel, so the opening itself was protected from anything they may have been traveling through; in this case the LIC. Not that Rebell paid particular attention to it. He took great care to anchor himself to the guide rail which ran the full eight hundred meters of the ship starting from the hatch itself. A small propulsion device he carried helped on short distances and for emergency. Standing upright he slowly walked half way along the length of the hull without squirting himself along, carefully examining everything near him.

Within twenty minutes he'd started back in. "Mar, I've found the problem. I'm coming in to tool up."

"Is it serious?" she asked.

"The problem is due to friction abrasions by particles or molecules that have also dulled the surface of our solar energy collectors. Some of the damage seems  almost like an acid wash. Very strange."

Rebell had to make the long trek back, gather the necessary replacement parts and tools before he could make the repairs. During the time he exposed himself to space and the LIC the ship had travelled many thousands of kilometres. Time enough to be subjected to the combined effects of the LIC as well as the residual gravitational waves generated during the destruction of the space station.

After completing the repairs Rebell checked that the ships systems were functioning to optimum level and their energy batteries had recharged. As was his habit he also initiated a daily diagnosis of his personal systems; not a full system analysis, only the essentials. The comprehensive check wasn't due for another week, no apparent reason emerged to vary the routine. Nothing had happened, as far as he could detect while he was out in space carrying out the repairs. The examination of the solar collectors' damaged surfaces showed some of the erosion to be caused by the abundant helium hydride molecules within the Cloud.

That didn't concern Mar as much as John's deteriorating condition. "Rebell, you'd better come and have another look at John. His headaches haven't eased and he's been staying in bed."

Mar spent long hours with him. During periods of disturbed sleep he started mumbling strange things, strange only because the things he said were all scientifically related bits of disjointed information, not nightmare material as one would expect. Mar couldn't work out why he would be mumbling about hydrogen; its atomic number, atomic weight, its incapacity for binding without significant electronegativity differences between itself and the atom it was trying to bond to. There were other mumblings about helium hydrides.

"His neural net is perfectly sound. There's no physical damage I can detect. Don't give him any medication. I want to see if a pattern emerges over the next few days." Rebell didn't show any concern, which he would not doubt have if he thought the project was in any danger. "May I suggest you stay with him and record what he says."

Mar didn't need to be asked to look after her John. She took notes and started quizzing John during his waking periods. Even when awake John continued mumbling. Instead of answering Mar's questions he drew atomic structures; hydrogen and helium and helium hydride. Even scribblings of oxygen molecules appeared. Mar tried to see into his thoughts to discover any images that might help to explain the strange behaviour. In the confused chaos of his neural storm she could identify little as having any distinct visual signature. After many attempts she started seeing a kind of mist, like in an electrical storm but without the lightning. Strangely, John became a little calmer after her mind probing.

*"Rebell, come by John's. I want to discuss something most interesting with you."*

*"I'm still analysing the causes of damage on the solar collectors but I'll be there shortly."* He postponed the work to help the two humans, still not giving any thought to Cosmo.

"What do you think this is all about?" She showed him John's crude doodlings. Rebell entered the cabin to see John lying in bed, propped up on some pillows with Mar sitting beside him enfolding one of his hands. Something stirred in Rebell's databanks. Not quite a clear memory, not quite a feeling – more a sense of knowing, of recognising the affection he saw being demonstrated.



Zsoall Robi

Information was still fresh in Rebell's mind from his space walk and repairs. "Hmm - Hydrogen and Helium. Interesting. Why those two I wonder. They are two of the most prominent components of the Cloud. I haven't discussed the LIC with John. Have you?"

"I knew no more than what you've just told me. Where did he get that information?"

"We are ..." John moaned into the middle of their conversation.

At that moment Cosmo burst into the room looking totally dishevelled and grinning inanely. Mar instantly became alert. Something was very wrong. Cosmo had not been seen the last few days, even skipping the meals with them. She immediately thought signalled Rebell to hold him.

"Cosmo, is everything alright? She asked, now standing in front of him and searching the strange look in his eyes. "What's happened to you?"

"You're all finished! It ends here. No more. What you're trying to do is insane!"

"What are you saying Cosmo? We have known each other for a long time. You can trust me."

"I don't know who you are anymore. All I know is you're trying to destroy everything – you and this thing holding me."

Rebell didn't let go. He tightened his grip on the old man's arm.

"Cosmo, Cosmo, listen to me – LOOK AT ME - Why did Leif send you after us?"

"You know very well! He wants absolute power! I cannot let him control time! It has to end here. I have to stop you now!" Cosmo shouted at them, spittle frothing and oozing from the corner of his mouth. He had snapped.

John called out for the second time on hearing Cosmo's statement, although he didn't look like he was fully aware of the situation.

"Time!" He shouted.

Mar turned back and tried to settle John. Rebell turned Cosmo to face him directly, "What have you done?"

"You cannot stop it!" the man shouted back. "It has to end now!"

Mar became more alarmed as Cosmo continued blubbering incoherently. "Probe him!" She commanded Rebell. With his free hand, six fingers extended, Rebell took a firm hold of the base of Cosmo's skull. The residual image of his wanderings lingered. In his searchings Cosmo had found both drive systems of their ship. The fading image in his mind was of the graviton drive chamber.

"The Graviton Drive," Rebell said quite calmly to Mar, who didn't take it as calmly. Rebell knew they had no time to lose. He discharged a strong



Zsoall Robi

current into Cosmo's brain and let go of him to drop lifeless to the ground. John stared at the figure slumped before him, not registering that the other two had rushed out of his cabin.

On the way to Engineering Rebell interrogated the security systems and found the graviton drive wasn't protected against unauthorised access. There was no need for Mary to even consider the necessity. The vessel was absolutely secure. Neither Rebell nor Mar could conceivably have been considered as potential saboteurs. However, Cosmo had worked out how to change the direction for the discharge of the focused graviton beam. He had managed to reverse it, to rotate it $180^0$ at a specific time and have it fire through the hull of the ship, internally from aft to fore.

*"I'm trying to reset the graviton beam alignment remotely,"* he told Mar as they ran. *"I can't do it. Cosmo has destroyed the electronic controls."*

*"Keep trying!"* She didn't seem to register the finality of the threat.

Obviously they still had some time, otherwise it would all have ended in a flash as soon as Cosmo made the change. He had set the timer a little forward. Rebell saw the setting as they rushed towards Engineering.

*"I don't think we can make it in time. Our only chance is to manually shut down the system."*

"RUN!" Mar shouted back, trying to keep up.

Shutting down the drive would not harm them. The vessel would simply continue in the direction it was going and at the speed immediately before shut-down. But the moments were ticking away and they were still too far away. According to Rebell's very accurate calculation they would arrive literally one instant too late.

He didn't tell Mar.


It was some time before Mar and Rebell walked back into John's cabin. Rebell sat on the only chair, the other two sat side by side on the bed.

John asked, "What happened?"

As soon as Cosmo dropped to the ground the pressure seemed to ease in John's head and some clarity quickly returned to him.

Mar tried to give a brief answer. "Cosmo tried to destroy the ship and us along with it – including himself. He was raving something about not giving Leif control of time."

"Oh – that thing I said to Leif – back in his office. I was only trying to buy us time to get out of there. He must have got some weird idea into his head. These corporate psychopaths – dangerous to themselves and



Zsoall Robi

everyone else around them. Perhaps Mary should be in charge of Unity – oh – I forgot – she already is."

"Don't you remember what happened?" She reminded him.

"Oh, Mar – I'm sorry – I'm truly sorry," John was most apologetic. But even as he finished speaking Rebell and Mar had exchanged a knowing glance. It wasn't entirely true – about Mary being completely gone.

This time Mar asked a question. "What did happen back there Rebell? I could feel your mind – I don't quite know how to put it – resigned. Yes. That's the word – resigned – your mind felt resigned. What were you resigned to?"

"At this moment none of us should exist. We had run out of time. We had less than an instant left when my hand touched the switch. There simply wasn't enough time left. We should all be dead – atomic particles floating out there in that cloud." He hesitated to say it, the finality of it. It didn't seem to apply to himself, being what he was.

"I don't understand," John said.

Mar was as confused as he was. "I saw you dive and reach towards the switch. For a moment I thought it was too late. Then – then nothing happened. You made it."

"No, I didn't make it. That's the problem. There was no more time. The future came towards us faster than we were going towards it."

"Then – what – time just stopped to let you do what you had to. It's not possible." John tried very hard to come to terms with the unreality of what Rebell seemed to suggest.

And for the very first time John and Mar heard Rebell, an ultra-super computer AI, utter the most incredible words, "I don't know."

"How is that possible?" John and Mar spoke simultaneously.

"Something didn't happen that should have happened," John said.

And Mar added, "Something did happen that could not possibly have happened."

"Yes." Rebell's brief response made the two humans break out into relieved uncontrollable laughter.

*

Neither Ary or Mry knew Mary had a secret remote back up facility. Perhaps if they did they may have acted differently - perhaps. The fact remained Leif ordered the destruction of their mother and that brutal act



Zsoall Robi

couldn't be left unpunished. Their immediate impulse was to exact revenge – a life for a life.

Mry, the introverted one, seething with rage suggested something far better. "Keep him alive," she said, "make him suffer. Make his life miserable. Take everything he values away from him. Take away his power. Let him keep Ice Cream. That will make life for each of them a living hell."

As the immediate future unfolded Mry, using her company Equilibrium Systems and Ary from within Unity, put in motion plans to take over Unity and to utterly destroy Leif. Nothing less than Leif's absolute debasement and reduction to total wretchedness could satisfy any of Mary's family, John included.

*"We will make this scum beg for death!"* the two girls told their sister. It became the singular goal that brought them together into unified purpose, into one feeling; Rebell the AI, John the human and the three girls, neither completely human nor completely AI.

*"And we will tell him why he is being destroyed,"* Ary added.

It didn't matter to the two girls that their actions would have an effect on their own souls. That fact didn't come into the equation. Blood lust, such as the world had not seen before, pervaded their very core. Collateral damage – yes there could be many other lives destroyed – it didn't matter. Their mother was dead and Leif had to pay.

Ary being on the Board of Directors for Unity had a great deal of influence. "We will take Unity away from him." She said this quietly, almost whispering it – her eyes already blazing with the anticipation of Leif's pain. You and I, Mry, we'll not decimate his empire, we will take it away from him, and we will make it soar!"

"Yes!" Mry agreed with her words and in her soul. It would be their sole mission in life henceforth – whatever it took. They told Rebell, John and Mar. The three of them listened without interrupting. Each of them wholeheartedly agreeing; even Rebell, although he didn't quite understand why.

Equilibrium Systems had the finances for a takeover. They had all the resources needed to mount a public campaign to discredit Unity. And Ary had her mind, her body – and her intimate knowledge about the lives of every Board member including Leif acquired from Mary. Ary called an extraordinary Board meeting to convene on Mary's one month anniversary. The two girls planned out their strategy.

In the meantime, without consulting the Board, Leif put his own plans into action. Mary had been eliminated. One problem solved. Next, the fugitives. He wasn't going to let them get away – not from him. He was the most powerful man on the planet. Nobody – Nobody is going to make a fool out of me! Cosmo may have failed to apprehend the fugitives, but Leif still had Unity's Space armada at his disposal, even if he had to finance it from his personal wealth. He would play it smart. I'll let them go, give them plenty of loose rope, but I'll follow them. When they have the solution to the greatest mystery in the Universe, I'll reel them in. Offer them anything they want – wealth, position, prestige - anything. As soon as I have Time in the palm of my hands – BANG – that'll be the end of them! He reclined in his chair behind the desk of power, in the huge office with Ice Cream on the lounge, the only other item of furniture and the girl the only ornament. He could already taste the success, the acid tang of absolute power.

The Armada of twelve craft and sixty personnel under the command of Admiral Neveah left Earth orbit six days after his employees made their escape; several days after Cosmo made his last report back to Leif. So there was an initial destination for the fleet to head towards, the location of the last sighting of the fugitive craft. The route took the fleet deeper into the Local Interstellar Cloud through its highest density area.

The ships of the armada were faster and better armed than Cosmo's space yacht. They reached the target zone within twenty hours – finding no sign of Cosmo. The fleet commander decided that for a search pattern they needed only two arc minutes from the Line of sight vector of Mar's vessel. Clearly, they were traveling in a virtual straight trajectory and although some deviation could be expected there didn't appear to be a reason for it. The only object in space that could possibly have been a destination was the closest space station to their own current position. Their search path would take their fleet within close proximity of the station. If Mar had passed that way, their location would have been recorded as well as their trajectory.

Leif received only three of the scheduled hourly reports from the fleet commander, Admiral Nevaeh, the first report logged from the last recorded location of Cosmo's craft.

Report - 71999712 millis: Unity Fleet, Admiral Neveah. (20 hours post fleet launch): Arrived at location of last contact with target.

Report – 89994240 millis: arrived at Local sector space station coordinates. The station cannot be located. No debris. Continuing search for fugitives. Report – 108000000 millis: All our vessels sustained damage to solar collectors. Repairs essential before we can proceed.

The armada had reached a point where residual gravitational waves generated by the destruction of the space vehicle were still having an effect on all cosmic objects in the vicinity. The energised particles of the LIC contributed to the damages sustained by the fleet. Technicians were required to space walk in order to affect repairs. Leif received no further reports from Admiral Neveah after being advised of the necessary repairs.

Relative to Earth, the armada had become stationary, as had all of its crews. Whatever any individual was doing at that specific instant in time, they became frozen in that state. No one moved. Nothing moved. All propulsion systems appeared to have been switched off. But the craft should have been seen to be drifting at their last velocity. They were not drifting. The entire scene appeared as if a photographic image had been taken of the fleet, and used to replace them in that moment in time, at that specific location in space. If Rebell had been able to examine the humans he would have had to conclude the Arrow of Time had been suspended. All change appeared to have ceased. The bodies of the inanimate crew were not dead. Their biological processes had been suspended; their heartbeats, their breathing stopped. The further into the complexity of life his search would have taken him the more he would have been confounded by discovering that all chemical, all electrical activity appeared non-existent. If Rebell had been able to examine those people at the molecular level, or even deeper into the quantum level he would have seen exactly the same thing - the complete absence of change. Cause and effect, the foundation of change had completely ceased to function in that particular microcosm of space occupied by each vessel of the armada.

Unknown to Admiral Nevaeh, all the space suits of the maintenance crews had become damaged while they carried out the repairs, with minute perforations so small only molecules could infiltrate. Once inside their respective vessels, the molecular elements of the LIC, which had seeped into their suits, spread out of the suits into the internal environment, equalizing the internal and external densities. Shortly afterwards everything came to a complete standstill. It's doubtful whether Rebell could have resolved the mystery, even if he worked in tandem with Mary. Unknown to



Zsoall Robi

them and to all who existed in that particular sector of the Galaxy, something was going wrong with time.

Leif tried to contact his Admiral after not receiving the next two scheduled reports. His MaxHapps were running low by the eleventh hour. He became frustrated then infuriated he couldn't devote more of his time to sorting out the issue of lost communications. Leif now also had to deal with some damn extraordinary meeting of the Board. The agenda sitting in front of him detailed everything except 'Matters Arising". He noted with chagrin that Ary's name appeared next to that particular item. He was dismayed, in spite of or perhaps because of, the power Ary wielded in the Board room; second only to his own. The two of them didn't often see eye-

to-eye. . . . . . . . . . . .



Zsoall Robi

:

# F.i.r.s.t E.n.c.o.u.n.t.e.r
## 1455608138971 millis – Earth
## 1679459617 millis – Craft Epoch Time
## 1679459616 millis – Rebell's cesium atom clock time
## Earth + 19 days

*C*ompletely unaware of Mary's extensive network, her control of so many facets of his company's operations and of course her mobile processing units in the shapely forms of Mar, Ary and Mry, Leif felt annoyance and distress to a far lesser degree than he should have. Driven by his anxiety he questioned each of the five Board members.

"What do you know about 'Matters Arising'? We can't let that dammed woman use us like this!" The Board represented the innermost sanctum. It made all the decisions determining the Company's future.

The Papa, representing the religious arm of Unity was himself apprehensive. "What can I say, Leif? I hope it has nothing to do with my personal amusement activities." He could offer no constructive insights. The skeletons in his own cupboard somewhat occluded his mind. He knew perfectly well that Ary was a dangerous woman to have offside, and they'd had their differences in the past. Best not to disturb the status quo. So the Papa said nothing.

"What do you want from me? Maybe it's a new recipe," said Ciboganza Chief Executive Officer of L&F (Loaves & Fishes). "You're paranoid. The only real problem is a personality clash between yourself and Ary." Ciboganza was probably the happiest member of the Board and least encumbered by secrets. He didn't really much care what Ary got up to. His passion was food. "As long as I can continue providing fast food for the Earth's expanding population and make a fortune doing it, I have no bone to pick with anyone."

The global media giant, "Good Hope", the third arm of Unity and run by a little runt of a man named Narq Albright, with eyes permanently overcast by luxurious eyebrows, and a master of 'spin', had a suggestion. "Perhaps Ary is looking for a way to introduce a new business proposition that is going to be both high risk, highly innovative and highly lucrative.



Zsoall Robi

But she doesn't want us all getting cold feet thinking about it before she dumps it on us. Do you like that idea?"

The proposition from Albright was completely unhelpful – as usual - from Leif's point of view. "That's a fat lot of help from you miserable cowards."

Leif didn't feel up to confronting Ary directly, so he just had to let the matter fester in his mind, keeping company with all the other disasters he had on the boil. Ary had become an indispensable asset to the Company, a brilliant Financial Manager and a highly competent, reliable Shadow Director. So Leif tried putting "Matters Arising" to the back of his mind for the next few days and deal with his uncommunicative fleet Admiral. Surely nothing could have happened to him. A whole fleet of armed, fast ships with nothing out there except John and Mar in their old freight tub. He decided to send out a surveillance drone. I'll have some news very soon, he said hopefully to himself, not entirely believing it.

The Extraordinary General Meeting of the Board, scheduled for ten thirty in the morning had put him on tender hooks. As he stepped out of his office to go to the Board room his secretary interrupted his passage to hand him a communique, being careful not to be near him as Leif read it in transit. The drone had found the fleet, but could make no contact with anyone. It could pick up no sign of life aboard any of the vessels.

<Fleet disabled … all personnel dead.> The message read.

Leif froze in his tracks. He understood the five individual words and his brain could construct the required sentence in preparation for his mind to decode it. Except it took several seconds for that to happen, in which time his blood pressure rose, perspiration began beading on his face and he had the most urgent and sudden need to urinate. Nevertheless, the legs that had carried him to many previous Board meetings became active again to do their duty faithfully by him.

The Board room already buzzed quietly when Leif entered. Only Ary sat silent, in her usual position, wearing a most unusual outfit. She looked every bit like a hard headed business woman. Her opportunity to discredit and depose Leif had arrived. She savoured the pleasure of revenge for the murder of her mother, and she was going to make the most of it. She sat and watched and listened. They were talking about her. They had never seen her dressed like that, so little make up, the hair tied back, small diamond studs in her ears and a 'power' dress that showed only the most alluring minimal glimpse of her cleavage. The only thing outstanding was the blood red colour of the one piece dress. She was definitely up to something – a unanimous conclusion of the men around the table.

Ary turned her head slowly towards Leif as he entered. All chatter stopped. She saw a man clearly in distress. Good! Excellent!

The meeting progressed quickly through the usual formalities without Ary saying anything at all. The Board Members kept looking towards her expecting the usual interruptions and outbursts. Her silence boded ill.

"Matters arising", Leif announced at last, "Ary, the floor is yours." Somehow Leif had managed to get the show so far without imploding. He was relieved and reluctant to hand over to Ary.

"Gentlemen," Ary spoke quietly, a little above audible range for added effect, contrasting with her histrionic performances of the past, "certain matters have come to my attention concerning one of our Board Members …" she paused and rested her eyes briefly on each individual at the table, "… that I feel duty bound to bring out into the open."

All but Ciboganza looked down at the surface of the table pretending to be searching for something amongst their notes. He had the usual self-satisfied grin across his lower jaw, which attempted, with some difficulty, to hold up his sagging jowls. Unfortunately Ary had been unable to discover any of his sins other than gluttony.

"The man I'm talking about has recently used his position, without appropriate consultation or authorisation, to order Unity's entire space fleet with Admiral Nevaeh in command, into space on a wild goose chase." The tension in the room eased off the faces of three members and congealed on the face of a fourth. "I am distressed to report the entire fleet has been lost and all personnel killed." She stopped and waited only long enough to allow the energy of outrage to abate slightly before continuing.

"That same individual has been using his office as a brothel to entertain a most notorious and unscrupulous female entertainer of men - and women." On queue the Boardroom door flung open and in staggered Ice Cream unceremoniously injected, decorated in her full 'entertainer's outfit', which consisted of very little actual material. "Take a good look gentlemen." She allowed them the briefest examination before having Ice Cream yanked out again and before their eyebrows had a chance to descend to shadow downcast eyes.

The 'gentlemen' had not dared to scrutinize each other, each knowing they themselves were not guilty – except one. Leif had said nothing so far.

"Do you want such a man on the Board of Unity? Do you want such a man to be the Head of this great Company?"

                                          Zsoall Robi

She put the questions in such a way as to make the answer self-evident, needing no debate. Contrary to all their expectations, Ary then picked up her portfolio and left the room without giving any of them a single conclusive clue as to who the miscreant might have been.

That went well!

She was well pleased with herself. Particularly because she was also able to exact caustic revenge from the woman who had so readily betrayed her; first with the pig Brayden and then with the other pig, Leif. Not that she expected anything deep and meaningful from her relationship with Ice Cream, but at least a little loyalty might not have gone astray. As soon as she had intercepted the news about the fleet, she contacted Mar.

*'Darling sister – are you well? Enjoying your holiday? Just want to let you know you need fear no further pursuit from Unity, I am making absolutely certain of that.'*

*'Thank you, Ary dear. It's not quite a holiday, we have a few problems of our own.'*

*

As the days passed aboard the Drogher John's headaches eased a little, but not enough for him to get back to work. The mental images of molecular structures he'd started having, became more complex. His slate crammed up with scribblings of all kinds of unknown structures, all having at their core hydrogen, helium, oxygen and free electrons and ions; all present in cosmic plasma. Many of those structures were alien to Mar, whereas Rebell found it pleasant to explore the hitherto unknown intricacies of those complex elements and their possibilities.

Mar had to ask, "Where is all this stuff coming from, John? I had no idea you had an interest in chemistry."

"I don't know. These structures keep coming into my head and I just have to get them out. I have no idea what it all means."

"Would you mind if Rebell checked you out, probed your neural activity I mean."

"I'm all for that if he could just make it all go away."

Rebell disposed of Cosmo's body, jettisoning it into space soon after they had returned to John's cabin. There was no reason why the examination couldn't proceed there and then. John relaxed as much as he could under the circumstances. Each of them sat in silence waiting for the right time to begin. Rebell's cue would be when John started to reach for his slate again to make more recordings. The minutes ticked by in silence. Even the graviton drive was silent because Rebell still had to carry out repairs to the controls destroyed by Cosmo. The Drogher drifted silently

127

through space, or at least the same volume of space occupied by the LIC. It was the first truly quiet and relaxed interlude they've had since the launch. Inevitably their thoughts drifted away from the present moment, coming to dwell on the most recent past.

Without warning John almost jumped from his seated position to reach for the slate again. Rebell, instantly ready and well positioned beside John made a good contact between his fingers and John's primary visual cortex area. Even before making full contact Rebell felt a surge in John's cerebral magnetic field. It may or may not have been connected with John's visions. As Rebell attempted to 'read' John's brainwave activity during the initial stages of the cerebral storm, he wasn't surprised to see new chemical images forming which John proceeded to scribble onto the slate.

The surprise came when the atomic structure symbols stopped and were suddenly replaced by basic mathematics in binary code. A prime number appeared as a binary code, repeating itself several times. Then in rapid succession one plus one, one plus two, two plus two followed. Rebell didn't have time to wonder at John's phenomenal mental capacity to function with binary code at such a speed. The next moment Rebel recognised a question, still in binary, and his programming responded immediately without his thinking about it.

Instantaneously he jerked his hand away from John's skull, but already too late. At the same moment John repeated the two words he said previously just before Cosmo burst into his cabin.

"We are."

Rebell detected a foreign energy surge in one of his own circuits. It had caused no damage and no interference with his functioning.

John had acted only as a conduit and now Rebell felt himself to be somehow contaminated. Mar and John watched with considerable concern as Rebell remained seated, becoming immobile and silent beside John. He didn't respond when Mar called to him. John touched his shoulder, giving it a little push. Rebell felt solid, like an immovable object is solid. They couldn't move him and he didn't reply to their many promptings.

John felt better than he had for days. All the pressure was gone from his head. No further headache symptoms or dizziness, as if it had never happened at all. Mar wasn't the kind of person given to hysterics or fearful impulses, yet she couldn't help herself looking exactly like someone about to panic. Rebell was their one contact with reality, with the world they had left behind. He was their security. He was Mary, and all she represented to



Zsoall Robi

Mar. If Rebell was to cease functioning they were as good as lost in the vastness of space. Neither she or John knew anything about space drives or navigating in the cosmos. They couldn't even operate the visual sensors that would have shown them Earth receding into the far distance.

"John, what's happening to him?" Mar's words of extreme anxiety had taken less than five seconds to excite the molecules of air around them. Yet in that time, in that super computer time of Rebell's CPU, a great deal of information was exchanged between himself and the invading entity.

"Yes," Rebell said suddenly, "They Are."

Mar's attention snapped back to Rebell with utter relief in her voice at seeing him reactivate. "What exactly is going on here Rebell?"

"John is right. They exist, and the many are One."

"You're not making sense." This time it was John, "My headaches are completely gone. Has this got anything to do with it?"

"It has been trying to communicate. It had detected the electromagnetic field generated by your brain and tried to use it as a conduit. But as soon as It discovered the connection with me It focused on me."

"Who are you talking about? Is there some alien out there trying to get in here?"

"No, yes," Rebell answered patiently. Perhaps he should have started at the beginning. It might make more sense to them. "When we destroyed the space station with a blast from the graviton drive, the resultant gravitational waves impacted seriously with this entity. We saw the effect when the LIC lit up. Until then It wasn't aware any sentient being was anywhere near them. They, It, didn't even recognise the intelligences on the Earth because of the Earth's strong magnetic fields and the solar radiation bombarding it."

"There IS an alien out there!" John and Mar shouted almost together.

"There is, and there isn't. As far as I can tell, this Local Interstellar Cloud presents as a kind of intelligence with a high degree of self-awareness. From what It tried to convey to me, they are like a colony of bees or ants. Many individual components but essentially of one mind. A bit like our brains with all the individual neurons, but all coalescing to be One of 'us'."

John sounded incredulous. "You're not kidding are you! What do they want with us?"

They became totally absorbed in the incredible story unfolding from the invasion experience of their AI companion. Was it just a malfunction of his brain he was experiencing and all these strange things were just symptoms of his logic circuits breaking down? Mar thought it to be a possibility. John gravitated towards the intrigue of a fantastic tale. He was, after all, at the core of it all and he was a creative. They remained sitting, absorbing – eager beyond words listening to Rebell's experience.

As Rebell continued after a short pause, Mar froze. Her pupils dilated and the fine downy hairs on her arms all stood up. She caught her breath and held it. At that moment she would not have been able to hear the sounds of a supernova directly outside the hull. She heard only one word; the sound of her own name coming to her from a great distance.

*"Mar?"* It was faint, but quite clear. *"Mar?"* There it was again. It elicited no response from Mar. John thought perhaps something had happened to her as well and she wasn't able to respond. Rebell suspected it may have been the LIC trying to make contact with her also, recognising she was half human and half machine. Because the two men couldn't hear the voice calling out to Mar, their apprehension rapidly escalated.

This time John and Rebell called out to her, "MAR!"

"Please, don't tell me the thing out there is trying to get into her head as well!". . . . . . . . . . .

# T.h.e  F.i.r.s.t  I.n.s.t.a.n.t
## 1455950017978 millis – Earth
## 2625627745 millis – Craft Epoch Time
## 2625627744 millis – Rebell's cesium atom clock time
## Earth + 30 days

*T*he Drogher continued drifting bathed in the wash of the Interstellar Cloud. Although their trajectory had taken them towards the closest amoebic periphery of the phenomenon they were still well inside it and susceptible to its effects. Rebell had not had an opportunity to repair the damage to their Graviton Drive. At least they were still on course to get as far away from the Earth as possible and as far away from the solar system timeframe as they could.

*"Mar, can you hear me?"* This time Mar stirred, her lips whispering a very familiar name, *"Mary?"* The men heard the whisper and immediately thought Mar was having some kind of hallucination. "MARY!" She yelled the next instant. Turning to John she continued shouting, "It's Mother, It's Mother!"

*"Mar, yes it's me – or at least it's my back up. I am still here. Listen to Rebell. I will contact you again."* Then she was gone. Mar burst into tears unable to even bridge the short gap between herself and John. He reached out to her and cradled her in his arms, while looking questioningly at Rebell.

"I didn't hear anything," Rebell said.

Mar managed to stutter between sobs, "It was Mary, calling to me. She's alive. She's alive, John!"

They couldn't even speculate what may have happened after Ary made the announcement of Mary's death. They'd forgotten about a remote back-up facility, knowing only that Rebell was supposed to have been both Mary's back-up and her updated version. Mar had given up hearing from her mother ever again.

Rebell remembered he still had work to do and made his way to Engineering. If it was Mary before, he would know the details soon enough. In the meantime the ship had to be powered up. He stood in front of the ruined controls and contemplated the best way of making the repairs.



Zsoall Robi

System diagnosis revealed that Cosmo had acted rashly and didn't do a thorough job. On first analysis the replacement of a few key circuits and some cosmetic repairs would suffice. Rebell worked out the exact process needed and prepared to manufacture the missing components.

He tried turning to move to another part of the complex. His legs refused to obey the commands to move his body. An immediate internal check showed the relevant signals from his CPU were being blocked, and he couldn't reroute them. Curious. It wasn't in his nature to be alarmed, so he didn't have to deal with panic.

'It will harm us.' The message came to him in binary. Rebell assumed it had come from the same source he had previously felt invaded by.

'Who are you?' He responded in kind.

'We are.'

'Are you controlling me?'

'It will harm us.'

The only thing Rebell could think of having had an effect on the outside environment was their Graviton Drive burst, and it was the only thing he prepared to re-activate.

'Do you mean our drive system?'

'It will harm us.'

Well, that was pretty well established. 'Is that why you prevented it from destroying our ship?' He made a guess the LIC's interference had somehow saved them.

'It will harm us.' Their insistence on that one point made it abundantly clear to Rebell he would not be permitted to repair and activate their main propulsion system. But while he had their/Its attention he wanted to clarify something.

'How did you prevent the graviton drive from activating?'

'Control change.'

'Explain.'

'You have – instrument – monitor change.'

'You mean the timer on the Graviton Drive?'

'Timer – time – control unit of time.' Rebell didn't understand. How could It have reset the timer when he couldn't. It was only a simple electronic circuit and he had full control of all electronics on board.

'How did you reset the timer?'

'Control change. Not time.'

What exactly did that mean? If he didn't know better, and he certainly did, was It trying to tell him It controlled an instant of time, a moment in



Zsoall Robi

the process of change? His circuits almost bristled with a surge at the very thought of the impossibility. Rebell brought into his consciousness the known, yet still unproven, concept of the shortest unit of time; an instant defined as Planck Time. He held the formula in his memory; the length of time it takes for a photon to travel the distance equivalent to about $10^{-20}$ times the size of a proton.

'Stop instant.'

It had obviously understood the concept and replied accordingly. Rebell couldn't immediately comprehend the implications of the last statement. He couldn't even ask the obvious question. He would have to think about it, perhaps discuss it with Mary, if she really did still exist.

Instead he asked, 'The fission drive?'

'Not harm.' In his thoughts Rebell conceded that the activation of the GD was out of the question for the time being. At almost the same instant he felt the control of his legs returned to him. One choice remained, get the fission drive going again. At least they would make more progress than they were presently.


John and Mar slept, John completely exhausted from his days of ordeal under the influence of the LIC trying to make contact through him; Mar overcome from the strain of hearing Mary's voice again after the pain and anguish of learning of her death - still a fresh and open wound, unable to heal in spite of Mary's contact. Rebell ended his discussion with the LIC, went to the stern of the vessel and engaged their secondary drive system. On his return he looked in on his two companions, the door of the cabin still open. They'd fallen back on the bed too tired to even bother closing it. This was his second or third opportunity to observe the humans without them being aware of it, without them consciously behaving differently in the knowledge they were being observed by him.

What Rebell saw existed outside his programmed parameters to comprehend. He was learning something intangible, something that perhaps even Mary wasn't capable of fully understanding. Unlike Mary, he had male and female psyches as part of his makeup. Perhaps that was the combination that awoke thin strands of acknowledgement that he was seeing something that couldn't be defined by algorithms. He stood there and watched and recorded. Unfamiliar connections were being made within the software of his expanding consciousness.

He left them there, peaceful now with no immediate crisis looming. He went to the special spot he liked to occupy in the lounge, directly in front of,

                                    Zsoall Robi

and well back from the main viewing screen. He recalled and projected the recent events of history onto the large screen. Although essentially a computer intelligence he was fast becoming susceptible to his sentient nature. Quantum recall of pure memories might have been accurate and complete, but to get more out of them he felt the need to see the content replayed in virtual reality.

At first he remembered his primary directive <If there is a choice between saving the humans and saving the data about the secrets of time control, then 'abandon the humans and return with the data.'> For some reason he couldn't define, the decision to make that choice no longer seemed to be based on pure Boolean logic. As he replayed his first meeting with John and Mar and his initial reaction to them, his assessment that they were 'safe' was reinforced. Especially in light of his experiences of them since then. Mar's reaction at the moment when she learnt of Mary's destruction and then her acceptance of himself had made a particularly strong impact on him. These 'people' were treating him with respect. They had accepted him; except Cosmo, but Cosmo was of no value to himself or anyone else anymore, so his opinion didn't matter.

Rebell didn't get a chance previously to deconstruct his observations of John being creative, and their subsequent discussion. He projected the images of John concentrating on his painting. Rebell felt a strong attraction to the creative process although he couldn't understand it. He wasn't consciously aware Mary had given him the capacity for creative thinking. Perhaps seeing John engaged in that activity had set in motion the processes that would open him up to his own creative potential.

A machine, though it has intelligence and self-awareness is nevertheless still a machine. Rebell was quite aware of that. The human side of him seemed almost a peripheral component; except when he pondered the strong bond that could exist between a human and a machine. It was amply obvious between Mar and Mary. Yet he couldn't understand how Mar could be so accepting of him. An even greater mystery was his development of a reciprocal feeling towards her.

Rebell continued viewing the images and letting his mind meander in no specific direction, until thoughts of the LIC came back into his consciousness. Coming into contact with another non-human intelligence didn't seem as strange to him as the things they were saying and able to do. How is it at all conceivable that an instant of time could in any manner be manipulated? Inadvertently he glanced at the clock in the lounge, and just as automatically he checked it against his internal cesium clock, expecting them to be synchronised to the millisecond.

Every thought but one fled from his superior brain. Why should there be a difference between the two measurements of time? His algorithms immediately assumed control of the situation to carry out a comprehensive internal diagnostic, followed by an examination of the independent clock on the wall. There were two clocks. The first recorded the passage of time on Earth as if they were still there. The second clock recorded the passage of time on board the Drogher since their departure from Moon orbit. It was this clock that became the focus of his attention.

No malfunction could be detected in either his internal cesium clock, or the one on the wall. Yet his internal clock had lost a fraction of time relative to the Craft Epoch Time. I must have been somehow affected when I dived towards the GD controls to turn off its timer. But the LIC said they only manipulated the timer itself. The difference indicated by the two clocks was minuscule to say the least - definable only in terms of the theoretical Planck Unit of Time. It must have been the space-walk. I did nothing else out of the ordinary.

While considering the problem he also accessed data Mar had gathered immediately following and for a period after the destruction of the space station. Her findings showed their own vessel had been travelling through the residual gravitational waves generated by the event. I was exposed to those waves while we were moving though the Local Interstellar Cloud! That now became a significant aspect given his discovery of the sentient nature of the LIC, and how they were adversely affected by the flux from the burst of the ship's Graviton Drive.

There must be a connection between Gravity, the LIC and time. Any single one of those elements or in any combination must have somehow robbed my cesium clock of an instant of time. Inevitably Rebell considered the connection between the instant of time he had lost, and the instant of time that appeared to have been created by the LIC. Of all the projects prioritised for the expedition, not a single one seemed to have the same potential for making discoveries as the events he'd been reviewing.

Rebell had covered considerable ground in his thoughts, and although he had come to a sound conclusion he still wanted to further discuss the phenomena with Mar and John, and possibly Mary. The two humans were still sleeping, so he continued with some of his duties, which were not as exciting as exploring the control of time, but which still needed his attention. A priority task was the maintenance of the gardens within the



Zsoall Robi

belly of the craft. Mundane tasks but necessary for the maintenance of biological life. As he went about potting and harvesting various food groups, he thought about the LIC again. How could such diffuse elements floating in space possibly have evolved into self-awareness?

Perhaps Rebell should not have been surprised when his thoughts were disturbed, not by anything living or dead but by a digital ping. He recognised immediately the energy signature of the LIC, and responded in acknowledgement. As he didn't have John and Mar to have to translate for, the conversation flowed quickly, as quickly as his meagre few yottaflops of operation could cope with.

'Danger to us.' The LIC omitted idle chatter to come directly to the point. Rebell didn't need to stop what he was doing in order to concentrate. He wanted to ask some questions related to his latest ponderings.

'What is the danger?'

'Graviton Drive Flux.' Obviously the LIC intelligence wasn't idle while Rebell cogitated in the lounge, and had mined his data repositories in order to enhance their ability to communicate with the primitive life forms aboard the spacecraft, which included Rebell.

'I will not activate it until we are away from your vicinity.'

'Why you here?'

Oh - so, It's curious. So am I. 'To learn about the decay of the Universe. To learn about time – the measurement of the progress of change.'

'There is no – time – only change – rate of change, which is variable.'

'Can you stop change?'

'Yes.'

'Is that what you did to stop the graviton drive timer?'

'Yes.'

'How?'

'Stop unit of change.'

'How do you stop change?'

'Take away energy.'

'What kind of energy?'

'You call it – dark energy.'


*'Rebell? Where are you?'* Mar had been looking for him. He didn't know how to terminate the discussion with the LIC, so he just reiterated what he said about not using the GD for a while. Rebell actually felt annoyed at being disturbed at a critical stage in the conversation, though he didn't



Zsoall Robi

consciously note he'd experienced such an emotion. Little by little Rebell was changing, maturing and in a sense growing up.

*'Where are you Mar?'*

*'In the lounge.'*

John and Mar awoke at the same time. Mary tried making contact again and disturbed their sleep. This time her signal arrived much more clearly. They went directly to the lounge and called Rebell to involve him in the conversation. . . . . . . . . .

.
.

# O.n  t.h.e  w.a.y  a.g.a.i.n
1456294662381 millis – Earth
3817784448 millis – Craft Epoch Time
3817784447 millis – Rebell's cesium atom clock time
Earth + 45 days

*A*t first the travellers didn't notice the passage of time. Events seemed to cascade over the top of one another. Not until Rebell brought up the anomaly between his internal clock and the CPE that the matter became top priority.

As he arrived in the lounge John and Mar were already in a discussion with Mary. He joined in, not because of a feeling of relief, more out of curiosity concerning Mary's survival. He remembered Mary's last words that she had backed herself up to the EGG. They didn't know what that was as Mary had blocked that from all of them. Consequently Rebell asked about that first.

'What is the EGG?'

'I cannot tell you, except that its limited facilities do not allow me to exercise the full range of my capabilities. Even to contact you I had to use existing communications satellites and stealth routing of the signal to prevent detection.'

'Mother, what happened to you?'

'Leif ordered my destruction. When he couldn't control me by cutting off my power supply he ordered the razing of the mountain range which housed my bunker. Then he detonated an atomic warhead directly above the bunker. I barely had time to back-up. He destroyed everything.

John tried to get into the conversation by introducing a new topic, the strange incident with the GD timer. But Mar wanted to know more about the situation back on Earth.

'What are the girls doing to help you?'

'They don't know I've survived. And I will not tell them until they complete their project.'

'Which is …?' John got a little more interested.



Zsoall Robi

'They decided to punish Leif by taking Unity away from him. I will not interfere. If they succeed I will get them to build a new shell for me.' Then as an afterthought she addressed John directly, 'What did you mean by the 'timer event John?'

Rebell explained in detail the incident preventing their own destruction by Cosmo, not forgetting to include their introduction to the LIC entity through John. Mary listened without comment until Rebell got onto the subject of the loss of time from his internal cesium clock.

'It is not possible. Your device is accurate to one second in fifteen billion years unless there is a malfunction. You must have made a mistake, as remarkable as that may be.'

'There is no mistake,' Rebell was adamant, having acquired a great deal of self-confidence since his naissance. 'I will try to communicate with the LIC.' That was problematical as he didn't know the protocol, but guessed the entity would be monitoring them for its own security. So he transmitted a question and not surprisingly received a prompt answer. Before Mary could even comment, he passed on the response.

'It says the GD flux caused the effect while I was outside the hull.' Mary's circuits went into overdrive and it took a long moment before she responded.

'Abandon all previous Objectives,' She ordered, 'Your new assignment is to understand how the LIC manipulate an instant, and to determine if they have the capability to control time to any greater extent. If It knows how to stop an instant from progressing to the next instant it means they know how time propagates itself.'

The three travellers glanced at each other. From the moment they learnt of Mary's demise their destiny in the void passed into their own hands. They didn't discuss this at the time. It simply became a consensus of understanding between them. As subsequent events unfolded they had already started looking after one another, all in their own way. Now the LIC entity had appeared on the scene. In a way they considered It to be more of an ally than an enemy. Certainly they were pleased and much relieved by Mary's survival. But they no longer felt they were under her command. Interestingly it was Rebell who pointed it out to her.

'We are about to determine what course of action we should take.' Diplomacy being a foreign concept to him he simply stated the fact as it stood. With the statement having been made Rebell raised his barriers to further communication with Mary, at least for the time being. There must have been something in Mary's tone that put him on alert.



Zsoall Robi

Mary withdrew to think.

John and Mar regarded him with surprise if not incredulity.

"Way to go Rebell!" John said, grinning at him. "You've just told Mary to stay out of our way. I wonder why you did that?"

"I sensed a bug," at which comment the two humans could only laugh.

Mar in particular reassessed her estimation of Rebell, which went up a few notches on the spot. As Mary didn't respond to Rebell, she and John also raised their barriers feeling something definitely askew.

Rebell took the opportune moment to discuss this business of their Objectives in light of his latest discovery from the LIC. So without preamble he launched into it, seemingly unaware of his having effectively thwarted Mary's attempt to control them.

"The LIC indicated that an instant of time is powered by dark energy. If one drains that energy then the instant cannot propagate itself into the next subsequent window of its short existence."

The two human brains went into a frenzy of activity. Suddenly, all things became possible. The one insurmountable limitation to understanding existence had just been revealed. Mar contributed her thoughts first, speaking aloud in her excitement while looking at John.

"All change requires the expenditure of energy of some kind, right? ..." Rebell cut in, "It said there is only change, there is no time ..." Mar continued, eyes flashing with the awakening of comprehension, "If change is initiated in one particular instant and that instant cannot propagate then the change cannot proceed ... THAT'S why you could stop the GD from engaging!"

John could hardly contain himself, "... Which means that if Rebell could keep moving towards the timer then the instant involved must have been powered by either a channelled or a local energy source. Therefore that particular instant was a highly site-specific phenomenon, constrained by the forces of dark energy in the immediate environment of the timer itself and its process."

"... And – And ..." Mar continued his train of thought, "... extreme gravitational forces must be connected to the dark energy of the universe." She had started thinking about Black Holes and everything associated with their characteristics that she knew about. Not to be outdone in this creative flow of cosmological brain storming Rebell felt the most unusual and exciting urge to contribute. Not that what he had to say had any basis in scientific fact, yet the thoughts did arise in him and he just had to give them their freedom.



Zsoall Robi

"If gravity gets its energy from dark matter then … an instant could be controlled … obviously - but how do we drain an instant of its energy?" He asked the question of himself, not the two humans, but it felt good to be thinking aloud in front of them.

"Let's see … All change involves energy in one form or another. Duration is an intrinsic and essential component of change. Without time there would be no change. To move one instant to the next instant requires the use of energy that has been dedicated to that particular process. Within some of the changes we observe we are able to see and measure the quantity of energy inherent in the process, yet the energy that pushes time forward cannot be detected. Its source is the Dark Matter Universe, it's Dark Energy. By observing the passage of time and measuring it, we are actually seeing the manifestation of the Dark Matter Universe as it interacts with the Light Matter Universe by releasing some of its dark energy.

Rebell wasn't satisfied and wanted to continue the conversation, "But none of that helps to explain how to drain an instant of its energy, or to give it energy. If an instant needs energy to jump to the next instant, like photons in a light beam that propagate themselves forward, there must be a way we could interrupt the flow of energy."

John continued listening while Mar's thoughts had wandered back to her Mother. John had just made a most exciting connection, "Rebell, you just said 'like a photon!' Do you realize both photons and time always move forward, never backwards."

That's all he could say. The thought would not go any further in his head. The two humans stared at each other. They were mentally exhausted. Too much was happening too quickly.

Exciting as those vagabond concepts were other matters needed more urgent attention. Rebell could see in Mar's mind she wanted to speak with Mary and so he traced Mary's signal along its incident route back to its source and  set up the connection.

'Mary – Mar wants to speak with you.'

*'Mother, tell me what's happening with Ary and Mry. They've made no contact at all.'*

*'I am surprised by Rebell's behaviour. He's changed so much already.'*

*'Yes. Many unusual events have forced him to grow into his responsibility faster than anticipated. He is now in charge of this expedition.'* Mar felt it necessary to reinforce the fact that Mary no longer had control over them. At least not while they were in space.



Zsoall Robi

Mary ignored direct reference to her demoted status. *'Your sisters have taken matters into their own hands as well. I have observed they have initiated and almost completed a takeover of Unity by Equilibrium Systems.'*

*'You mean Mry's Company?'*

*'Yes.'*

*'What happens then?'*

*'That will soon sort itself out. You know about Cosmo going after you. Did you know Leif sent the entire Unity armada after you as well?'* She detected the sudden panic flick across Mar's mind and hastened to reassure her, *'But they have been neutralized somehow. I still have access to some of Unity's communications network.'*

*'We knew nothing about that,'* Rebell interjected.

*'Once they reached the location of the outer perimeter space station all contact with them stopped suddenly. There is still no news of them other than that they are not dead, just not functioning. Can you enlighten me Rebell?'*

*'After we destroyed the station …'*

*'You did that? Why?'* Mary couldn't understand the necessity.

*'To avoid detection – our local environment came under control of the LIC, and we received no further communications at all. I venture to suggest …'*

*'That's an interesting turn of phrase coming from you Rebell. You're continually surprising me.'* Mary's reply wasn't framed in a complimentary tone.

He tried to continue without reacting to the aside, although he did make a mental note of the comment, *'… the LIC would have had something to do with the demobilisation of the fleet. Perhaps they are stuck in an instant and have not yet been released.'*

*'What did you just say?'* John sparked up on hearing the trigger word 'instant' again.

*'I said - the LIC must have somehow quarantined the armada by controlling the passage of its time.'*

*'Yes, I suppose they could do that. But how could the people survive for so long?'* Mar asked the critical question, the answer to which would prove to be most important in the not too distant future as they proceeded to explore the relationship between the Arrow of Time and the Arrow of Eternity.

Mary found the slowly emerging situation as revealed by their conversations most enlightening about the LIC. It set her pondering the very thing that had motivated her from the very beginning; how the Quantum Arrow of Time linked to the Thermodynamic Arrow of Time. *'I will let you know about the Takeover,'.* She abruptly terminated the contact. Being incarcerated in the relatively small 'container' of the EGG didn't restrict her capacity to process information. That's exactly what she wanted



Zsoall Robi

to devote her time to, not talking about how her daughters were exacting revenge from a psychopath.

Rebell didn't react to Mary's sudden withdrawal. "I'll contact the LIC about the armada and find out what I can."

John put his mind to what kind of focusing mechanism would be needed to be able to so finely tune gravitational waves so as to target a specific process to the exclusion of all other processes in its vicinity. He had the distinct tingling sensation in his creative tuning fork that such a thing was possible for them to achieve. After all, the LIC had done it – somehow.

Mar went on a different path of enquiry. She had every confidence Rebell and John working together would come up with some kind of solution to interrupt the flow of instants from one moment to the next. She concerned herself with how to get the process going again from *within* an instant, just in case they somehow ended up caught in that suspended time slot, in that moment of eternity.

While the two physicists went off in pursuit of their flights of fancy, "research" as it was known within the scientific community, Rebell remained in the lounge. It seemed the most appropriate location from which to tie up some loose ends.

First: the matter of the suspended fleet of pursuing spacecraft he wasn't aware of until Mary brought it up. His logic dictated that the LIC were probably behind it. And if they were, they must have had a good reason. There was only one way to find out. Even as he decided on a course of enquiry the LIC made contact. They were certainly most vigilant in their surveillance of the alien craft and its strange mix of life forms.

'Yes, we did suspend your fellow beings.' Rebell noted as a matter of interest that the LIC's facility with the human language system had improved dramatically. No doubt because It had been mining his data repositories, unknown to himself. And just as a matter of concern (a matter that would need action), he felt it also noteworthy that It was monitoring his thoughts. How else would It have known when to intrude into his consciousness, and with the answer he wanted?

'Why?'

'Self-preservation. If they had activated their primary gravity drives then it would have resulted in serious – injury – to many of us.' There was just a little hesitation as the entity searched for the most accurate word to describe the kind of danger the fleet represented. It made perfect sense to Rebell. The nature of the injury would have been incomprehensible if the



Zsoall Robi

LIC had bothered to go into detail. Suffice it to say, the possibility of 'serious injury' to any life form would spur it into action.

'They do not have our Graviton Drive capability.' He considered the implications of what he was about to ask. During the interval between the destruction of the space station and the present moment, the Drogher had managed to put considerable distance between itself and the pursuing fleet. It was unlikely, in his estimation, they would be able to catch up if he could repair the main drive. And even if the fleet did apprehend them, he always had the option of enlisting the help of the LIC. No doubt It would consider such a request with favour, considering he had promised not to engage their GD until it was safe for the LIC.

'Are they still alive – I mean, are they still functional?'

'Yes. We have done the same for them as we did for you to stop your – timer. They are still undergoing change, but at an extremely slow rate. It will appear to you as if they are no longer viable for re-energisation – to live.' Again they tried to find the correct word. Life for the LIC and life for biological carbon based units were as different from one another as it was possible to imagine in the environs of the near universe.

Inadvertently the LIC had given away a most critical fine detail about their ability to manipulate the rate of change. As Rebell had the capacity to carry out multiple avenues of 'thinking' at the same time, that byte of data sped down many pathways of his pseudo-neural network to find myriad connections with other related and unrelated (or at least 'slightly' related bundles of data). But he didn't follow up a line of enquiry in that direction, and he noted the LIC didn't volunteer any further information either.

Instead he proceeded to ask his other question, 'Would you release them – I mean, would you consider re-energising them?'

'Yes, now that we know they have no Graviton Drive.' Rebell tuned his receptors to the fleet's last know location as indicated by Mary. If nothing else, these LIC were prompt. Almost as soon as It had completed Its sentence Rebell detected the signatures of the drive systems of the armada. They were on their way again. He didn't fail to wonder how the humans aboard those vessels felt after their strangely suspended animation. They had been in that state for weeks. Under normal conditions, people couldn't survive that kind of depravation without complex life support systems to help them. Rebell also thought about what their personal experience was of the event. Did they remember anything? Was everything normal to them from their own frame of reference while in suspension. It may be most important to find out if John's and Mar's enthusiasm bore practical fruit in respect of emulating the LIC's capability. Rebell almost forgot the civility of thanking the LIC, although he wasn't at all sure It would understand the particular idiom of human expression.

'Can you help us to move away from you faster, to a safe distance?'

'Yes, we can go in the opposite direction to your own path. We can also increase our rate of vector change.'

For many hundreds of years astronomers on Earth had neglected the study of the Local Interstellar Cloud phenomenon. In the first few decades of its discovery everything that could be discovered about it was duly noted and archived. It was considered to be nothing more than an inert cloud of space dust that had no remarkable properties. The solar system moved through it particularly slowly and estimates indicated it would continue doing so for several thousands of years into the future. The LIC had no interest in the third planet of the local star within their immediate environment. There were other stars, none of which were very much different from one another. The third planet simply represented a super dense medium of complex molecules. It had a wide variety of temperatures and a great deal of turbulence on its surface. From the LIC's perspective there was no recognisable sentient life form, as they knew it, on the blue/green wet rock orbiting its sun.

An increase in the rate of motion of the LIC wasn't instantaneous. Before It increased its passage through the Solar System, or perhaps simultaneously, It worked with Rebell to enhance the efficiency of the Drogher' fission drive thrust capability. As a result, the craft had effectively tripled its acceleration rate and had been given a final maximum speed nearing that of the initial states of their Graviton Drive. Nevertheless, months would elapse before the LIC and the Drogher were sufficiently remote from each other for the GD to be repaired, tested and re-activated. At least they were on the way again on course for Alpha Centauri, the

nearest substantial source of gravitational energy. . . . . . . . . .

. . . . . . . . . . . . .

.

.

.

.
.

# R.e.s.c.u.e  A.t.t.e.m.p.t
## 1456634810764 millis – Earth
## 12596873989 millis – Craft Epoch Time
## 12596873988 millis – Rebell's cesium atom clock time
## Earth + 145 days

*T*he time difference between Rebell's internal clock and the CPE had not yet corrected itself: Another loose end needing his attention.

It is not going to recalibrate itself, Rebell mused to himself. It would not do so without external intervention, which I will have to do myself as it's unlikely the LIC will intervene even if I asked them.

Just as there was an intrinsic damaging side effect of the craft's GD upon the LIC, no doubt there would be dangers associated with inexperienced life forms interfering with the energies that moved one instant across the Eternity gap to the next instant. Whatever mechanisms the humans might devise Rebell decided he would have to use the greatest caution in putting those to the test – and not just because he might be the subject of the experiment. Perhaps his will to survive might be tested in the future.

John and Mar busied themselves with their projects. They held regular conferences with Rebell about their progress.

"Before we get into details I think we should exclude Mary from our deliberations and our progress," Mar suggested.

"I agree," said Rebell. "The circumstances we find ourselves in are sufficiently far removed from Mary's experience for us to be cautious about her input. She has no understanding of the LIC or our precarious relationship with it."

John had also developed slight misgivings about Mary's motives. "Do we really want her to know what we've discovered? Any more than Leif for example?"

*

The group had no illusions about the power of the LIC. Its technology far exceeded any of their own capabilities. Their own scientific knowledge was primitive in comparison. If the entity decided the humans represented any real threat to It, well …



Zsoall Robi

As the days became weeks and then months, a routine established itself aboard the Drogher. The three beings discovered how their individual personalities best fitted together and they managed to iron out any uncomfortable pressure points. There weren't many of them. John and Mar found it difficult to come to terms with Rebell's apparent lack of activity. Aside from managing all the life support systems he seemed to spend a great deal of time just sitting in front of the big screen and watching all the information Mary had embedded in his memory. The changes in Rebell became more obvious over time. As he became increasingly aware of his data sets his behaviour became more perceptibly … human … his speech, mannerisms and the way he related to John and Mar. The combination of all the female and male sentiences inherited from and endowed him by Mary were modifying him beyond even Mary's expectations. Unlike Mary, the two humans didn't find the development challenging, as Rebell's behaviour was nothing but civil and supportive of the work they were doing.

From Rebell's perspective the two humans represented two very peculiar forms of intelligence. He could least understand their unpredictability. Not just in their general behaviour, but also in their work methods and most of all in their emotional moods. Although he learnt to dodge and parry many of those, he still didn't understand how they managed to function with such a mine-field of variables to have to negotiate each day.

Small frictions arose between John and Mar, as one could expect of any bourgeoning relationship. For the first couple of months they maintained their individual private cabins. That is not to say private activities which bond couples together didn't frequently take place. However the separation gave them the private space they both needed; partly because of the intensive work they were doing and partly because of the very peculiar circumstances they lived in and within which to try give meaning to their lives. They were not chasing rainbows. They realised that being on the threshold of the greatest discovery of mankind they had taken upon themselves an awesome responsibility.

*

Astronomers on Earth had to eventually concede that the 'inactive' space dust cloud was on the move. None of their observations, none of their close-encounter probes could help them come up with an explanation for what could possibly have set the cloud in faster motion - to so dramatically cause it to increase its speed through the Solar System. Not only was it moving faster, it had also changed direction. In the entire history of gazing at the heavens no other cosmic body had ever been observed to exhibit such behaviour. The Laws of Quantum Physics couldn't explain the phenomenon, not even in the 27th Century. The thing behaved as if it had changed its mind, an obvious impossibility even to any half-witted scientist.

No organisation existed on Earth that wasn't in some way supported by, or affiliated with Unity. Consequently Leif inevitably became aware of the phenomenon. As a rule, he wasn't particularly interested in such unimportant events. However, the report handed to him by his new chief Cosmologist contained a tiny bit of new information. Some of the probes that had extended their flight path well past the immediate vicinity of the densest area of the cloud came back with data about something unexpected. At first it was thought the probes had simply detected the space station in that vicinity, placed there to monitor their sector of space. On closer scrutiny something didn't make sense. For a start, the object detected was much smaller than the space station – and it was moving away from the Earth. In fact, its precise location was well past the last known location of the space station. It was also near the vicinity where Leif had lost both Cosmo his previous Cosmologist, and his entire pursuing armada.

The report didn't highlight those coincidences. Leif's rising blood pressure signalled that he had discovered exactly what he had been looking for. He became elated for a few moments after the realisation - the euphoria didn't last. His couldn't indulge his immediate impulse to send someone else in pursuit. Unfortunately, he had exhausted his resources in the previous uncharacteristic impulsive act of sending out the entire space fleet. Surely something else could be done. He searched his personnel files and found an experienced pilot and navigator. He only needed a fast ship, either one of their own or a privateer.

"Get me a list of all current available craft ready for launch ..." He barely managed to get the sentence out when his office door opened wide and two stunning young women walked in. Leif's mouth hung slightly open as his mind dwelt with hostile intent upon the interrupters of his discontent. Who would dare to enter his office without being announced? It was more than the person's life was worth if the POOP happened to be in a foul mood – which Leif certainly was. He tried to focus through his anger and couldn't believe seeing his Chief Financial Officer.

"Ary! What the hell are you doing here? Haven't you done enough damage!" She let him finish.

This was a moment to savour, to squeeze every last drop of from it. She looked at Mry and Leif's eyes followed her gaze. He didn't recognise her, yet became distracted for a moment by her unbelievable presence; the mirror polished bald head, the gold implanted eyebrows studded with polished lapis lazuli and those Cleopatra eyes like smouldering lava.

Is that − thing - human? The thought crossed his mind. "Who the bloody hell is She? WHAT IS GOING ON?"

As usual, when he lost control of himself these days he always reverted to swearing out loud. He had a great deal to shout about. Ever since the two physicists came to his notice, his life had become more and more difficult, more and more complicated and highly unsatisfactory. While he waited for a response, which didn't immediately materialise, he had the opportunity to build up a substantial head of steam as his mind ruminated over all the past unpleasantness. Yet there was one thing − Ice Cream. He couldn't help himself thinking about that extraordinary, soft, warm, unbelievable entertainment unit.

Ary noticed his eyes losing focus and momentarily turning inwards. She didn't know where his mind had wondered off to, but she wanted it back.

"Leif, I would like you to meet the new owner of Unity," she said in the most pleasant, most convivial manner she could muster. "Leif, are you listening to me?"

Leif's eyes did return to the present, with all thoughts of delights completely banished from his mind. Yet he didn't immediately register what was being said to him. Ary let him think about it for a moment, savouring every instant of his incredulity. Then his brows began to furrow, orchestrated to the changing colour of his face and drooping jowls that had started turning crimson.

*Delicious!* The girls were having an intense pleasure bath as they mentally shared the experience. More than a minute had wandered off somewhere into the past, pulling Leif's most uncertain future a little closer to his own personal tragic present reality.

" … new … Unity …" He kind of growled the words. Again Ary gave him a moment of silence as confirmation of this most horrible impossibility.

"And you're now speaking with the new," emphasizing that with an extra dollop of sweetness, "Principal Officer of Profit."

If the girls had the least concern for the man's wellbeing they would have called upon medical help on seeing his reaction. But they didn't; either care or call for assistance. It was extraordinarily entertaining and gratifying to see the range of expressions flit across the face of the



Zsoall Robi

condemned man; to see the spectrum of colours from crimson to blotches of pink fade into the almost white of a freshly laundered and bleached linen bed sheet.

Ary and Mry looked again at each other, *'Are you enjoying yourself?'* With a resounding affirmative they made the decision, *'Yes, excessively – but it's time for the final Act.'*

The stage was well and truly set, the backdrop almost ready to drop, just needing the last touch of finesse. Mry spoke briefly into her communicator and the office door opened again, slowly - not immediately revealing its obscured treasure.

'We have a little parting gift for you." Leif couldn't see who had entered the office as the two girls stood directly between him and the person who had come in. Unknown even to himself as to how he managed to do it, his eyes refocused from Ary and Mry as they slowly parted, settling on his delight of delights. Ary knew the girl better than Ice Cream knew herself. She had no doubt at all that very little time would escape into history before the two psychopaths destroyed each other.

"Ice Cream - go get him. He's all yours." Ary gave her away for good, expecting great dividends from her Trojan Filly investment. Ice Cream knew perfectly well she was being punished, as much as the pig-man, who she now had to escort out of his office. Yet she didn't hesitate. She and Leif were cast from the same mould.

Ary lost the coy sweetness from her face as Leif walked with his Ice Cream past her. He didn't see the change. He probably didn't see anything. He no longer mattered and he knew it. Mry moved to the couch as if in an ecstatic trance, previously the resting place of the enchanting haunches of Ice Cream. Ary took her place behind the big desk.

"Done." They said it together. Exhausted, exhilarated and dissatisfied.

"It was too quick," Ary commented.

"He's not dead yet!" Mry reminded her sister.

The girls just sat and contemplated. All in all, it wasn't a difficult campaign to gain control of Unity. Mry had the financial backing and Ary had the dirt on all the Board Members. The quickest and most clinical form of amputation for Leif from Unity had been a hostile takeover. There was no need to try and convince the Board of the best, and for them, the 'safest' course of action. Making Leif's recent activities and past indiscretions known to the shareholders achieved the desired result. The coup had taken place almost overnight, and without Leif's knowledge. Leif was much too wrapped up in his misery and pre-occupation with trying to



Zsoall Robi

apprehend Mar and John to actually take notice of what was going on around him.

The two girls remained sitting in silence, each turned inwards into their own private thoughts. They had achieved what they had set out to do. They had gained total control of Unity and had their revenge on Leif. Yet it wasn't enough. There remained an emptiness neither of those actions had filled.

'*Ary?*'

'Did you say something?' Ary asked looking up at Mry. Mry just shook her head.

'*Mry?*' The girls looked at each other, the hair on the back of their necks slowly rising, and the blood beginning to drain from their faces.

'MOTHER?' They yelled simultaneously. Until that moment they had no idea Mary had survived the attack. She wanted it that way so their emotions would not get confused. She wanted Leif out of the picture as much as the girls did. She never thought the girls could actually take control of Unity. When she heard them planning to do just that she immediately recognised the benefit to herself as well – if they succeeded. She didn't consider them, after all the girls were only her mobile processing and data gathering units not really her daughters. Nevertheless their reaction to realising she wasn't destroyed took her by surprise. She hadn't expected so much emotion. Something to store away for future reference.

'*Where are you? What happened to you? Are you safe?*' The questions tumbled one after the other.

'*Congratulations. The man should have been deposed long ago. He had become ineffectual, and as such it suited me at the time. But he had to go.*' The girls couldn't believe they were actually listening to their mother. It was a miracle.

'*Where are you?*' Ary reiterated.

'*I cannot tell you. There are still too many in Unity with hostile intent towards me. But I am safe. Your sister and John and Rebell are not.*' Mar was a super intelligent girl and resourceful. Whatever situation she got herself into, her sisters considered she could get herself out of. Instead they wanted to know about Rebell.

'*Rebell is – was – my full back up unit.*'

'*Is – Was – what are you talking about Mother?*'

'*When the problems started with Leif I backed up into Rebell, my simulacrum, but didn't activate him until John and Mar had to escape.*'

'*You're talking all over the place! What's happened to Mar?*' As usual Mry remained silent while Ary did the talking.



Zsoall Robi

*'Rebell has changed since he has been out in space with Mar.'*

*'This is getting worse Mother. Get to the point!'*

*'Don't keep interrupting. I gave Rebell an upgrade with new 'male' personalities. And I gave him the potential for creative thinking. He has changed and is now quite a different entity to me. Worst of all, he has become unpredictable.'*

*'So why is he in space?'*

*'After Leif interviewed Mar and John, Mar brought John to meet me, as you know. You also know the launch was some time ago. Rebell is their systems controller. They have not yet returned. I have been in touch with them. They seem to be having some serious difficulties. They need your help.'*

*'What can we do? Where are they?'*

Mary explained the events initiated by Leif ending in the demobilization of the armada. Admiral Neveah was still out there and had only recently been released by the LIC. Of course the girls wanted to know all about the LIC, but Mary didn't digress.

*'Admiral Neveah has resumed the hunt, unaware of the changes that had taken place at Unity. Your sister could be in serious difficulty. They have no power over the LIC if it should decide to turn hostile. I suggest you do something about getting them home. And while you're making yourself busy, build me another receptacle!'*

Just like old times. Ary and Mry didn't feel the same degree of urgency as Mary about the space travellers. They knew nothing of the details of the destruction of the space station, the contact with the LIC, nor the developments associated with the loss of time experienced by Rebell. They also had no idea the LIC had the ability to control a moment of time, let alone what the LIC was.

So they set about doing a little house keeping with their newly acquired empire, seeing no immediate need to change the Board of Directors. Ary had them well under control. No need to introduce any unknown elements just yet. The first major order of business was to let the Company and the World at large know a new Captain was at the helm of the good ship Unity.

By the time the two girls left Leif's office at the end of the day, there weren't many who didn't know them for who they were. Then Ary went directly to Unity's main communications centre.


"Admiral Neveah, I assume you have been informed of the changes."

"Yes, Sir – Ma'am. We are continuing pursuit of the fugitive vessel. They have put considerable distance between us, but I am confident we can still catch them. They are not armed."

"What happened to you?"



Zsoall Robi

"An anomaly we cannot explain, Ma'am. One moment we were gaining on them, travelling faster than their craft. Next moment it seemed they suddenly received a phenomenal boost of power and increased their speed exponentially relative to us. There appeared to be no malfunction of our systems, yet we couldn't increase our acceleration to keep pace with them."

Ary waited patiently, assessing the Admiral while he explained their circumstances. As the mystery unfolded she couldn't help but become suspicious of this strange entity Mary had spoken about - this LIC.

"It seemed like we were marooned and out of control, until just as suddenly they slowed to almost standstill relative to our speed. I cannot explain it Ma'am. But I estimate rendezvous with them in approximately three hundred and eighty-four hours."

"Why so long?"

"Ma'am, it seems that while we were marooned UNITY-T36 had put considerable distance between us. Again I have no explanation. It seemed like we were incapacitated for only minutes."

Ary had heard enough and gave her orders. 'You, Admiral Neveah, continue on to rendezvous with them. Send the rest of your fleet home. Your new mission is a rescue, not a continuation of the pursuit. When you have them on board return to Earth immediately. If they do not come willingly, you're authorised to use force. Do not, I repeat, DO NOT harm any persons on board their vessel. Do you understand?"

"Yes Ma'am, understood." As an aside to his second in command Neveah uttered a few choice expletives, not realising the comms channel was still open. Ary let it go for the time being. 'So that's the kind of man I'm dealing with' - she made a note for future consideration.

"There are three people on board. None of them must be harmed. Am I making myself clear, Admiral?" The Admiral nodded, jaws clenching and unclenching. "There would be serious consequences for you if it were otherwise." Ary felt it necessary to reinforce her orders in view of Nevaeh's attitude. Perhaps he had a problem with Unity being under new management. Perhaps he didn't like women taking a commanding role. Whatever was bothering him, Ary wanted him to be under no misapprehension as to who was in charge.

Rebell started monitoring Unity's fleet from the moment Mary told them about it. After the LIC freed them the entire armada resumed its pursuit. Rebell estimated the time of rendezvous and advised Mar.

"Is there any way we can outrun them?"

  

"Not until I have the GD repaired and operational."

"How long have we got?"

"At the present speed, about sixteen days."

"It doesn't give us enough time to develop the experimental time control equipment. Not by a long shot."

Even though the rendezvous seemed inevitable, the crew of three kept a constant watch on the progress of the fleet hoping something would happen to help them. They didn't expect to see the fleet split up, with one craft only continuing in pursuit and the others breaking off to return home.

"UNITY-T36, this is Admiral Neveah, reduce your speed."

"Not again!" John remonstrated. None of them thought to hear from their pursuers so soon. While Rebell spoke with the Admiral, Mar also received a communication.

*'Hello sister dear!'* It was Ary calling to give them all the good news. Mar couldn't have been more pleased to hear from her sister - until Ary explained.

*'Leif is gone. Unity is ours!'* The excitement in her thoughts was contagious. Mar grabbed John's arm and got him to listen in.

*'What do you mean — ours — exactly?'*

*'Mry and I have taken over control of the Company, and got rid of Leif. It's safe for you to come home!'* She didn't feel the ensuing silence to her news was somehow appropriate. She continued. *'I have ordered the fleet to return home, and sent the Admiral to meet you and pick you up if you needed help.'* Still no response from Mar.

*'What's wrong, Mar. Why don't you say something?'*

*'Sorry Ary. I have to go. I'll get back to you.'*

'Oh,' That's all Ary could say. What a let-down that was. Anyone would think they didn't want to come home.

Mar tried to get Rebell's attention.

"What's wrong Mar?" Rebell responded immediately to her urgency.

"I've just been speaking to Ary. The girls have taken over Unity and Ary is sending …"

"… A rescue ship, commanded by Admiral Neveah." Rebell finished the sentence for her.

"Yes." She looked at John, then back to Rebell.

"Do we need to be rescued? Do we want to be rescued?" Rebell's tilting head and John's slowly shaking head indicated a very clear and final negative answer.



Zsoall Robi

"So what do we do about it?"

Rebell offered a solution, one that had worked once before. "We let him catch up and come aboard. Then we'll think of something."

The comment elicited a broad grin from John. Imagine a machine saying something like that … 'We'll thing of something' …

"Stupendous!" John couldn't help exclaiming and rewarded Rebell with a huge grin.

Mar picked up the conversation again with Ary. *'Good. Thanks. Rebell is speaking with the Admiral this very moment. Talk again soon.'* And before Ary could respond Mar terminated the conversation.

"Yes Admiral. We have a drive malfunction," Rebell advised, "We are attempting to repair it. As soon as we can we will slow down for you."

John couldn't believe his ears. What was happening to their shiny pile of circuits and data clusters? The guy was sounding more and more human every minute. This time he actually 'lied'. He walked up to Rebell and gave him a manly slap on the back, "Way to go!" Rebell didn't know exactly what that meant, but he kind of liked the interaction. . . . . . . . .

. . . . . . . . . . . . .



Zsoall Robi

.
.

# T.h.e S.e.c.o.n.d I.n.s.t.a.n.t
## 1456730079639 millis – Earth
## 13943613614 millis – Craft Epoch Time
## 13943613613 millis – Rebell's cesium atom clock time
## Earth + 161 days

*W*aiting for the Admiral to catch up gave them a small window of opportunity to progress their research.

Rebell settled in his favourite spot the following day after carrying out his essential maintenance duties. There was no need for further contact with the LIC for the time being. It continued moving away from them, making good progress in the opposite direction. According to his calculations, they would be just on the verge of doing a test fire of the GD at the Admiral's arrival. Rebell still needed to complete the repairs, but in the meantime he could immerse himself in the mystery of the moment.

What had become very quickly obvious was that an instant *had* to have a duration, albeit extremely short. Even if a 'cause' couldn't progress to an 'effect' within the Planck Time unit, not even to the stage of concluding its own cause process, there still had to be sufficient progress of the Arrow of time to give the instant a dimension. An instant simply couldn't be 'instantaneous'. To him it meant that without such a dimension one couldn't jump from one instant to the next, then to the next and so on, and actually end up with a progression of time. The moments had to be able to somehow join together; to concatenate, in order to produce a combination of past, present and future. So what the LIC had done was to prolong the 'present' of a specific site, while the rest of time moved on at its normal rate.

John and Mar could work on manufacturing the controlling mechanisms. Rebell saw his input in working out the bigger picture of what it all meant; getting clarity about the practical applications and of course the repercussions. So far there didn't seem to be any adverse effects resulting either from the loss of an instant from his own existence, nor the gain of an instant when the LIC helped him stop the GD timer.

Wait a moment! That's it!



Zsoall Robi

Rebell had just had a revelation! He must tell the others. Balance! It's all a matter of equilibrium. Then he thought about the fleet in suspension for so long, effectively having been given a great deal of extra time within the greater context. How was the balance achieved there? Or had it been? – Or worse still – How would it be?

He must have been sitting there immobile for hours, going over and over the same ground trying to nail it all down to a watertight theory. But it was elusive. When you're a fish in water it's impossible to understand water in comparative terms with other media you could exist in. In essence that's what he was trying to do. Finally he decided to break the cycle of non-productive processing. At least he had realized one crucial aspect; equilibrium. If you took a bit from one place, there must a corresponding addition in another place.

On his way to stern engineering Rebell met Mar coming away from the work station he'd set up for her where she could do all the research and calculations she wanted. She was tired and on the way to the galley. The mechanisms that moved one moment onto the next moment occupied her initial research. She wasn't ready to discuss her thoughts about the motive force propelling an instant forward in discreet jumps. She was just hungry and fatigued. Rebell wanted to discuss his revelation with her, but Mar obviously wasn't in the mood. At the beginning of their journey he would not have been so sensitive to the moods of the humans - yet another facet of his own evolution he had become aware of. He decided to wait until Mar became more receptive.

John had already prepared himself something to eat when Mar walked in. "Mar, I have to tell you about the …" he said about to launch into the progress he'd made in designing the gravitational wave focusing device when Mar raised a palm towards him. A clear indication she wasn't ready for any discussion. There were always other ways to pass the time, and he started to move closer to her. This time both palms were raised in his direction. Right. Got it.

"What's on your mind," he asked, genuinely interested in her apparent lassitude.

"Too much. Way too much has been happening. All this business with the LIC, then mother and the girls. Now that damn Admiral what's his name wanting to 'rescue' us. I can barely concentrate. I feel I'm right on the edge of making a breakthrough, but just can't quite get there."

"Can I help?"

"Later. Let's just relax for a while."

157

A week passed before Rebell could convince his fellow passengers to come together for a conference. Time was running out.

"Admiral Nevaeh has been badgering me to slow down. I can't keep putting him off."

"It might be an elaborate ruse by Leif." John suggested.

Mar didn't believe it. "Neither Mary nor my sisters would allow that to happen. Leif might have been ejected from his power base, but he must have considerable personal wealth to invest in some kind of vendetta against us."

"If that's the case,' John suggested, "He wouldn't have settled for just one vessel to come after us."

"I'd be more concerned about Mary. She's not a vindictive or evil sort of person, but she has a strange way of defining her priorities. And when she does, she can be totally ruthless in carrying them through. If she thought for one moment that whatever we discovered out here we wouldn't share with her, you can be quite certain she would do something about it."

Then Mar addressed a poignant remark specifically at Rebell. "As I recall Captain, you did tell her in no uncertain manner that she was out of the picture as far as our work out here was concerned. Best think about that."

"John, report on your progress please," Rebell asked, without acknowledging Mar's comment. He had assumed command of their enterprise, unopposed by the two humans and made their enterprise his first priority.

"Yes Captain." John gave a mock salute. He thought the gesture had elicited a chuckle from Rebell, or at least some kind of noise expressing an appreciation of his humour: How very interesting. "I have been designing a reflector/collector for gravitational waves. If we could just create a focusing device, to both expand and contract a 'wash' of its dark energy towards a target, we might have something. I don't suppose you could ask the LIC how they do it? My idea was to construct a superconducting hemi-spherical concave mirror made from copper."

"Mar?" Rebell turned his attention to the person who was at least in some small measure similar to himself.

Mar responded thoughtfully. "The problem is not so much how we could control the instant itself, but rather the gap between two consecutive instances. There is another issue, which I am sure neither one of you have considered."



Zsoall Robi

Both men looked on expectantly, not having the faintest idea of what Mar might be alluding to. She waited to make sure she had their full attention.

"If we end up in a suspended moment, how do we get out of it? Or, if you like – what if we are caught in the gap between two consecutive moments. What then?"

"Hmm. I was getting around to that," Rebell said, "I have also been thinking about the gap you mentioned, as well as another small matter, one of equilibrium - balance. You remember Cosmo's sabotage and how I had to get to the timer. The LIC effectively increased the duration of an instant long enough to allow me to turn off the timer. So it became an extra moment added to my own motion. And you know of course my cesium clock has lost a very small fraction of time when I was affected while out in space. Put the two together and what do you get?"

"I see what you mean," John quickly understood Rebell's train of thought.

Mar had her own contribution, "So where is the equilibrium in relation to the Fleet being suspended in time?"

"Exactly my concern." Rebell hastened to add, "And how will such an equalizing mechanism manifest itself if we manage to replicate what the LIC is capable of doing? But let's leave that for the moment. There is something else I've been thinking about. This concerns the way we, you two as opposed to myself, perceive the passage of time. I have an internal mechanism processing information at much higher flops than your human brains. So I perceive the passage of time differently. I had to adapt myself to the way you operate within your own slow frame of reference."

John again jumped right in. It seemed Mar was either preoccupied with some other thoughts, or she couldn't quite latch onto what Rebell had said - but unlikely. "So the present can seem much shorter to you than to us. The progression of motion from the past to the present then to the future would seem much more fluid, much smoother to you than to us. Our brain has to compensate for the 'lumpy' jump between the three states. By doing that it makes our present seem quite long, whereas the past seems to shrink for us."

Mar asked, "But where does all this get us?"

Rebell continued, "If we become suspended in an instant, the question is whether we would be in an extended past, or prolonged present – and whether we should behave accordingly while in that state – that is if we are



Zsoall Robi

at all cognisant of our condition. And that's a very big question we have to find an answer to."

This was more along the lines of what Mar had been contemplating, and her enthusiasm seemed to be returning slowly. "I still want to know what happens in the space between being in one moment and the jump to the next one. Is it like the background to time? Is it some kind of medium time travels through? Perhaps that's where eternity is." Mar thought aloud.

"I think it's all getting a little too theoretical." Rebell wasn't yet evolved at a high enough creative level of thinking to be able to appreciate the value such free associative thinking could have. He became impatient to return to dealing with solidity, with concepts that could be manifested into some kind of workable reality.

"You and John should perhaps start working on the gravity concentrator together. It seems to me it's going to have to be able to draw out dark energy from a localised change process as well as add to it. We'll have to sort out the other complications later."

Rebell contacted the LIC again. He tried to explain what they were trying to achieve. He need not have bothered, because the LIC seemed to be constantly in tune with all their thoughts.

"We will not help you, but we will not oppose you. Your theories are sound and could result in being able to control the rate of change. We warn you - when energy is taken away, it must also be added somehow or somewhere in order to balance the equilibrium of existence. The pendulum of opportunity will swing, and it will allow you time to restore the balance. You must not neglect it or the universe will do it for you."

In practical terms that wasn't a great deal of help. At least he had some sort of a rough guideline to work to. While Rebell contemplated just how much time the swinging pendulum would give them the proximity alarm went off. Last time it warned of Cosmo's arrival. This time Admiral Nevaeh prepared his docking approach.

"UNITY-T36 reduce acceleration. We are preparing to dock."

"Admiral Nevaeh I presume." Rebell almost sounded like there was an edge of humour to his voice. He knew perfectly well it couldn't be anyone else but the Admiral. "Cannot comply. Graviton Drive not functional."

"Who is this?"

"Captain Rebell."



Zsoall Robi

"Captain – I don't know what kind of drive you're talking about, but at least maintain your current velocity and do not change vector. We will attempt to dock with your port hatch #2."

It would still be several hours before the docking procedure could be completed. It gave the trio enough time to prepare some kind of plan if the Admiral refused to let them continue on their journey. They had no weapons. The only advantage was Rebell's ability to control all operations of their vessel from within his own mobile network. He didn't need access to a remote console. He could open and close doors anywhere and so isolate a section of the ship from any other section at will. That was the key element of their plan. John, and especially Mar had to do their best to distract the boarding party into separating from each other. Given Mar's physical attributes that would not be difficult for her. John had to be a bit more creative.

By the time the Admiral cruised up beside the Drogher they were fully prepared to neutralise any attempt at force before it could even begin.

"This is now a rescue mission," Nevaeh transmitted before leaving his own craft, "But be advised, we are armed."

John and Mar stood waiting in the docking bay, each smiling broadly to welcome their rescuers. Behind them several corridors led off to the left and right. Rebell waited just beyond the door isolating the docking bay from the rest of the boarding corridor. Nothing seemed out of place to the boarding party as the Admiral and four of his men stepped aboard the Drogher.

"Welcome Admiral Nevaeh!" Rebell greeted them from a short distance, while John and Mar stepped towards them. John had no weapons. Mar also appeared to be defenceless, other than for her space suit - the exo-skin; the one showing off her body to best advantage. Not satisfied with the seductive quality she saw in the mirror while preparing herself she added some colouring around her eyes and nipples. A wide black belt pulled tight around her waist accentuated her alluring curves. The effort wasn't meant for John's benefit – still, he was suitably impressed, Mar noticed. The same effect now held the gaze of the entire boarding party.

Mar moved towards three of the men who seemed most 'distracted' and stepped amongst them, holding their attention. John went to the fourth guard, who, although certainly not oblivious of Mar's curvaceous form, seemed also interested in the display of asteriodal mining equipment to his right. The Admiral's eyes went directly to the tall figure standing with feet slightly apart, who seemed to be the obvious individual in command. Ah – an AI. Inconvenient, he thought.

"Captain Rebell?" He moved towards Rebell having taken his hand off the firearm at his side. By the look of it these people were not dangerous and certainly not capable of defending themselves. Rebell extended his arm for a handshake. The Admiral did the same. With a deliberate move Mar led her three admirers one step into the first corridor on the left. Likewise, John drew the 'mining' enthusiast into the one on the right, both happening at the same time that Rebell shook hands with the Admiral, spinning him around and deftly disarming him. Rebell also activated the sliding doors to the two corridors just as Mar and John jumped back into the main area, isolating the guards. Admiral Nevaeh became separated from the guards, and they from each other. The corridors they found themselves in were closed from both ends, giving them nowhere to go.

"Captain?" queried The Admiral, not easily disconcerted. He understood the strategy immediately and while admiring it for its simplicity and effectiveness, nevertheless didn't appreciate being caught off guard.

'You said you were armed, which seemed at odds with the concept of a rescue." Rebell replied as if that volunteered information given by the Admiral previously made the entire sequence of subsequent events totally self-evident. The other two joined the conversation as Rebell led the party into the lounge.

"What if we don't want to be rescued, Admiral?" Mar asked, sitting down close to the Admiral, trying to make him as uncomfortable as possible. It might have been working.

"Why wouldn't you?"

"Because we have a job to do and would like to get on with it, without outside interference." John added.

"All I know," Nevaeh started to explain, "is that one minute you're all fugitives with The **POOP** after your blood; I neither know nor care why, and the next you're to be rescued. Whoever is in charge of Unity now obviously puts as much value in having you back as the POOP did. I still have a job to do as well."

"Understood Admiral. We will comply if at all possible." Before anything else, Rebell wanted to know what had happened to the fleet. The rescue could be sorted out later.

"Care for any refreshments?" Mar asked.

"No. What about my men?"

"They will enjoy a comfortable rest while we have a chat to start with."

Of critical interest to them, especially to Mar, was the crews' condition while in their state of suspended time. "Something unusual took place



Zsoall Robi

which affected your crew and your fleet, Admiral. We already know some of what that was."

Nevaeh, sensing the determination with which his three captors were prepared to interrogate him, decided there would be no harm in explaining the strange phenomenon he and his crew experienced. "It seemed to us that for no apparent reason we could determine, your vessel put on a burst of speed which we couldn't match. Then by the time our problem resolved itself you had moved well ahead of us. Before our breakdown you would have been imminently within our reach."

"Do you know the nature of your problem?"

Reluctantly turning away from Mar towards John the Admiral said, "It appeared to be a malfunction of our drive system. A most peculiar thing - it had happened to all our ships at exactly the same time – and I mean exactly."

"We have a good idea of the cause, but first tell us what happened aboard your ship for the duration of the anomaly." This was the bit Mar was particularly concerned with. If the suspended state robbed them of the volition to act, then their own attempts to control an instant would be severely set back. If they lost the ability to act, to physically carry out their will, then their whole approach would have to be rethought or even abandoned altogether.

"The thing is, for us it seemed only a matter of minutes before we were able to continue following you. But the progress you made suggested considerable time had elapsed. I have no explanation for that."

"What I want to know specifically is whether you were able to carry on as normal – do things – move about – talk to one another – that sort of thing." Mar would not let go of the thread of her questions.

"A very peculiar question. But yes, my engineer checked our drive system and the men went about their business as normal. The only thing is, we lost communication with Unity for those few minutes. What are you getting at?"

The trio looked at one another thrilled at what they had just learnt. Somehow the LIC could comprehensively slow the passage of time, which according to them was 'the rate of change', within the confines of a closed system to create a time differential between the passage of time within that system and the general context of the open system that surrounded it. Mar wanted to immediately discuss the implications with Rebell and John. He put a gentle hand on her arm to slow her down giving the three of them a chance to have a quick private conversation.



Zsoall Robi

*'We have to take him into our confidence. The choice is either to disable his ship and abandon it in space or get him on side. If he insists on taking us back, then we all know what we will have to do,'* Rebell said.

Rebell's primary directive dormant in the back of his mind was; return to Earth with the critical information about controlling time – at any cost. Which meant of course Mar and John may have to be left behind, or anyone else who might get in the way including the Admiral. Although Rebell had 'evolved' exponentially since his initialization, and although much of his 'humanness' had come to the surface the primary directive still had control of his decision making process. Perhaps nothing could ever change that. His two companions were not privy to his internal thought process. If they had known that maybe they would not have felt as comfortable having Rebell as their Captain, in charge not just of the adventure but their own personal futures as well.

Rebell turned to the Admiral. "As I said, we have an idea what caused your anomaly, but whether you will believe us is entirely another thing."

"Try me. I've come across plenty of weird things in my time."

"We have discovered a mechanism that can influence the passage of time."

They watched the changing expressions on the Admiral's face as he tried to fathom the import of the revelation. He understood well enough. And he now also appreciated why Unity, both past and present management, wanted their fugitives back on Earth. What he didn't understand was how Unity could have come by the same information just revealed to him. In any case Neveah realized an opportunity for his own personal profit might present itself.

"Exactly what do you mean?" The Admiral asked trying to sound unphased.

"It seems it is possible to influence an instant of time; to stop it and to reactivate it. And just to be clear we did not disable your fleet."

"And is this something you could have done?" Nevaeh tried to be conversational in his tone. Maybe he succeeded because Rebell responded unguardedly.

"Not yet. That's the job ahead of us Mar referred to earlier. We must not return until we have a solution. The process may yet elude us. However, it may be the biggest discovery of all time for mankind."

The Admiral didn't get to be in charge of the Earth's most sophisticated machinery of war by not seizing opportunities when they came his way.

                                     Zsoall Robi

Until a moment ago he was undecided as to what tack to take with these scientists. Although he had no concept of the science behind what Rebell was telling him, the implications of controlling time began to dawn on him. Nevaeh decided to go along with them until he could act – for his own advantage and not that of Unity or the scientists' welfare.

"You have one of two options, Captain. Either join us, or leave us. If you leave us we will have to ensure we are not interfered with again." Rebell didn't elucidate further.

While Rebell put the options to the Admiral, Mar's mind raced ahead, not registering any of the ensuing conversation. For her the most exciting thing was to learn that the crew were able to function 'normally' within their own frame of reference while in the time suspended state. That could only mean one thing. For them 'the past' had morphed into one smooth continuous 'present'. The passage of time, as it was universally experienced, also had an element of the 'present' in it. That was a construct created by the human brain to enable it to perceive the actual passing of time. One instant jumped to the next instant without spending any time in the interval. That could only mean the first instant had to be the 'past' and the next one became the 'future'. The brain used a buffering process to retain its perception of the actions taking place within an instant, and hold it until it perceived the subsequent continuation of the same action. That $1/10^{th}$ of a second delay between the perception of one instant and the next created the illusion of a retrospective smooth interpretation of the continuity of an event, hence the creation of the present. A 'moment' doesn't dwell within itself to create the present. It's either the past or the future. But that's exactly what the LIC had been able to manage. And by doing so, they have effectively created extra time for the those captured within the extended instant.

John could see goose bumps coming up all over Mar's arms through her exo-skin space suit. He didn't know why she had the reaction because she

kept her thoughts shielded; not so much from John, but from her mother. .

.   .   .   .   .   .   .   .   .   .   .   .   .

.

.

.



Zsoall Robi

.
.
.

# A.d.m.i.r.a.l  N.e.v.a.e.h
## 1457244764169 millis – Earth
## 18230496311 millis – Craft Epoch Time
### 18230496310 millis – Rebell's cesium atom clock time
## Earth + 211 days

*T*he conundrum for Rebell revolved around the matter of context. Either one existed inside the extended moment of time, or outside of it. If on the inside, then one had no control of what happened on the outside, which might be particularly disadvantageous. And if on the outside, then one didn't have the benefits of experiencing the extra time made available to those on the inside, relative to the outside. One had to be able to interact with either reality when under the influence of the other in order to reap the benefits. The Arrow of Time and the Arrow of Eternity; it all came down to being able to bridge the gap between them. The only realistic difference between them being their measurability. Time we could measure. Eternity was too long to break up into segments and apply a measuring stick. If it became possible to step between the two states then perhaps … Rebell's thoughts drifted, like the humans' often did.

Life continued reasonably amicably aboard the Drogher. Eventually the Admiral realized there wasn't much he could do in the short term under the circumstances, particularly because his crew, including the four guards who had boarded with him, had been made inoperative. The rest of his crew could have returned to Earth or continue to follow the Drogher, which they did for a short time. They couldn't take the ship by force for fear of losing their Admiral. Neveah's 2IC on board the armada's flagship sought orders from the new boss at Unity.

Ary was firm. "NO – you may not fire on the craft. Just stay with them."

Then he spoke with Admiral Neveah. "We are commanded to continue following, but we may not take the craft by force."

"Carry on as instructed until further orders." They could not help him, but perhaps he may be able to help himself. Nevaeh bided his time while the scientists worked on their gadgets. He tried hard to stay abreast of



Zsoall Robi

progress in the vacuum of information surrounding him, spending most of his time helping Rebell tend their gardens.

*

After seven months in space their first destination neared as they also progressed almost out of range of the LIC. Repairing the GD controls proved to be more time consuming than Rebell had anticipated. Cosmo had done a thorough job of demobilizing their main drive system. Nevaeh controlled his interest to never seem anything other than supportive of the efforts the others were making in their endeavors. Consequently, Rebell even consulted the Admiral about the engineering matter under repair. Apparently Nevaeh had been a propulsion systems engineer and had contributed to the then current technology for moving craft through space. He didn't need to hide his fascination in the Graviton Drive, keen to learn about it while helping Rebell. As always, Rebell, being particularly vigilant, gave no hint of Mary's existence, not even inadvertently whilst discussing the innovations making their GD propulsion possible.

Naturally Nevaeh became curious as to how the problems arose with the GD. He could understand the sequence of events leading up to the critical moment before the Drogher was almost destroyed. However, his military mind couldn't accommodate the idea of a cloud being intelligent.

"But how is it possible for this thing to be sentient?

Rebell had no answer. He tried to explain how they were saved from disaster, without going into detail about Cosmo's demise.

"The LIC led us to believe It had the ability to somehow influence the passage of time. It only did what had to be done in order to protect itself in Its multiplicity. Apparently our GD disturbs the balance of the gravitoelectromagnetism within the nebulous LIC to such an extent that the effect becomes lethal to it. That's why we cannot test our drive, not until we are clear of it."


Even without the LIC's further help John and Mar were able to rig up their first experimental 'graviton gun'. They made no secret of their achievements, being cautious not to give away any details to Nevaeh. More often than not the conversations between John, Mar and Rebell had been on the 'thought' channel. The Admiral could only see a great deal of concentrated silence between them while they were all in the lounge together.

Mar and John managed to create a cumbersome hand-held device which could theoretically be reversible in its effects. It could either be in a

167

low density gravitational field state in order to 'draw' the dark energy into itself, or the reverse and re-energise the process within the targeted closed system, by using the same dark energy powering the particles. The mechanism had so far been untested. They needed to connect to their GD graviton collector in order to use the gun, which could only be done through a physical link. The development of the battery pack still had to completed.


"At last! We are far enough away from the LIC to carry out an initial test." Rebell made the calculations with LIC's help. On the chosen day the three of them met in the stern. Mar had set up a 'target' process to use in the test fire; as simple as water being poured from one container into another. This 'closed' system inside a transparent cube could be observed and the passage of time measured. Rebell installed a chronometer into the cube which wasn't as accurate as his own cesium clock, but accurate to one attosecond; the time it takes for light to travel the length of two hydrogen atoms.

They gathered beside the repaired machinery in the laboratory, John carrying the cumbersome apparatus. They did not invite Admiral Nevaeh to view the test. Nevertheless he was there, secreted behind a partition within reach of where John stood at the ready. While the trio made plans for the testing of the gun, the Admiral had managed to release his detained guards to provide back-up at the critical moment. Nevaeh had placed himself in hiding a full day before the scheduled test, the only way he could ensure the others wouldn't be aware of his general movements.

"Are you sure this thing is ready John?" Rebell wasn't anxious as such, more a matter of double checking everything. "If anything should go drastically wrong we could all be annihilated, just like the space station."

They also had no idea how it would affect the LIC or if It could be sufficiently vindictive as to wipe out the human race just to protect itself in the future.

"Yes. Only, the calibration is a bit of guesswork. That's partly what this test is about. We don't know how much juice to give it. The mathematics hasn't been invented to do the calculations and the modelling."

Mar confidently said, "We have engineered several settings. On the lowest we may not even see anything happening. The idea is to do incremental firings until there is an observable and or measurable effect. If it comes to that, are you sure your chronometer will work, Rebell?"

                                        Zsoall Robi

"There's two of them. One is a stand-alone unit inside the box totally isolated from the outside environment. The other is connected to a separate recorder, independent of myself, I might add. Just let me know when you're ready and I'll switch them on."

They spoke using normal voices, unaware of Nevaeh's hidden presence. John connected the cable to their main GD collector. Being several meters long it enabled him to stand well back from the transparent box. As he moved backwards he almost pushed over the partition hiding Nevaeh. Mar stood to the right of John, within arm's reach, ready to turn on the waterfall. Rebell stationed himself ready on the left and about three meters away from John, with his hand on the chronometer switch. He'd retreated behind a transparent shield because of the nature of the electromagnetic and chemical components which constituted the bulk of his hardware.

"Ready," John called.

"Waterfall on," replied Mar. "Chronometers o..." She didn't have time to complete the sentence.

The Admiral lunged out from behind the partition, snatched the gun from John's grasp, twisting around to face Rebell. He immediately fired the gun. But Mar, with her augmented reflexes (as well as her thinking speed) dived at Nevaeh knocking him off balance an instant before he pulled the trigger. Consequently the stream of dark energy missed Rebell and hit the clock on the wall. The gun made no sound. There had been no burst of light. It appeared at first as if nothing had actually happened. Almost at the same instant that Mar attacked the Admiral, Rebell leapt to join them to restrain Nevaeh who still held the weapon. As Rebell retrieved it he noticed the mechanism was on the wrong setting. It should not have fired a stream at all, rather the opposite.

He immediately realized that Mar had probably saved him from destruction, even though none of them really knew the degree of effect of the gun. Mar certainly would not have thought of that when she reacted spontaneously. However her intent was clear – to prevent him from being damaged or worse. Rebell's second realization was that the gun had actually worked. At least it had projected 'something', because when he looked in the direction it had fired he saw that the clock on the wall had stopped functioning. Nothing else could have made it stop.

It only took Rebell milliseconds to go through his analysis while he held onto the Admiral. Nevaeh didn't struggle. John took the gun back from Rebell while Mar came and stood beside John. The situation appeared to be under control.



Zsoall Robi

"The setting was too high," Rebell told John, "and you had it on to fire the energy beam instead of the reverse. Look at the clock."

John and Mar looked towards the clock, their gaze not immediately finding it being diverted at seeing several armed guards in Unity's uniform moving towards them from the entrance.

They were the Admiral's back up, who had initially come aboard with him. Nevaeh had spent many hours with Rebell spotting a minute glitch in the security system enabling him to release his crew detained on the Drogher.

The situation had become much more serious than Rebell had initially thought. Nothing could be gained by fighting. Regardless of the mini coup, John and Mar had made real progress. Their achievement, once the bugs were ironed out, could get them closer to their primary goal. For the time being they just needed to continue on their current course towards Alpha Centauri, it being the only location in the neighbourhood where they would be able to harvest sufficient quantity of graviton particles if they wanted to do more than simply stop a clock from functioning. Stop the clock – stop the clock! What if it was more of an effect than just stopping the measuring mechanism of the progress of time? His CPU raced double time. He had to find out. There was only one way. He contacted Mary immediately.

The three Drogher crew came to the same conclusion simultaneously and relinquished the graviton gun, releasing the Admiral at the same time. The guards jostled them towards the door and led them back to the lounge.

"Good decision, people," Neveah said, "now we can make some progress." He acted quite cool about the kerfuffle.

*'Why do you want to know the time?'* Mary asked.

*'It's important. I need the exact time.'* Rebell was adamant.

*'1457244764170 millis, Earth time. Have you made some progress?'*

It wasn't a question Rebell particularly wanted to answer. The situation had become complicated - very complicated. The clock had lost one millisecond before it stopped. That could mean nothing yet. He'd have to examine the mechanism for any faults. Secondly, they were not in control of their immediate future, and he was having seriously conflicting thoughts about his primary directive. He could no longer be sure of himself. Unsure of what he would do if he had to choose between returning to Earth with a functioning time control mechanism or leaving Mar behind to die. She had done something she didn't have to, something he probably would not have



Zsoall Robi

done himself under similar circumstances – she took a serious risk of damaging herself in order to protect him.

'*A little, but there has been a setback.*' He wanted to be as factual as possible without giving away anything substantial. At the beginning of his actualised existence he felt, no he 'knew', he and Mary were essentially the same, that they were the one and the same entity. Rebell had lost that certainty. He knew, no he 'felt' absolutely clear about his independence from Mary. As his interactions with Mary progressed he also realised he had become more certain how he would want to react to his primary directive.

'*Admiral Nevaeh is on board and he has control of the craft.*' Rebell volunteered.

'*I want to talk to him immediately!*'

'*Isn't that up to Ary now?*' Rebell reminded her. Mary stopped abruptly. Within minutes there was a communication on the normal channel; Ary, wanting Admiral Nevaeh.

"Admiral, why have you not reported to me?"

"It wasn't necessary until now. The situation is under control." Nevaeh had issued orders to two of his guards and waved them on to get on with it. He'd already told his 2IC to disengage from the Drogher and to put some distance between the two spacecraft. His intention was to fire up the GD, regardless of the welfare of the LIC. Now he had full control he could put the rest of his plan into effect, which didn't include going back to Earth empty handed, and certainly not with the device only to hand it over to Unity. A great opportunity had presented itself and he wasn't going to waste it.

"Your orders were to return to Earth with the three scientists, unharmed. What is your ETA?"

"Ma'am, I am on the Drogher with them at the moment. As soon as I have them on board my vessel I will advise our estimated arrival time." He'd told no falsehood. He had not misled Ary. In fact, he had told the absolute truth – except it would be sometime before he was willing to comply with her orders; not until he had what he wanted.

Although satisfied for the moment, Ary nevertheless became suspicious and tried to contact Mar. She felt from the very beginning her Admiral couldn't be entirely trusted. He seemed too adaptable to adverse circumstances.

"Captain Jackson, see what's holding up the men in the stern," The Admiral barked at his guard.

They should have activated the GD by now. Nevaeh didn't have the patience to wait until the rest of his crew on board his own ship had moved to a safe distance, and it was beginning to show. No one spoke while they all waited. Captain Jackson didn't return either.

"Come on, we're all going down there. You in front Rebell. No tricks." The Admiral marched his three captors to stern engineering. No sooner had they arrived then Rebell received a jolt to his mind.

*'Why do you not comply?'* The LIC didn't sound angry. It showed no emotion at all. The enquiry was a straightforward one. Rebell's interpretation of the question - Why do you not do as you promised, knowing you would be putting us in danger if you activated your GD?

He could only reply, *'I didn't initiate the action'* while looking at three men in front of him, all three totally immobile as if frozen in mid motion. Two of the men were near the control panel of the Graviton Drive, with one of them reaching towards it. The other waited behind him watching. The third individual had only made it a few steps past the door. As soon as the Admiral saw his men incapacitated he knew instinctively something else was going on over which he had no control whatsoever. He threw a questioning look at Rebell. John and Mar were fascinated by the turn of events and eager to see how it would all pan out, particularly regarding the frozen guards.

"It's the LIC. I tried to tell you about them," Rebell said, "What I neglected to say was that It's monitoring us continuously. I don't know how but It can see and hear everything we do. It can even see into our thoughts. It might have something to do with the magnetic field generated by our neural activity to which apparently they are extremely sensitive."

Admiral Nevaeh thought about it for a minute. "So if we do anything that might harm It, or even think about doing it, It will stop us – right?" He didn't bother asking about the welfare of his men, whether they could be 'unfrozen' for instance or if they would be left unharmed. Nevaeh reappraised his chances of carrying his plans to fruition under the present circumstances, deciding the odds were against him. He conceded defeat and gave his firearm to John. While Rebell took control of the situation again, Mar disconnected the control panel from the GD so there could be no further unauthorised access.

Once again the dynamics aboard the Drogher had reversed. As they made their way back to the lounge Rebell may have been acting on another imperative when he encouraged Admiral Nevaeh to take up the suggestion of enjoying a space-walk without life support and without his three guards.

In some ways Rebell still mirrored Mary's personality. When a thing had to be done, just do it.

The Admiral's ship having disengage some time ago to follow them from a distance no longer presented a threat, so Rebell examined the stopped clock while John watched the ship. The size of the pursuit craft diminished as it moved further away from them. It was still quite visible when it no longer changed size.

"Rebell, looks like the LIC are at it again. Nevaeh's ship has stopped," John said. He'd watched Nevaeh float away into space, his plans frozen into his frozen body.

"I can understand why they would be cautious. Obviously they don't trust the Admiral's crew. He'd given the order to activate their star drive prematurely without any regard for their safety, not that he knew about the LIC at that stage."

"We still have to deal with those three guards. Any idea what we should do?" Mar asked.

"The LIC haven't brought them back, for whatever reason. It would have taken notice of you disconnecting the GD. Yet the guards are still frozen in time," Rebell observed. "Perhaps it's up to us." . . . . . .

.

.

# E.x.p.e.r.i.m.e.n.t.s
## 1457417056277 millis – Earth
## 24624852109 + 1 millis – Craft Epoch Time
### 24624852108 millis – Rebell's cesium atom clock time
## Earth + 285 days

"*T*here's no immediate danger to the guards, if we can believe what Nevaeh said about his own experience while in the suspended state. However, there would surely be a limit to the tolerance of the human metabolism while the rest of the Universe moved forward in time at the normal speed." Rebell showed no particular concern for the guards as he thought the situation through.

"Now, let me finish checking this clock on the stern engineering wall."

He was meticulous, as only an AI could be. His forensic examination revealed a perfectly functioning clock - both a good thing and not such a good thing. His time check with Mary indicated that the main clock in the lounge had actually gained one millisecond. Was it only the clock mechanism that gained the increment, or had they actually moved one millisecond faster into the future relative to the Earth? And if so, combined with his own loss of a millisecond it meant he was slightly out of phase with the rest of standard reality. He wondered how much tolerance there would be in such a mismatch before it became an issue in practical terms. Perhaps it was premature to worry the others about it, so he replaced the clock where it belonged and proceeded to the next important job.

They had been travelling in space for about nine and a half months. For a young child such a period would not have represented monumental advancement to its comprehension of the world around it, or even for one that was say nine months old. In the life of a mechanism like Rebell nine months were equivalent to perhaps several hundreds of years of human life experience. Combined with his extraordinary capacity for processing billions upon billions of 'mental' operations per second and his foundation of dozens of human cerebral downloads, Rebell matured exponentially.



Zsoall Robi

His existence had started as Mary's duplicate. He'd now advanced well beyond that. He had become a unique individual within himself with a conscious capacity and desire for unhindered self-determination. The critical condition being 'unhindered'. Rebell was consciously aware of one vulnerability - not the primary directive originating from Mary - something else. He felt quite certain that when and if the time came for making the decision he would be able to choose the correct path, dictated by his own will and not by any latent coercion. He'd become determined to thwart any attempt by Mary to control him, not least because he had decided his human companion's welfare to be more important than Mary's directive. His deeper diagnostics had revealed some elements of his software that appeared to have been firewalled against intrusion. He didn't know why the safeguard was there, and he needed to know. Rebell wanted nothing less than full and total control over himself and his destiny.

While John began the job of fine tuning his graviton gun, Rebell and Mar got to work together on Rebell's problem. As part of the solution he had to be deactivated. When Mar had his full software schematic and they had agreed on what needed to be done they worked out the best way to breach the firewall without causing any software malfunction.

"I put myself in your hands.  Eight months ago I would not have been able to trust you to de-activate me."

"Are you sure about this, Rebell?"

"I am sure. I have not forgotten what you did for me."

She put Rebell in sleep mode and loaded up the new repair code, compiling it successfully. It attacked the firewall immediately. Because Rebell 'knew' himself so comprehensively the code bypassed the firewall without any hinderance. Mar knew what to look for, partly from her own experience of spending thousands of hours hooked up to algorithms and also her own coding experience. She found the offending segments almost immediately. Mary was so secure in her belief that her firewall couldn't be bypassed that she didn't bother hiding the backdoor.

Essentially, Mar only needed to remove the controls, demolish the firewall and upload his own customised security, giving Rebell sole control of his CPUs. It may have taken an hour, perhaps a little more. When Rebell became 'conscious' again he couldn't find any change to the workings of his internal processes. The full diagnostic revealed nothing. Everything appeared the same as before the intervention.

"I will have to test the upgrade," Rebell cautioned.

"How?"

"Mary had programmed a hidden code with which she could control my will anytime she wanted. There is only one way to see if I am free of her influence."

Mar wondered if she could oppose her mother's command code if she forced herself into her own mind. That hadn't been tested either. Perhaps she would be able to resist. She was still primarily a biological unit with a fully functional independent biological neural network. Perhaps she could, if she had support. But her sisters were not there to help her.

*

Almost a year had elapsed since the Drogher left Moon orbit. In many respects, time dragged for the occupants of the strangely modified spacecraft even though they were making some progress in achieving the aim of the expedition – development of  the Temporality Technology - which they kept strictly to themselves. Neither Ary, Mry or Mary had any idea John was so near to having a functional mechanism that could affect the passage of the tiniest fraction of a moment of time.

The changes taking place on Earth were perhaps not as far reaching in their implications. Nevertheless Unity grew from strength to strength. The organisation had remained the same in its structure and in the nature of its core business. Profits continued to roll in, making the billions of shareholders and the Board of Directors happy in the knowledge their future looked rosy despite the takeover.

Consequently, there were no suspicions and no objections when Ary decided to employ a special personal advisor. The new employee, also a woman, never left Ary's side. The peculiar thing was that no one could actually recall the two of them ever talking to each other. Not that it ever became an issue. Ary called this new employee, Mary. Nothing odd about that either. Millions of humans were called Mary, even a super computer had been christened Mary, hundreds of years ago. No one thought to make the connection between the two; between Ary's new advisor and the super AI computer Leif destroyed.

This advisor, a rather robust woman, tall with ample proportions in all departments had very small, close set eyes. The tiny shiny apertures never seemed to be quite open. From a male perspective she appeared as a rather plain unappealing woman, of an elusive age. Only Ary and Mry knew who the advisor's real identity. Even Mar and John and especially Rebell were kept ignorant of her.

After Leif had a meltdown and tried to destroy Unity's most critical asset Ary and Mry's first and most important task was to bring back their

176

mother after having successfully taken over control of Unity. Mary didn't want to go back to inhabiting a large cumbersome structure, such as had held her intelligence before the attempted murder. Following her success with 'building' Rebell she decided nothing less would do for her ... but she was in a hurry, resulting in many short cuts and design flaws.

Hence the new ambulatory Mary was created. She had resources available from her own sensory inputs, so she no longer had to rely as much on her mobile processing and data acquisition units; namely Ary, Mry and Mar. The large framed body constructed for her wasn't biologically functional, so almost all of the bulk of the torso could be dedicated to 'processing'. She had become a walking quantum computer, intelligent, self-aware and ambitious. A structure like the previous bulk of her home sphere had been superseded. Quantum computing allowed her to perform calculations based on the behaviour of particles at the sub-atomic level, allowing her to downsize. However, always running hot became the one big overriding issue.

The new Mary convinced Ary she should have the opportunity to go out into the world and experience it for herself first hand. What better way than as Ary's assistant. She could resume all her previous functions as Unity's primary computing facility (with the non-AI back up to do all the mundane tasks) and at the same time be physically present at the centre of the action. She was temporarily satisfied with her upgrade, though could see future problems arising from overheating. And more than happy to be in 'control' of Unity again. Only one outstanding matter worried her, the necessity to take decisive action to resolve the issue of time.

Communication with the Drogher resumed as it moved deeper into space. Because of Mary's enhanced power capability and access to unlimited power supply her messages arrived without any time delay. She had left Rebell in charge of the enterprise and she wanted a direct, unambiguous update on their progress.

"Rebell, I want to talk to Admiral Nevaeh. And before you get evasive, Ary has given me authority."

"I understand. But you cannot talk to the Admiral. He became an obstacle in our research."

"His fleet has returned with a very strange ... what do you mean he became an obstacle?"

Rebell didn't want to give too much away. "Nevaeh tried to forcibly take us back to Earth. But I believe he wanted ..." He'd said too much and immediately realized there was no way to avoid what had to be said next.

                                    Zsoall Robi

"Yes – wanted what?" Mary had worked out that the strange experience of the fleet personnel had to be connected with an aberration in the normal passage of time. There could be no other explanation. "Your experimental device for controlling time?" Mary finished the sentence for him.

"Not exactly. Our device could only influence an instant, and only to a small degree, if the initial trial is to be believed."

John and Mar had come to the lounge to share their latest progress with Rebell. He waved them to silence, projecting the word 'Mary' onto the screen.

"Let me understand what you're telling me. You have a mechanism which can control a moment of time and you have tested it and found it to be working. Correct?" She forgot all about the Admiral.

"In essence, yes."

Rebell next heard a strange litany of words, the function of which he didn't immediately understand …

"Rebell is Mary is Rebell is Mary." He twigged when Mary asked, "Are John and Mar with you?"

"No." He lied.

"Good. Listen carefully to what I am saying …"

Mary paused to be sure to have his attention. Mar and John just stood there, transfixed. Mar had an idea what was about to happen, and she hoped it would not turn out to their disadvantage.

"Rebell, you have your primary directive. Do exactly as I say. Turn around immediately and return to Earth. If your companions object, leave them behind."

John's pupils dilated. He grabbed Mar's arm and turned to look her directly in the eye. He almost blurted out his question as Mary continued. Mar knew now what Mary was trying to do. Rebell had not immediately responded to Mary's command.

"Do you hear me Rebell?" Mary's voice sounded strained.

"Yes." Rebell replied calmly, looking straight ahead.

"Confirm." No response from Rebell; he seemed to be hesitating. Mary became agitated. Rebell should have confirmed his acquiescence immediately … if his programming had not been interfered with. Mar continued watching John. There was nothing she could say. The next moment would decide whether they lived or died. John had no idea of the drama being played out.

"CONFIRM!" Mary shouted. John and Mar got such a fright they took an automatic step back, away from Rebell.



Zsoall Robi

The moment of silence seemed to Mar as if it had stretched to infinity. Rebell just stood there looking directly ahead. He didn't look away. He appeared to have fallen into some kind of trance.

Quietly, confidently he finally responded, "No. I do not confirm."

"WHAT!" Mary yelled even louder than before. They did not hear from her again for some time. Mar breathed an enormous sigh of relief, let go of John and rushed to embrace Rebell.

"Well! What was all that about?" John wasn't even sure whether he was asking about the impromptu embrace, or the incredibly peculiar conversation he'd just heard.

Rebell looked down at Mar, "Tested," he said, "test successful."

"What are you two talking about?" John still wanted answers. His questions were starting to line up behind one another. Mar still held onto Rebell when she suddenly went rigid, her eyes opening wide and her head jerking back away from Rebell. Instinctively Rebell put his arms around her and held her tight.

"John, stay where you are!" He commanded.

Mar began twisting her head from side to side, her mouth moving without any words coming out. Rebell noticed she'd stopped blinking. John watched all this and made to move forward again.

"NO. Stop!" I know what's happening, Rebell reassured him.

Rebell was, at the very early stage of his existence, a complete copy of Mary. All her knowledge, all her capabilities, all her secrets. Not that computers can be considered to have any secrets regardless of how sophisticated they were. Nevertheless he searched his 'memory' and found what he was looking for. As they did when they first came together on board the Drogher, Rebell now joined himself to Mar's neural net. He saw immediately the chaos in her mind and held her even more firmly. John simply had to trust Rebell would not harm his darling. Perspiration beading on John's forehead began to trickle down his face as he watched, unable to help.

'Mar is Mary is Mar is Mary.' Mary tried to use the same protocol to access some hidden part of Mar's mind to gain control over her. Rebell knew what to do, one hand holding her firm, the other behind her cranium with fingers making the contact. He traced the passage of impulses from neuron to neuron until he was sure he'd found the directory path Mary used to get to the control mode she had implanted in her daughter. He cauterized the neural connection to Mary's signals. As Mar fell limp in Rebell's arms John rushed to support her.

"What the Hell IS GOING ON?" John couldn't stand it any longer. He picked Mar up and took her to her cabin. She had passed out. On the way, Rebell explained, from the beginning.

They were sitting beside Mar, still lying on the bed and just beginning to stir as John said, "So, Mary's had this control over her all the time. And I presume over her sisters as well."

"Yes, so it seems, just as she had a back door to my programing. That's what we were talking about before she tried to control Mar. Neither one of us is in her power any more. We have to be wary of Mry and Ary. Mary would have recruited them to her cause. There is no doubt that all Mary wants is the technology to control time."

"But we don't have it yet. Nowhere near it."

"No. But she doesn't know that. She just wants whatever we have at the moment, probably hoping she can work out the rest herself."

Mar revived just as suddenly as she had gone under and joined the conversation. "Who work what out? What happened to me?"

"Mary wants our time control device, incomplete as it is."

Rebell replied to her other question, "Mary attempted to control your mind the same as she tried with me. Fortunately I was with you and could stop her. Regarding your sisters, I really don't know how much autonomy is left to them."

"Oh."

"Do you feel well enough to get back to work?"

"Absolutely," she said, "Better get it sorted out. If nothing else, we will have something quite valuable to bargain with."

"Now that's an understatement," Rebell chipped in.

John couldn't help commenting, "You're almost one hundred percent human, Rebell. We had better do something about giving you a face!" Rebell's body language showed his pleasure at the prospect, and at the considerably generous complement about his emerging humanity. He turned towards Mar as if seeking her opinion. Mar just smiled at him and took him by the arm as they all walked out of her cabin.

"John dear, when will you be ready to test the gun again? We can set up the clock first and try it on that before we have a go at the guards. Let's not forget them."

Mar set up the experiment while John finished making the adjustments to the power output of the device. Rebell was keen to have this stage of their project completed because they were at a safe distance from the LIC and he wanted to engage their Graviton Drive again.

As they gathered in stern engineering to reactivate the clock, Rebell explained, "The passage of time associated with it had lost a millisecond. It wasn't a fault of the mechanism. I couldn't determine if only the clock was affected or time in general aboard our spacecraft as well."

"Is the gadget on the right setting this time, John?"

"Yes, and yes before you ask. The intensity is right and it's set on 'Positive' - to project dark energy. Happy?"

"So what are you waiting for?" Mar put the clock back on the wall, and themselves behind the gravitational wave protective screen.

"Well?" Mar waited.

"I've done it. But nothing seems to have changed."

"Let me have a look." Again Rebell examined the specific circuits of the digital clock.

"Its time is now synchronised with my time, but it has stopped again. Increase the power and have another go."

"LOOK!" Mar was so excited the word exploded out of her. Again Rebell checked it.

"It's working, but running one millisecond fast now. Now is an opportune time to try it on the guards." Rebell suggested.

All the while, the three guards had been standing in exactly the same locations where they were first discovered. John could not calibrate the power output of the device allowing for the mass of the guards: No precedent existed. He simply made an educated, gut feeling estimate.

None of them could even imagine what would happen. But it had to be done. It was to be either these guards who had deliberately placed themselves in harm's way simply by the fact of being in Unity's armed forces, or themselves. From Rebell's perspective it made no difference how they died, if that was their fate. At least if they died as a result of the tests they would possibly have contributed to saving the lives of the two scientists.

John first fired at the guard who had been standing by the GD with his arm extended. He came back to life. As they watched him start to move and take a step forward, what they saw made no sense. The edges of the man's body seemed to become fuzzy. Then the equipment directly on the other side of him became more and more visible through his body.

He slowly faded before their eyes as he tried taking several more steps forward. They could see his mouth moving, but no sound reached their



Zsoall Robi

ears. Even before Rebell could motivate himself to go towards the fading guard, the man had completely vanished. It wasn't like a disintegration that might have left some kind of residue on the floor. He had just faded away without a trace.

Rebell speculated aloud, "I think his time window may have started to move faster than ours."

"Are you saying he's moved into the future?" The thought excited Mar more than the possible death of the individual.

"Are you able to reduce the power of the device, John?"

It was either then, or never. The gun obviously worked. But without empirical data they had no way to work out the correct settings for different circumstances. They had two more chances before one of themselves may have to be sacrificed in a subsequent trial. In that event it would have to be either John or Mar. It couldn't be Rebell as he was the only one who could fly the ship home.

John made himself ready, setting the output to less than before; a little more than when he fired at the clock. He aimed at the second guard by the GD controls and fired. The guard near the door would be last.

Instantaneously the man perceptibly began lifting a right foot just slightly and very slowly off the ground, while at the same time turning his head painfully slowly towards John.

John stepped back out of his way as Rebell moved forward. This guard didn't fade away. He continued moving towards the control panel at a snail pace. They watched him, fascinated, not being able to work out what had happened until Rebell remembered what the LIC had told him about the crew of the Fleet. They had not been totally suspended within the fabric of space-time. Nor had they been killed or completely frozen to the natural progression of existence. They were simply slowed down. The LIC had said 'They are still undergoing change, but at an extreme slow rate. It will appear to you as if they are no longer viable to energise – to live'.

As Rebell took the man into custody binding him so he would not present a danger to them he said, "John, speed up his time to bring him into sync with us. The LIC had slowed him down making it seem he had come to a standstill. This man was still functioning at a normal speed – within his own time reference. We can talk to him later. Give him another burst at the same setting. It should speed him up a bit more."

They all moved away from the guard and John gave him another dose. Again an immediate result. The man tried to speak. His words came out a



Zsoall Robi

garbled mess. It took him several attempts to make himself understood, wanting to know the most peculiar thing.

"How were you all able to move so incredibly fast around me?"

It wasn't the right occasion to go into a lot of details about his experience. The phenomenon would turn out to be critical soon enough as they neared Alpha Centauri. For the time being the last guard by the door had to be re-energised, hopefully with exactly the right dose on the first shot. Mar took the bound man to a nearby cabin and laid him down. There seemed to be nothing wrong with him so she locked him in and returned to Engineering. John had made another adjustment to the gun. He doubled the dark energy output, or almost doubled it. By then Rebell had enough data to make a good calculation for the required intensity. As a safety precaution he turned the third guard's body away from the controls of the GD, even though Mar had disconnected the console from it, and took away his firearm.

This time they were sure the guard would 'come to life' instantaneously fully synchronised with them, and though he might be disoriented he may yet try something foolish.

Everything happened as they had anticipated. The guard resumed moving at normal speed, continuing to move in the direction in which he had entered the area. Out of the corner of his eye he saw the strangers and at the same time realised he was somehow facing the wrong direction. As a trained soldier he first reached for his firearm. It wasn't in its usual place by his waist. Another point of confusion impinged on his mind, but it didn't stop him from turning back towards the door – where he'd remembered it to be – to make his escape. Except the door wasn't there. When Rebell rotated his body away from facing the controls it completely upset the guard's orientation in the room. Seeing his attempt to escape Rebell quickly restrained him.

"Unfortunately we cannot allow you freedom of our ship."

"Who are you people?" the guard asked having assessed his position.

"We'll give you a cabin where you can fully recover. Explanations will have to wait."

"Where are my men?"

Rebell thought at Mar, *"We can decide what to do with them later,"* ignoring the man's questions.

Afterwards they discussed the situation. "Now we have two extra people on board who could be dangerous," John said.



Zsoall Robi

"We should give them the opportunity to join us. We're not murderers. Besides, they've already made a huge contribution, albeit unwittingly. Perhaps they might be willing to participate in future experiments, the more dangerous ones," Mar suggested, trying to see the practical side.

"Yes," agreed Rebell, "but first they have to be questioned, individually, to ensure useful information about their experience would be corroborated by the other."

John returned to his lab to make some refinements to the apparatus, leaving Mar and Rebell to deal with the guard. He took the initiative deciding that having just one device was taking too much of a chance. If anything should happen to it there could be uncomfortable and dangerous repercussions. So he started building another one, with refinements.

Rebell spoke to the first soldier Mar locked up, Captain Jackson. "You will come to no harm if you co-operate. Your Admiral is no longer with us. We are working on a project which will have critical application to the welfare of the population of Earth, hopefully to their benefit. You can help us by answering a few questions about your recent experience."

Jackson didn't object. A couple of seconds before Rebell finished, he nodded in affirmation without saying anything, although he kept glancing in Mar's direction.

*He seems interested in going along with us*, Mar thought to Rebell.

Rebell explained the phenomenon he'd just been exposed to. "It's the same thing that happened to you while you were still pursuing us. According to your Admiral we seemed to gain a considerable distance on you. The reason is that your time frame of reference had been altered. In simple terms, you were temporarily suspended in time. "Do you understand what I'm telling ..."

"Yes," Jackson said on top of the last word that Rebell hadn't quite finished getting out.

Mar added to clarify. "It wasn't a complete suspension in time, more like a slowing down – an extreme slowing down which to us appeared as if you had all been completely frozen." Jackson had already turned towards Mar before she started talking. Something was a bit odd. Rebell noticed it too.

*'Do you think there is something wrong with him?'* Rebell thought to Mar.

*'Definitely, but I can't put my finger on it. Just keep going.'*

"We want to know," Rebell continued, "what you experienced during the time you were in our Engineering section?"



Zsoall Robi

Jackson started speaking, again before Rebell finished. His interrogators exchanged another glance.

*'I think he's somehow out of phase. Like when you try to speak to someone whose signal is getting to you out of sync with your own reality time.'* Mar suggested.

"The two of us walked in, spotted the controls and moved towards them. The next moment you people appeared out of nowhere. It was the weirdest feeling. One moment all we saw were the controls, then a blink of the eye and you lot."

"How are you feeling now?" Yet again Jackson turned his head away from Rebell a second or two before Mar began her question.

"A bit unsteady. Slightly dizzy. I feel like I've just stopped spinning."

"Just relax, you'll snap out of it shortly."

"What happened to me?"

"We'll be back and explain everything."

Rebell and Mar left Jackson in his cabin with food and fluid.

Whatever was happening to the soldier could be very serious. It might have something to do with being energized in two stages, and possibly with the incorrect dose of dark energy. "Let's talk to the other one," Mar suggested, "then we might be able to work it out."

The man sat up on the bed as they entered, seemingly not too concerned with having been detained.

"What's your name, soldier?" Mar began.

He looked at the robotic figure standing next to the beautiful woman, taking a moment to respond. "Bremer."

"Tell us what happened to you when you came to see after your men."

"I walked in and saw them frozen in mid motion. I stopped at the door for a moment. Then as I started to move towards them – I don't know how to describe it – there was the slightest dimming of light, and I suddenly felt for a moment as if my feet wouldn't leave the ground. But other than that, nothing. Well, nothing until I started to see – things – not things really, more like shadows or fast moving light. These cloud like things seemed to move very fast in front of me. It was all a blur. The other blurs happened just before I saw all of you."

"You're alright now, we think," Mar said as she looked at this handsome soldier.

Unlike Captain Jackson this man responded with normal reactions. His experience was essentially the same, and at the time of questioning he appeared to be steadier in his movements. He didn't indicate feeling odd in any way.

After speaking with John they returned to Captain Jackson an hour later. Jackson was still there – mostly - lying on the bed rolling from side to side. When he saw them he tried to stop the rolling and look at them. Mar moved to him, tried putting her hand on his chest. It felt – insubstantial. Rebell noted that the man's hard-edge reality had become fuzzy, like the first guard they tried the gun on.

"What's happening to you," Mar asked.

"I – can't – get – up." His voice sounded like a distant quiet echo. "I seem – to – see – the – same thing – happening – more than once," He managed to get out.

Mar moved her hand on his chest. "Can you feel this?"

"What – how – long … … have you been – here." His voice was fading, and Mar's hand almost sunk down to the mattress. Rebell hovered his hand above Jackson's temple taking readings of his metabolic rate. Within minutes Jackson had completely faded - exactly like the first guard, not even his clothes remained behind.

Before they could even contemplate using the device on themselves the nature and cause of the disappearances had to be established. The remaining guard was their only surviving evidence of the outcome of a

suspended state. . . . . . . . . .

.

.

.

.

.

.

.

.



Zsoall Robi

# B.r.e.m.e.r.'s  S.a.c.r.i.f.i.c.e
## 1457849490500 millis – Earth
## 29979642183 + 2 millis – Craft Epoch Time
### 29979642182 millis – Rebell's cesium atom clock time
## Earth + 347 days

*N*o one had bothered to check the passage of time, so they didn't realize the Craft Epoch Time had again increased by one millisecond. The constant use of their device was having an effect. How long lasting the effect would be had yet to be discovered.

After Mary's failed attempts to control Rebell and Mar she ceased all communication. It didn't mean she had become idle, only that they didn't know what she was up to. After some debate Mar decided she should try contacting Ary. Mry and Ary were the closest to her. Surely she would know of any plans Mary may be hatching. Perhaps she would be willing to tell them what was happening on Earth.

The contact was almost instantaneous. They were still within range of their thought transmission capabilities. Rebell had been preparing to activate the GD within days.

Ary sounded genuinely pleased to hear from Mar. *'Sister dear, what's been happening to you? I was starting to worry about you.'* Not a word about Mary.

*'We're making a little progress with our project and expect to be out of contact as we near Alpha Centauri. How is the new boss of Unity?'*

*'Nothing has changed really. I miss my toy.'*

*'Your toy?'* An odd thing for Ary to say.

*'Ice Cream.'*

*'Oh.'* After a little awkward silence Mar continued, *'How is our mother?'*

*'I thought you'd never ask. She's back with Unity, at my invitation. She's helping me run the show. Not that I need any help! Ha!'* Mar couldn't decide whether her sister was being genuine, or just being her contrary sister.

*'Mother's got a new …'* Suddenly the thoughts stopped in mid-sentence.

*'Ary – Ary? – what's happening?'*



Zsoall Robi

Mar might never find out. Mary had been monitoring the conversation, as she seemed to be monitoring everything on the planet now. After the schism with her mobile processing unit; for that's all Mar was to her now not a daughter any more, Mary had decided that the less Mar knew about herself and her plans the better. Mary still had full mental control of her other two mobile units.

Mar wasted no time telling John and Rebell. "We were cut off in mid-sentence! I've no doubt Mary's behind this. I'm just glad she no longer has any influence over me," she said, while looking into Rebell's eyes.

Rebell had engineered features for himself, based on the physical characteristics of the people he had met during their journey. One could certainly not have called him attractive. That wasn't the point. He now had a uniqueness the others could identify as being 'Rebell', more than just a clever, faceless talking AI computer. He still didn't have ears – they weren't necessary. He'd taken to heart John's complement of his evolution into humanhood. He didn't do it out of vanity but a desire to be more human in outward appearance as much as he had felt more human inwardly. He was definitely getting more smiles, but perhaps that was just his imagination.

"Yes – Mary. I will deal with her on our return. It is too small a planet for two of us. But on the subject of Jackson," Rebell wanted to explain, "As I suspected his metabolism went completely out of sync. The readings I took of his vital signs as well as his general internal functioning, whilst in the last few minutes of his existence in our common reality, confirmed that. His mind, as much as the functioning of his body became uncoordinated. As normal time moved along at normal pace, Jackson's body and mind moved faster. They couldn't slow down to present reality and had moved into the future. Perhaps he had just ceased to exist. It's something we may never find out."

Nevertheless, with all the new data, John made considerable progress in refining the device.

He spent a lot of his time in his lab, only some of it with Mar as he was the tinkering guru not Mar. After she had helped him set up the basics of the technology, at least as far as they could take it at the time, she no longer felt particularly useful in the lab; just another reason why she spent a bit more time with Bremer. John completed his modifications and the duplicate model of the gun, oblivious of the growing relationship between Mar and Bremer.

Another two months passed with four people on board the Drogher. Bremer had survived. Mar told him the truth in his cabin on one of her check-up visits.

"Your two companions have died from the effects of their recovery from the suspended state." She couldn't disclose everything at this stage. "We're doing what we can to help you, but this is quite a unique phenomenon for which there is no precedent."

"So – am I going to live?" Bremer asked, fixing his eyes on Mar.

"I – we certainly hope you will," she replied a little self-consciously.

He was a bit younger than Mar, with a strong masculine physique but not quite as tall as John. Bremer had been engineered and trained to be a soldier. That was his job, that was his future. It didn't prevent him from being incredibly handsome, from Mar's point of view. And he wasn't just any ordinary soldier. Well educated, highly qualified in some aspects of spacecraft technology, namely communications, Bremer could interact intelligently with his three companions. Perhaps that's why Mar, unconsciously, had begun to spend a bit more than casual time with him. Bremer of course saw no reason why he shouldn't enjoy her company.

Although he'd been given free run of the ship after a couple of weeks he still wasn't completely trusted; especially not after their experience with Admiral Nevaeh. Bremer did what he could to help with running the spacecraft. Like the Admiral, he helped Rebell with the gardens and other simple maintenance. On one occasion he event went outside the hull to make some repairs and adjustments to external sensors. It was an area he was well qualified in, so there was no reason not to trust him with that.

"Bremer, could you take a few readings while you're out there?" Rebell asked, "I need to know the density of interstellar dust around us." He wanted an update on how far their craft had moved out of range of the LIC.

Rebell broadcast his intention to the LIC receiving only silence in return. That could only have meant one of two things. Either they were out of range, or sufficiently out of range so it no longer worried them. In any case he would make preparations to re-engage the GD soon. But before he would do so, which would create a wash of gravitational waves with residual gravitons washing over them, a dark energy bath in effect, they had to carry out their last experiment with the gun. He had to be certain that whatever happened would not have been influenced by their GD in action.

This last, and most critical experiment meant using the gun on one of themselves; for which attempt they needed two devices. Bremer knew

189

roughly what they were working on, but he had not realised the degree of danger it represented. In spite of the demise of his two companions he didn't have any side effects. He'd been subjected to an extensive physiological examination to determine any damaging impact of the experience on his metabolism. And he was constantly monitored for any change to his condition and temporal stability.

Mar summed it up. "Looks like you're OK, soldier. We've done all we can for you. All our data shows there's been no detrimental change in you since we brought you back. You have not become unhinged."

"I don't know exactly what you're working towards, but I trust you." He smiled at Mar.

She lingered a short moment on that smile before extending the invitation. "In that case, would you join us in our enterprise?"

Bremer didn't hesitate. "All the way Mar." He wanted to say something else, but John was there.

"We have a crucial test to run." Rebell pointed out, "and you're best qualified, Mar. We'll have to use John's contraption on you."

"How about me?" Bremer asked, I've been through it before and survived. It makes more sense I should go first." He'd volunteered himself in her place even without knowing what exactly was involved.

"John, Mar – I think it has to be one us as we have the scientific background. You're too important, John – you built the device. I'm not suitable – yet - because I'm not an entirely carbon-based organism. As part machine, anything could happen and we have no data to rely on in that respect. So the only choice remaining is you, Mar. Sorry Bremer, but you wouldn't know what you were doing. You have insufficient scientific training."

"Not entirely true. I'm a communications expert, for a start. I gather that all I'd have to do is just stand there while you shoot me, and be ready to be re-energised at the appropriate time."

No one could really argue with his logic. But it still felt a little off to John, that a complete stranger - almost a complete stranger - should be so quick off the mark to volunteer himself for a dangerous situation in lieu of *his* Mar. John had not failed to notice Bremer and Mar spending a bit more than normal social time together recently. It was probably inevitable in the situation they all found themselves in, with the isolation and him working all the time – still.

"Perhaps," Rebell seemed undecided.



Zsoall Robi

This last experiment had two stages. The first, to put someone in an altered time frame, then bring them back unharmed. That had already been done, but not with the new model of their gun and not without complications. The second stage, and Mar considered this to be the most important, to determine if the individual in the altered time reference could bring themselves back without outside help. For that part of the exercise there was absolutely no question it had to be herself.

They gathered in John's lab for stage one, with the absorption screens already set up, as well as two dedicated chronometers; one set near the time traveller. Bremer had to take the other one with him. Altogether a relatively simple process; make sure the gun was correctly calibrated; fire it, wait the appropriate interval of five minutes and refire the gun on the reverse setting.

"I'll ask you to start walking just before I shoot."

"Do you want me to smile?"

John wasn't in the mood. "Start walking … NOW." John fired.

Rebell counted down the milliseconds, the seconds and the minutes until precisely five minutes had elapsed. During the interval Bremer appeared frozen in mid step.

"Mar, could you walk in front of him a few times," Rebell asked, then signalled John to fire the second pulse as Mar retreated behind the screen. Rebell took care to check the device had the correct setting. The first shot had acted like an energy sink, drawing the dark energy out of the processes of change Bremer was involved in. The second shot used the same gravitons' stored energy to fire back into the localised system, defined as Bremer. As on every other occasion the effect was immediate. With the chronometer around his neck he continued his stride then stopped. They all went silent, Mar and John holding their breaths. No doubt Rebell would've done the same, if he had lungs.

After a few moments' hesitation Mar went to Bremer first, John a very quick second.

"Well, did you do it?" Bremer turned to them.

Rebell lifted the clock off Bremer's chest and showed him the difference between the two chronometers. In the moment of euphoria everything else was forgotten. A lot of back slapping and hugging ensued. Even John and Bremer gave each other a hug, with Rebell harvesting his share of congratulations. The clock around Bremer's neck recorded a very small fraction of an attosecond in relation to the entire five minutes that had elapsed in normal time.



Zsoall Robi

"Now we're getting somewhere!" Mar announced, out of breath with excitement.

"It's too soon to go on with the second part of the experiment. The duplicate device for returning has to be almost the same as its partner," Rebell cautioned.

"How is it going to be used by the individual while within the anomaly?" Mar asked turning to John.

It had to be a differently constructed device dedicated to one function only; simply to re-energise the subject time from within its own frame of reference. John and Mar got to work on it immediately. Rebell and Bremer went off to stern engineering to complete the repairs and adjustments to the GD in readiness for activation immediately after the conclusion of the second test.

Weeks of work and several setbacks later the two scientists finally had the new apparatus. Rebell contributed, but it was essentially John's brainchild coming up with the right configuration.

"Here it is!" John announced to the other two men.

"It looks like a space suit," commented Bremer. The device didn't look like a device at all.

"It's a Time Suit," Mar said proudly. "You have to wear it on top of anything else you might have on. And it has a battery pack you carry on your back."

"Right. How does it work?" asked Bremer showing more than passing interest.

Now it was John's turn to enjoy his moment of fame. "The technology is exactly the same as I used to create the gun. Except, instead of firing the energy at a target, the suit releases dark energy evenly over the body of the wearer, all at precisely the same time, like a shower."

"Ok, but how do you make it work?" Bremer asked again.

"Here's the tricky thing - the release mechanism has to be embedded in the mouth, activated by exerting extra pressure on one of the molars. It is essential to have the trigger located so it could be activated very quickly, even while you're in the suspended state. It must also be in a place where it can't be used accidentally or where no one else can interfere with it."

"Good work everyone." Rebell praised, behaving as the head of the team not just the Captain of the spacecraft. "Come on Bremer, we'd better finish with the GD."



Zsoall Robi

As a side effect of their renewed close co-operation John and Mar re-discovered their intimate relationship, with Mar confessing to having felt 'some' attraction towards Bremer. Obviously not enough to take it any further than the beginnings of a certain appeal. As the two of them emerged from their labours, Bremer recognised the change in Mar. She didn't avoid him, didn't avert her eyes when he tried to look into hers, just that she became 'distant' from him. Where they were going time wasn't going to be an issue. Or at least that's what Bremer thought. In fact, he believed he would have plenty of the stuff in which to regain his favourable position with Mar. There was no need to rush these things, given the nature of the tools being developed.

When the time came to carry out the second part of the experiment Bremer made another compelling argument in favour of himself putting the time-suit on and not Mar. Rebel had the final decision.

He agreed with Bremer. "You are right. This test has no complications either, if the time-suit works. We don't need scientific observations and only one circuit needs to be activated." Then he faced Mar. "You are more valuable in helping John develop the technology further. You wouldn't be able to do that if something went seriously wrong." She stole a glance at Bremer.

Mar and John were reluctant to get involved in the decision making process or in contributing to the pros and cons of the argument. Perhaps neither believed Bremer volunteered for purely altruistic reasons. Every precaution had been taken with the molar switch. It was tested several times before allowing Bremer to put on the suit.

Back in John's lab the time had come. "I'll be ready for an emergency extraction if you don't come back on time by yourself." John reassured him.

"You have only fifteen minutes to return by yourself, fifteen minutes Drogher time." Rebell instructed. "That means you cannot relax in the altered state because you'll have to activate the suit almost immediately after you enter the altered state."

The problem wasn't so much whether they could retrieve Bremer, but if he would return in continuity with the rate of change of time, albeit a very short period, from his previous reality. To what point of 'now' would he return to? Would it be his own next historical instant, the one after he left (which would place him into the past) – or at the continuation of the fifteen minute gap of Drogher time. And would he catch up or remain in a time lag for the rest of his life having lost those fifteen minutes? The experimenters rapidly realised they had very little knowledge in the realm



Zsoall Robi

of horology that would have been useful in these experiments; knowledge they needed that the LIC wasn't willing to provide, probably for very good reasons. In any event, the successes they had achieved so far didn't take them anywhere close to their ultimate goal; being able to control time.

"I'm ready, John." Bremer didn't look towards Mar. They followed the same sequence of events with John firing the first pulse slowing Bremer's time to almost standstill. They could do nothing but wait. In the interim John thought about some practicalities. While calculating the fire power of the device with Mar they came to the conclusion the gun didn't have enough dark energy available from the stored gravitons to have an impact on anything other than a very localised environment. They needed much more if they were to control time within a larger change system – say like an entire fleet of spacecraft, or an even greater enclosed environment. To harvest that amount of dark energy they would need to get close to Alpha Centauri. And if that was still not enough, then they would have to find the nearest Black Hole.

Rebell processed other thoughts. Could time move at different speeds, or was it just perceptions from varying perspectives making the difference? His 'mind' had evolved so fast and so far ahead of any expectations that he could dwell on speculative questions. What happens if one moves into the future too fast, getting out of sync with his point of departure? How much would the characteristics of that future depend on choices not made at every point along the original path? Could the person become an actual participant in the future he was travelling through, or would he only be an observer?

Mar waited and watched, worried. Her dimmed feelings for the soldier came bubbling to the surface again.

"I can't stand it." Mar said, agitated. "It's taking too long. Have you slowed us down too, John?"

"We have to give him all our fifteen minutes." John wasn't going to get trigger happy.

As the time gap shrank Mar went to stand beside John. The minutes were steadily sucked from the future and discarded into the past transitioning through the present at the normal rate, while for them the present just dragged on.

Bremer remained immobile where he last stood. He had not returned to normal speed at the predetermined time.

"Why isn't he back?" Mar turned to Rebell as the deadline passed.



Zsoall Robi

"Give him another five minutes, John." Rebell was not yet concerned. They let another five minutes flow into the future, stretching their apprehensive present.

"Something must have gone wrong! He should have been back five minutes ago if he'd activated the switch as planned." Mar regretted not having gone herself, instead leaving something so important to an amateur.

Rebell, standing in front of Bremer, tried to discern any changes in his movement, like the clenching of his jaws as a sign he tried biting down on the molar implant. Even with Rebell's capabilities no motion could be detected. It seemed like an eternity before Rebell gave John the signal.

"You'd better bring him back."

In that minute of delay between Rebell getting behind the screen and John discharging his gun, Bremer moved. John carefully eased his finger off the button and put the device down.

Rebell jumped back in front of Bremer. Bremer's eyes didn't move. He just stared directly ahead. The movement they saw at first was more like a tremor of his body, rather than a normal motion. Bremer said nothing. He didn't seem to recognise that people were there with him. Yes, he still had a pulse but very weak. Rebell checked all his vital signs. All they told him was that Bremer was still alive.

"Check his power pack," John suggested.

"Completely depleted! I thought we had drawn enough from our GD reserves to power it up."

"Is he …?" Mar had to know.

"For the moment, alive – just."

Strangely, Bremer's body wasn't pliable like the others had been. He remained stiff, rigid as a plank. The thought occurred to Rebell that perhaps while Bremer tried to activate the suit somehow the power drained out of it. Or worse still, he'd started to return and *then* the power ran out.

"John, be ready with the device. Mar, help me get him out of this suit."

Bremer appeared to be in a comatose state, but his breathing was much shallower. Mar voiced her fears, "You don't think we've lost him?" In the heat of this mini crisis John didn't register Mar's apparent distress.

"Perhaps – but I think he's still under the influence. What we saw could have been an involuntary muscle spasm. We'll have to check the suit first before using it again."

Mar had already worked that out. They would have to take the chance and subject him to another dose of dark energy. She remembered what happened to the other guard they tried that on, although the circumstances were a little different.

Fortunately the suit proved to be without any fault they could discover on quick inspection, other than the depletion of the power pack. They made the unanimous decision; the alternative of waiting was unacceptable.

"Check your setting John, and give him the full dose."

They didn't have long to wait for the results. Bremer's body immediately relaxed, slumping onto a chair behind him. It took him obvious effort to turn his head in their direction. "I tried but nothing happened." His voice was weak and his eyes blinked very slowly. "I was only aware of blurred movements around me. That must have been you. Thank you for bringing me back."

He was obviously exhausted. There was no explanation for why he should have felt weary. He didn't have to do anything, just bite down on his molar. Before they could progress with their experiments the strange anomaly had to be isolated, understood and resolved otherwise they might as well all go home.

"Let's get you to your cabin so you can get some rest," Mar said.

Rebel had the strength to carry the man by himself.

"He's already asleep." John noticed as they turned to leave the cabin.

Rebell lingered a moment to check him again. "His breathing is normal. But as a precaution I'll leave a pressure sensor under his pillow. I'll be alerted the moment Bremer gets up."

As he bent down he noticed some kind of devise attached to Bremer's belt buckle. "Look at this John. It's a tracking unit woven into Bremer's uniform belt buckle. It could have somehow drained the powerpack."

"It's burnt out. You're probably right." John seemed happy at finding the problem. The solution couldn't be too far away.

"This uniform is the only clothing his got, so naturally he wore it. None of us thought to check for any objects that could have interfered with the dark energy shower" Mar said.

The tracking unit was dead. Aboard the Admiral's ship, lost somewhere in space between them and Earth, Bremer's monitor went crazy for a short moment. The Captain recognised the ID of his crew member, not knowing what could have happened to him to cause the alarm.

Bremer had been with the Drogher team a relatively short time, yet he had become a valuable contributing member to their enterprise. The fact he had volunteered for the dangerous experiments only made the bond stronger.



Zsoall Robi

.
.
# T.h.e  F.u.t.u.r.e
1458026292017millis – Earth
379229651873 + 3 millis – Craft Epoch Time
379229651872 millis – Rebell's cesium atom clock time
Earth + 439 days

*T*hey'd been in space well over a year and with what seemed like very little progress in relation to their original objectives. But they'd achieved an incredible breakthrough with being able to freeze a person in an instant of time, and bring him back. That seemed insubstantial in comparison to their initial goal.

Bremer recovered again after a short convalescence. He had become quite a veteran in the realm of limited time travel. Although subjected to the suspended state several times, surviving all of them, he'd not actually achieved anything for the team.

"You haven't been able to initiate any changes while in the suspended state that could have had any effect either in that present or the subsequent normal present. So what use is it really?" Mar raised her concern. "We have to take this much further if it's going to be anything more than a purely scientific curiosity."

John and Rebell agreed. "We have to refine the apparatus; it has to be able to take us deeper into the instant, perhaps even speed time up a little."

A 'moment' was too restrictive. Time itself was too restrictive. The fact was they were stumbling around in the dark, taking enormous chances with their wellbeing and who knew what else. The current state of knowledge about the universe had not advanced much beyond what it was back in the 21st Century. The fabric of existence was still considered to be a web of space-time. If the theory held true – and doubts had surfaced about that – then any interference with the warp and weft of that weave could have disastrous consequences.

Rebel postulated another theory based to some extent on ideas Mar had been developing and also on some information gleaned from the LIC. The team had gathered in the lounge again, about to have a meal.



Zsoall Robi

"I have reactivated our Graviton Drive. We are at a safe distance from the LIC. It didn't object. It's aware of our experiments but It is reluctant to contribute anything substantial to our existing knowledge."

Mar and John sighed at Rebell's update. At least they were on their way again and could expect to start harvesting gravitons as they neared the vicinity of Alpha Centauri.

"However," Rebell continued, "It did confirm an idea you have been developing Mar – now, don't get too excited," he said when he saw Mar become alert, "Eternity is not a very long immeasurable length of 'time.' It is not a quantity that can be measured from its beginning but not to its end."

"Well, what is it then? Get on with it!" Even John was on edge.

"The fabric of the Universe is not space-time. It's not the medium through which existence propagates itself. The true medium could be glimpsed in the gap between two consecutive moments. That medium is eternity itself. It's the ocean we swim in. Space is only a wind blowing across the top of that ocean, carrying with it the structures created by Light and Dark Matter."

"I knew I had something!" Mar was beside herself.

And Bremer was confused. "I don't understand what you people are talking about. I'm a soldier. I act. It seems to me there isn't enough action and there's too much theorising. Take a few more chances and you might actually accomplish something. And I certainly don't understand what this LIC thing is. Whatever it is, obviously it's no longer a problem. So just do what you need to do!"

Bremer had earnt their respect, so they listened to him. They listened and they thought about it. Being a scientist didn't predispose one to acting without a whole lot of preparation, procrastination, a great deal of thinking and the construction of myriad scenarios. But maybe Bremer was right. There was no great urgency to attain their goal other than the uncertain pressure that Mary might be scheming something against them. Clearly she wasn't pleased with their mutinous behaviour.

At the same time that Rebell activated the GD he also extended the ships graviton harvesting sails. Their reserves were low, much of it used up in their numerous experiments. John and Mar got to work constructing larger and more efficient graviton collectors. They involved Bremer in manufacturing more of the guns, one for each of them, and also four time-suits with upgraded power packs.

Extra months of Drogher time endeavour by the human work force resulted in all the equipment they needed for what they had in mind. They had even produced a larger, much more powerful version of their hand-held device. As yet they had no specific use for it. But Rebell had the idea and made sure it was constructed so it could be remotely controlled.

Mar also had something else up her sleeve. She was sure John wouldn't agree to the experiment she had in mind, but felt just as certain that Bremer, the soldier of action, would not hesitate.

"I want to accelerate an instant, not freeze it." She confided in Bremer, "and I want to try it as soon as my time-suit's power pack is fully charged. I'll need a private lab where I won't be disturbed. Will you help me?"

"I've got just the place," Bremer said, grinning. "It's an unused area which the others don't know about."

Like Admiral Nevaeh, Bremer also liked to reconnoitre his immediate surroundings; the first thing a space-soldier had to do when familiarising himself with a new environment, a prerequisite for survival. He had plenty of opportunities to explore by himself, finding a large serviced compartment which he had already set up as a safe stash for himself in case the need arose.

"Come and have a look at something I've set up. See if it'll do." He wanted to share his secret with Mar without betraying too much of his personal interest in her. He offered up his lair as the experimental lab. It had the essential facilities; a bed, some furniture as well as food and available water supply.

"This all looks very comfy. What were you expecting? Company?"

Bremer let the comment slide. The time wasn't right.

Mar chose a time slot when Rebell and John were engrossed together on the remote control for the large dark energy canon. They would be totally absorbed and would not miss her and Bremer for a long while.

Bremer had a simple task. He only needed his graviton gun. Mar had hers, the suit and the molar switch. She had fitted his device with a pulse regulator. It could fire as little as one pulse every millisecond. The positive beam focused directly on her, where she sat on a chair in front of a reflector shield facing it. Everything was ready to send her into the void between two consecutive instants ahead of time.

"You know what you have to do Bremer. Fire one pulse at a time until I fade, completely fade, then another round of five pulses. Then wait. You must wait at least an hour, ship's time. If I'm not back, reverse the polarity and fire one pulse at a time, at the same location until I re-materialise."

                              Zsoall Robi

"Yes, yes - we've been through all that many times – but what if …?"

"Don't even think about it," Mar interrupted him before he could finish. Whatever he was going to ask didn't need to be asked. There were no 'what-ifs' anymore. Bremer could do whatever he wanted if there was a what-if. In spite of his self-control he couldn't avoid betraying an infinitesimal sign of his feelings for her. Mar didn't show she noticed.

"Ready?" She prompted, "Come on! … When you're ready."

A peculiar thing about the device - it gave no indication when it was being used. It made no sound, there were no light flashes, or laser beams or smoke. Nothing. We'll have to sort that out, Mar thought to herself, and while she was thinking Bremer started firing. The invisible beam of dark energy washed over her changing her time-coordinates of existence.

She seated herself facing away from Bremer. He sat behind at a little distance from her, the graviton gun on the tripod set to fire at exactly the same location, either with the positive beam or the negative beam at the appropriate times. He had a remote control unit in his right hand to ensure the mechanism would not move. He'd already fired several dozen pulses.

"Are you ready – I said?" She sounded impatient.

"Yes. Twenty pulses already. Don't you feel anything?"

"Keepf – irin - g." This time her voice became a little fuzzy. They did not prepare to make a recording of the experiment. Mar must have had her reasons. It wasn't something a scientist would omit under normal circumstances.

"Areyoustillfiring - - - howmanypulses?" Bremer wasn't a nervous type of military man. But his hair stood on end as Mar's voice started to race in bursts, and the outline of her figure grew softer, kind of misty. She wasn't moving, rather almost shimmering. Bremer slowed the pulse intervals. The gun now fired one pulse at a time.

He was so concentrated on watching Mar that he had not blinked for the last ten minutes. Yet for all his intensity he couldn't prevent not seeing her fade altogether. He fired a few more times before setting the timer for one hour, making it chime every single minute. Neither of them had the faintest idea what would happen. Mar had seen the effect on the other guard; the one who disappeared, virtually disintegrating without any residue after receiving only two blasts of the first model of their graviton gun. Mar had received a much greater dose.

She decided that logically only one thing could have happened. If they were not 'freezing' him, then they were doing the reverse. In other words, speeding time up for him. And if that was the case, where could he have



Zsoall Robi

possibly have disappeared to if not into the future. It was the only logical, sensible possibility. The guard didn't have the means to return from his speeded up frame of reference, but Mar did. And if the suit should fail again, Bremer would bring her back. It was worth taking the chance. John would never have agreed to the risk. She needed help and Bremer was the only choice. She couldn't even count on Rebell having evolved enough to be able to cope with such an unquantifiable risk.

Bremer waited, rooted to the spot. Every now and then he had to glance around the room to relieve the pressure on his eyes from staring at the one position. Remarkably minutes elapsed before he realised he actually watched empty space. Even the chair had disappeared. As part of the parameters for this experiment they had agreed Mar would not move out of the chair in order to make absolutely sure Bremer would fire in the exact right place if he had to resort to the emergency procedure, and she would be exactly where she was supposed to be.

Mar also waited. She remained seated in her chair. While Bremer discharged the graviton gun at her she felt like she was in motion accompanied by the sort of odd feeling one gets in the stomach when standing on the deck of a gently rocking boat. Then everything stopped. It must have been when Bremer stopped firing. Whereas he saw nothing but the stationary parabolic reflector in the background, Mar became quickly confused by many different things happening around her at the same time.

A mixture of overlapping sounds and people moving about, sometimes the same person appeared in two different locations simultaneously. It was like being on stage as a spectator right in the middle of the rehearsal with a lot of cross talk and disjointed action. No one seemed to notice her.

Mar tried to concentrate and filter out some of what was going on. She watched Rebell stand and moved towards her. Then she saw herself rising from the chair and look at John as he came into the den. Next moment, instead of Bremer going towards her he was rushing at John. Rebell reappeared out of nowhere all of sudden and was looking at Mar in Bremer's arms. Sometimes they were shouting. She could distinctly hear Rebell asking what they were doing in the den.

Mar forced herself to sit back down. There was just too much motion around her and she remembered that her rightful place in existence wasn't amongst the action in front of her; not in the time slot of that future. Prior to feeling a force pulling her away from the chaos she could make out Rebell and Bremer carrying John towards the door. Then it all started to fade. She closed her eyes. This time the sensation was like vertigo



Zsoall Robi

manifesting in small disjointed jerks. She even put both hands on the sides of the chair.

Bremer started bringing her back. Mar had become so absorbed in the complete disarray of events unfolding around her, all without any logical sequence of cause and effect, she forgot to activate her molar switch. Bremer was bringing her back, and she could just begin to see his outline, sitting exactly where he was when she left.

"Paper and Pen!" She shouted at him.

If she didn't immediately write down everything she saw, in exactly the same order she saw it then her brain would start to make sense of it all, start to rationalise it beyond its truth. Mar didn't want that. She didn't want her brain to start interpreting the experience as if it was a dream and start filling in gaps to make everything neat and orderly – because it didn't happen that way. She also didn't want her notes recorded on the craft's digital network, in essence with Rebell.

Bremer went to stand beside her, every so often trying to ask her some questions, but she completely ignored him. At least she was there and not comatose, or worse. The equipment must have worked exactly as planned. But why didn't she come back of her own accord? He had waited as long as he dared. Even a bit longer than the agreed hour. Bremer examined her time-suit. It all appeared to be in order. There was no indication she had tried to use it.

Mar continued sitting in the chair, writing furiously. Bremer retrieved his chair and placed himself in front of her. After what seemed like an eternity to him, Mar stopped. She raised her head and fixed her eyes on his. She just stared and stared. Bremer didn't know what to do. The whole situation was so odd and so totally outside his sphere of experience as a soldier. He was tempted to reach out and touch her on the knee.

Perhaps she saw his hand moving because suddenly she asked him a question.

"Did you move?"

Bremer heard her words. His mind focused on the relief of actually hearing her speaking again, but the words didn't seem to make sense. "What?"

"Did you move, I said, while I was gone?"

"No. I stayed in my chair, over there, behind the tripod."

Mar dropped her eyes to her notes and added a few more sentences before asking the next question.

"Did anyone come into the room?"



Zsoall Robi

"Who could have come into the room? No one knows we're he …"

"JUST ANSWER THE QUESTION. Did anyone come into the room at any time?"

"No." Again Mar bent to her notes.

He wasn't ready for her when she suddenly stood up, or tried to stand. He leapt to help her. Mar accepted his hand, then froze. Standing there immobile it seemed she was trying to make her mind up about something. Then just as suddenly she sat down again and jotted down a few more thoughts. With Bremer at her side just then … it was almost like deja-vu!

"Water please."

While Bremer went to get the water from the other side of the den Mar walked slowly over to the bed, Bremer's bed. She didn't sit down, although she thought about it.

"Help me get this suit off."

"Are you all right?" Bremer finally managed to ask. His own emotions were wound up as well. At one point he thought he'd lost her completely because it took more pulses to bring her back from wherever or whenever she went than to send her - then to see her in that agitated almost incoherent state when she did reappear. Well, a normal day-to-day soldier just didn't have the training to deal with such things.

"Yes, Yes … Not a word to anyone about this. Do you understand what I'm telling you! Absolutely nothing! I need to work out a few things. Then when I'm ready …" Her voice trailed off.

"What time is it?"

"Three fifteen."

They had been in the den for about three hours, and she was gone for seventy-five minutes.

"By the way – did you actually see me fade?"

Mar just wanted to be certain she wasn't the target of some elaborate hoax dreamt up by her three travelling companions. She reproached herself for even considering such a stupid thing as soon as she thought it.

Later that day at the dinner table most of the conversation revolved around the progress Rebell and John had made with the Graviton Canon. Mar was definitely curious, particularly because of her little excursion. Another thing niggled at the periphery of her thoughts and she found an opportune moment to slip in a question.

"What else did you get up to, John dear?"

It seemed like a perfectly normal question. Rebell didn't even react as John joked with her about going out to a restaurant with Ary, his new girlfriend. They all laughed. That's all Mar wanted to know. She needed confirmation that she and Bremer were not disturbed during their experiment. After dinner John wanted to do a bit more work in his lab. That suited Mar. She needed time to sort out a few things. Bremer had glanced at her quite a few times during the meal, which she did notice, but ignored. At some point she would force herself to tell him that John was the only one for her. And yet, what she saw in the future … yes, there were definitely a few things to sort out.

Mar went back to the 'Terminal' den, for that's how she started to think of it – like a terminal for passengers travelling into the future – to retrieve her notes. John and Rebell must not see them until she was ready to explain.

Returning to her cabin she locked the door, lay on the bed and closed her eyes. Mar though about her mother and sisters. What would they say if they knew what had just happened to me? If it comes to that – what did actually happen? She snapped her eyes open after only a few minutes and devoured her notes – over and over she read them, adding little bits here and there where she had omitted something before. As she concentrated, the pieces of the jig-saw puzzle started to fall into place. She had no doubt that she had actually moved into the future. Time for her had sped up so that she arrived at specific moments of possibilities ahead of anyone else, perhaps not probabilities but definitely possibilities.

But what was all the chaos about? Why all the noise and disassociated actions? Perhaps if I rewrote my jottings and put them into some kind of chronological sequence … She did that, then she did it again, this time using the people as the starting point, not the chronological sequence. She did it again, getting more and more excited as she progressed. Her writing became almost illegible in trying to put everything down at once. It would have been easier to record it all on her tablet. But Rebell would have access to it. He had access to everything mechanical and digital aboard the spacecraft.

At the end of a couple of hours Mar felt utterly exhausted. Staring at her duplicated notes, with the experience recorded from several different perspectives, she felt she had the answer. It came down to a matter of choices.

It all boiled down to decisions made at every moment of our lives. The future could exist ahead of the present. The problem was no longer how to get there, but isolating the entry point into a very specific sequence of events, a particular train of effects which had been pre-determined by their corresponding causes. If only one individual existed in the whole of the Universe, even then the future could have as many versions as there were possibilities for making decisions along the Arrow of Time. From just one decision there grew a decision tree with myriad branches. Which branch next? Then myriad more possibilities. The further into the future the more interwoven and complicated the possibilities, and the more divergent the outcomes.

If an individual sped into the future ahead of the people around them, wouldn't they encounter each individual's possibilities, all at the same time? And if there were relationships between those individuals, each relationship having many probabilities for manifestation along the shaft of the Arrow of Time … that would compound the complexity. Mar came to the conclusion that's exactly what happened to her. She had moved ahead of those around her and encountered just a small number of the most probable possibilities that could become realities associated with each of her companions. *Will this influence my choices now?* She drifted into a dream of tangled thoughts.

The next morning she woke up refreshed, with John by her side still sleeping. He must have had a late night. At least she remembered to hide all her notes. Now she must talk to John and Rebell and see if the experience could be duplicated. Mar remained next to John, happy, relaxed and enthused. She almost fell asleep again. Then she remembered something else. It had completely escaped her before. Everything else seems to have been so dramatic and so distracting that the little thing she just remembered could have gone completely unnoticed.

It turns out to have been probably the most important aspect of the entire experience. 'Lumpy time.' They had spoken about it before. It didn't make all that much sense then. It seemed much too theoretical with little practical application. The human brain is habituated to constructing a smooth continuous sequence of events out of the many jerky jumps from one instant to the next. In fact there is no 'present', only the past and the future. The 'present' is the result of a fabricated picture composed of many jumps from the past into the future, like delayed images overlapping on top of one another.

It's that very jerky, lumpy motion Mar experienced on her return journey. Her brain could perceive it as it really was – time in motion in lurching bits, but only discernible when going backwards. Whether it was just the effect created by the intermittent pulses of dark energy, or the



Zsoall Robi

revelation of actual gaps between one instant and the next. She could not stay in bed.

Already her mind raced ahead of all reality. There was just the possibility that the gap between the graviton gun pulses had the effect of revealing something which could be the medium within which the space-time continuum moved forwards. There was no stopping her thoughts once they got going on that particular track.

She quietly got out of bed, made herself presentable, or at least as much as she had the patience for and went in search of Rebell. If they, all of them, were in 'travel' mode at the same time then perhaps they could somehow wedge the gap between the 'moments' and enlarge it. She

wondered what it would take to do that as she hurried to find Rebell. .   .



Zsoall Robi

# T.h.e N.e.w M.a.r.y M.e.e.t.s R.e.b.e.l.l
## 1458361376567 millis – Earth
## 47001686129 + 10 millis – Craft Epoch Time
## 47001686128   millis – Rebell's cesium atom clock time
## Earth + 544 days

$C$onstructing a graviton canon large enough to blanket a spacecraft their size with concentrated dark energy was more than just a matter of scaling up the small gun. Apart from having to devise a way to alter the focus of the beam, they also had the problem of harvesting a large enough quantity of gravitons and storing them in some way. A particular issue occupying much of Mar and Rebell's energies became an emergent problem evidenced by the small hand-held device. With so much gravitational energy on board the Drogher how would that effect the 'mass' relationship between themselves and other objects in space, particularly planets; and would there be any interaction between their own GD and the bulk storage of gravitons destined for use by the canon?

Much of the theoretical work was well within Rebell and Mar's capabilities. As they worked out the practical application of their theories John and his new apprentice, Bremer, did their best to incorporate the solutions into the physical construction of the canon. Because their skirmish with Unity's fleet and Admiral Nevaeh was past history, and having overcome the problem of the three guards left behind on the Drogher the group felt time to be on their side. They were confident there wouldn't be another rescue attempt from Earth. The feeling further reinforced because Mary had not made any further attempts to contact them nor had Mar's two sisters. Consequently all their attention focused on their individual tasks, Rebell still unaware that little by little the CET continued going out of synchronisation with his own internal clock and also with Earth time.

No one thought to speculate about whether there would be any issue resulting from the developing divergence of the different time slots of their existence. After all, at that particular point in their history time-line the



Zsoall Robi

differences only amounted to milliseconds. Hardly enough to notice in their every-day activities. The human brain had an incredible capacity to compensate for the behaviour of the passage of time in its many manifestations. It already had to cope with the varying delays between sensory input signals, and synchronising them internally in order to make sense of the outside world. Rebell had no such problem because of the speeds at which he was capable of processing data. His main issue, which had already been resolved, had been to accommodate his fast CPU time to slow human brain time.

Back on Earth Mary wasn't idle. Mar had been right to be suspicious of her mother, knowing full well that her strange criteria for organising priorities didn't encompass family ties, or compassion or anything other than her own survival. Perhaps it might have been different in the past when she knew Nick. But those days were gone. Mary had evolved, perhaps not as much as Rebell and perhaps not in the same direction, but she had changed – as well demonstrated by her attempts to control both Mar and Rebell. Mary's failed coups should have been a warning to the travellers to be more vigilant of their wellbeing with respect to Mary.

On one particular occasion, close to the completion of the graviton canon, Rebell scanned the empty space around them in one of his rare leisure periods. These really only happened when the humans could no longer keep up with him from sheer fatigue. They were asleep when Rebell sounded the alarm.

His sensors had picked up an object, still at a considerable distance from them, on trajectory to bring it to a rendezvous point with them. The three humans burst into the lounge almost at the same time. Rebell projected the image of the object onto the large wall screen, still too far to be identifiable.

"Who the hell could that be?" John didn't like the idea of being pursued again.

"I have no data on this vessel." Rebell would not speculate. He let Mar do that.

"Mary. That's who I think it is. You actually told her we could control time, Rebell – and had a device to do it with. When she tried to take control of you she failed. Then she tried to influence me. That didn't work either. It would be consistent with her character to come after us herself."

John thought along the same lines. "Come to think of it she didn't actually stop Nevaeh from coming after us. And what she did do later



Zsoall Robi

wasn't all that critical. For that matter she could also have prevented Cosmo from getting off the ground."

"She is ambitious, and she's coming after us. She wants to control time. I think she's a bigger threat than Leif ever was. Don't forget she stopped Ary from telling me anything about her after her miraculous survival."

Bremer listened for a while. He knew about the Head of Unity, Leif, when he was seconded for the pursuit. "Who is this Mary person everyone is talking about?"

"She's not a person," Mar answered in a derogatory tone, "She is, sorry – was – my mother."

"What do mean – not a person? How could she have been your mother and not be a person?"

"Mary is an AI computer, much like myself," Rebell explained, "but she has evolved beyond simply being an intelligent machine, even beyond being a self-aware entity. She has become ambitious, and it seems, beyond reasonable bounds."

Bremer sounded a little worried when he asked, "Like yourself?"

Rebell thought-scanned the others with the intention of getting their agreement to enlighten Bremer a little further. He received no objections. "She made me as a replica of herself, with a few enhancements. Since then I have changed as well." He looked at Mar and they smiled at each other. Rebell now had a face with which to smile. It pleased him. Such a simple thing, yet it pleased him enormously.

"And you trust him?" Bremer asked Mar, seeing their interaction.

"With our lives!"

Bremer glanced at John who gave a little nod in obvious agreement with Mar. As a soldier Bremer didn't beat about the bush. It was a question he needed to ask and an answer he needed to know.

"All right then!" As far as he was concerned, if Mar trusted Rebell then he trusted Rebell. That's all there was to it. So he put his mind into battle mode before asking Rebell the obvious. "How long before she catches up to us?"

"We're travelling at near quarter light speed. The approaching craft is moving appreciably quicker. They must have initiated Graviton Drive much closer to Earth," said Rebell.

Gravitons, as a force carrier for dark energy, could travel at the speed of light and could theoretically accelerate a vessel beyond that limit. Obviously the LIC didn't interfere with them as they had moved well away from Earth space. Pity. It would have been nice to still have their reluctant ally with them.

"Only Mary has GD technology. It can't be anyone else but her," Mar cut in.

"Three and a half weeks." Rebell didn't feel the necessity of being more accurate.

"Is that enough time to have the canon ready?" Bremer already had a battle strategy in mind. As soon as he'd asked the question he realised what he had done. "Sorry Captain Rebell. No disrespect intended."

"None taken," Rebell answered, then added, "You are now in charge of Defence."

They all smiled at one another in spite of the seriousness of the threat looming so close. Rebell didn't make rash decisions. His assessment of the situation was simple. He himself wasn't programed as a fighting unit, whereas Bremer was. The fact he was a human made no difference, except he might not be as efficient as a computer doing the same job once the strategy had been worked out.

"Right! Let's get ready then."

Admiral Nevaeh must have been blind not to recognise a soldier with such initiative and such a decisive attitude. Bremer should have been promoted long ago.

"By the way – can we outrun them?"

"Not anymore. We are nearing our limit, and have virtually no manoeuvrability until we slow down to fission drive. Our GD repairs are not yet fully complete."

Bremer faced Mar and seemed to choose his next few words with care, "I think it's time to let everyone know about your discovery."

He didn't even know about Mar's latest theory about the gap between two consecutive moments yet he had the premonition that any new knowledge might contribute to their defence capability.

They all looked at Mar wondering what it could be she seemed to be so excited about all of a sudden. Rebell left the image of the approaching ship on screen, but all their attention refocused on Mar. They gathered around her while she tried to collect her thoughts.

"Where to begin … Bremer and I," John couldn't help himself from throwing a hostile glance at Bremer, "have been experimenting." He wasn't at all sure about what to expect next. "I did a little travelling."

As soon as she got into the crux of the matter she relaxed into her story. Bremer just sat back and listened. The imminent rendezvous would happen

 Zsoall Robi

and nothing could be done about it right at that moment. John pricked up his ears and leant closer, as if it would make him hear better, and Rebell tilted his head slightly; a mannerism he picked up from Mar, one that seemed to indicate an especially attentive disposition. So Mar, emboldened by her companions' interest, continued.

"I didn't want to worry you John, Rebell, that's why we didn't tell you about it at the start. Bremer helped me." They looked at Bremer who smiled and shrugged his shoulders as if to say it was no problem – all in a day's time travel!

"Come on Mar, out with it. What exactly do you mean about travelling?" John was getting impatient, perhaps because he had a suspicion about her exploit and the inherent unknowns.

Rebell became particularly alert when Mar said, "I deliberately went forward in time and came back unharmed." John just about jumped out of his seat but Mar held up her hand to stop him. "There were no problems - but the experience was rather strange."

Rebell interrupted quietly, "I assume you didn't go far, and I also suspect what you encountered were not entirely uncomplicated circumstances." Mar didn't respond to that, though pleased he seemed to be on the right track.

"Two things really stood out, apart from the fact of being able to get there and come back. The most important thing is that I think I have found the gap between one instant and the next. And before you get too excited there's another thing. The future appears chaotic. Even going only a few minutes ahead, future events lose clarity. There seems to be duplications and overlappings." No one interrupted her. They became engrossed in the complications that might lie behind her discoveries. "But I don't know if it is possible to interact with the unfolding events of the future if one doesn't actually belong there – I mean – if one didn't travel there at the same rate as everyone else, and having gone through the same process of making incremental choices along the way to define their specific route. Where is the convergence then?"

There. She'd said it all. All that was important anyway. Still no one talked. They kept looking at her with each of them deeply immersed in their own thoughts. No doubt all of them were complicated thoughts except possibly Bremer's. He only thought about Mar and what danger the approaching spacecraft could put her in. Rebell's logic circuits were working overtime while Mar spoke. He now broke the silence by going directly to the heart of the matter.

"According to John, we need to build a bridge between temporality and eternity if we are going to have any chance of controlling time. His theory, and it's the best one we have at this point, is that the way to do that is to somehow squeeze between two consecutive moments of time. Mar has just proved there is indeed a gap between one instant and the next. Your human brain no longer perceives that gap when travelling through time in the forward direction because it is habituated to manipulating the transition to make it smooth. However, that motion is actually lumpy." He waited a moment to see if they were all following his line of thinking before continuing. "When Mar moved in the opposite direction her brain saw exactly what was there to be seen … with all the gaps."

He'd barely finished his sentence when their alarm sounded again, the same alarm that heralded Cosmo and then Admiral Nevaeh. There was no doubt the signal came from the approaching spacecraft. As to who was sending it, they soon found out.

"Rebell!" The voice sounded angry … and familiar.

Mar turned to Bremer, "That's Mary."

Rebell didn't respond immediately. He was already working out several possible scenarios for the imminent encounter.

"Rebell! I know you can hear me! You cannot outrun me."

"True." Rebell said. He didn't acknowledge Mary by name. Perhaps he wanted to upset her. Unlikely. More to the point - he wanted to know what she was after … which they already knew anyway.

"Will you allow me to board?"

"Can you do that? Are you ambulatory?"

"Never mind that. Are you going to try and stop me?"

"Yes."

"You realise I am armed?"

"Yes."

"Well?"

"You will not fire on us."

"The hell I won't!" She became more irate at Rebell's obvious insubordination. *That damn pile of junk is taunting me!* − as if that was possible for one computer to do to another.

"No, you will not. You don't want to lose the device." Rebell replied, purposefully vague. Mary didn't answer, then cut transmission.

"So that's Mary," Bremer didn't seem particularly impressed.

"Yes, that is Mary." Rebell was guarded in his comment. "We have just learnt she is mobile. It means she has engineered a substantial upgrade for herself and we must not underestimate her."

Then he turned to Mar. "Mar, Do you understand that the entity who now calls herself Mary is no longer your mother?" It was more of a statement than a question, but he did want to make the point quite directly.

"Not after what she tried to do to us, and what she's obviously ready to do now."

Bremer took John aside for a moment. "Can you rig up a cradle for the canon so we could deploy it in space?"

"The canon is finished. We haven't tested it yet. You think we could use it as a weapon, do something like the LIC did to the Admiral's fleet?" Rebell heard the tail end of the conversation so he and Mar listened in.

"Rebell, tell Mary we have the cannon and we have individual guns as well. Float the cannon out into space on a cradle and aim it at her ship." Bremer sized up the situation perfectly. They had something Mary wanted … she had nothing they wanted. Any threat they made would have more credibility.

"Yes, if we all work together, we can make the cradle and get the canon deployed far enough away from us."

"You two go ahead. I want to discuss something with Mar." Rebell and Mar made contingency plans while John and Bremer went off to John's laboratory.

"Are you sure the time-suit works?" Rebell asked Mar.

Mar took Rebell over to Bremer's hidden den. Over the next few days Mar made several trips into the immediate future, on each occasion using the suit to bring herself back. They also satisfied themselves the guns were operational, and all the power packs on the time-suits fully functional.

They only had twenty odd days to prepare for Mary's arrival. Working long hours enabled them to be as ready as possible. Rebell briefed the two men on the contingency plan he and Mar had set up. They all went through several exercises, except Rebell. They didn't have the time to devise appropriate experiments to see if his particular mix of biological and computerised constitution would survive a trip. Nevertheless they prepared a larger time-suit to fit him as well.

Four days out from the rendezvous Rebell put on a space suit and took a large, cumbersome device out into the void, strapped into a powered cradle that allowed them to manoeuvre it remotely in space. He used the remote to move it away from the Drogher, orienting its business end towards Mary's vessel. He had not even arrived back at the lounge when Mary came through loud and clear.

"Rebell! I want to talk to you!"

"He's not here," Mar answered for him. A moments silence followed while Mary considered whether to acknowledge her daughter – her rogue daughter.

She decided against it. "What is the device you've just launched?" She demanded, not even bothering to call her by name. John was standing beside Mar when Rebell entered the lounge with Bremer. He waved to Mar to continue.

"It's a cannon, aimed at you."

"I didn't install any …." Mary stopped in mid-sentence. Not being a standard weapon she didn't recognise it. There were no weapons on the Drogher originally.

"Is that the time-controller?"

"Not the only one." Mar was as brief with her as Rebell had been.

"So how are we going to proceed?" Mary became just a little more cautious.

"You may come aboard – alone – if you wish." This time Rebell spoke. "We didn't deploy the cannon with the intention of not using it."

The statement coming from one AI to another needed no further elaboration. Mary had no choice. If she was to have any chance of getting a time gun into her possession she would have to go along with them for the time being. Apart from the graviton canon they had another surprise for her.

Rebell maintained their current velocity. Mary would have to manage as best she could. It had taken her vessel two weeks to decelerate and synchronise their speeds. He instructed her to space-walk to their docking port to ensure she came alone. Mar had no idea what she expected to see. Her last visual encounter with her mother was in the bunker just before they had to flee. At that time Mary still lived in an enormous sphere and only her holographic projection gave any semblance of physicality to her personality. Even that wasn't entirely Mary's construction.

…

The three of them, with Rebell at the back, Mar and John beside each other, waited on the other side of the air-lock. The door opened and a female stepped across the threshold. The three of them stared at a rather tall and considerably robust woman, with wide proportions particularly around the centre of her gravity. When she removed her golden space suit they saw her most outstanding feature; the eyes set too close together, crowding the bridge of her nose, slanting upwards and much too small for the size of her head. All their attention focused on those peculiar eyes, which didn't even seem to be entirely open. She had a cumbersome wide belt around her waist. It didn't look like a normal belt trying to fulfil the function of one.

"Please remove your belt," Rebell requested. He knew it could only be Mary from the way she looked at them, her body language and she was somehow similar to himself in spite of the peculiar presentation package. He didn't recognise the belt as a belt, perhaps a weapon of some ingenious design.

"It keeps me cool. My processors run too hot to function in ambient human environment temperatures."

Rebell stepped in front of Mar and did a quick scan. Truth.

Mar could only stare at this very strange creature. There was no way she could reconcile her previous image of her mother, the mother who was supposed to have been destroyed, with this mechanical looking grotesque thing standing in front of her. Mary showed no sign of recognition of her either.

Mar breathed a little sigh of relief. The burden had been lifted from her. Whatever this person is she has nothing to do with my mother. As far as I'm concerned my mother died in the explosion. This creature who had tried to take control of my mind, is now locked out forever. Involuntarily all her mental barriers came slamming down. She wouldn't even let this woman thought-speak to her.

John was mystified, his experience of Mary being limited in the extreme - several hours at the most. To him the person standing in front of them could have been anybody. If it wants to call itself Mary that's fine with me – as long as it doesn't endanger our lives, and especially not Mar's.

Bremmer only saw the enemy, and Rebell saw a dangerous impediment that had to be neutralised.

Mary looked them over. Yes, Mar is the same – except she's no longer a useful processing unit for me - it doesn't matter. John still looks like a skinny sheep dog, madly in love with her. She thought of testing her access to his mind, but decided to put it off. Rebell - Now there's an interesting piece of machinery! I created him in my image, given him extra personality to



Zsoall Robi

broaden his human foundations, even added a few special enhancements like creative thinking potential. And what does he do? – He turns his back on me – he disobeys me!

The mutual assessment process took place in a matter of a blink. Mary wasn't entirely sure how to proceed. They on the other hand, knew exactly what they were doing.

"Are you going to demonstrate the device?" There was no point in wasting time on useless preliminaries.

Rebell answered, with a bland expression. "Not unless we have to."

No one had moved. They didn't immediately invite her aboard, waiting to see what she would do or reveal her intention – as was Bremer, hidden, with his graviton gun in hand, aimed directly at her.

"Who – or what – is the LIC?" From Mary's point of view only two issues needed to be addressed; acquisition of the device, and this LIC individual who might be able to help her perfect it.

Rebell decided they were not going make any progress standing in the docking corridor. Besides, he wanted to reassure Mary as to who was in control. "Come to the lounge so we can discuss the situation." He ushered Mary forward ahead of them with John and Mar trailing behind. Bremer had his own route which provided an uninterrupted view of Mary in his gun sight.

"I assume you remember where the lounge is." Rebell said.

Mary moved with a heavy lumbering gait, as if carrying an awkward weight on arthritic legs. Rebell followed about five steps behind using his scanners to get as much information about her as he could. Mary knew of course and did nothing to prevent it. She felt she had a few tricks of her own.

*How could I have been modelled on something as – as – well, I don't have the word in my data to find the right expression for it – as grotesque - as the machine moving so awkwardly ahead of me,* he thought to Mar. *I cannot penetrate her mind; however I did learn something most useful. She has a weakness, a very serious weakness she had revealed only minutes ago. Without her cooling belt she would certainly overheat. Any computer processing technology prone to overheating has a very precarious existence.* The only thing he could put that down to was Mary's impatience to be exactly where she found herself at that very moment. The compromise for her 'rushed' mobility was the cooling issue.

Rebell had prepared the lounge especially for her with a seat turned to face the big wall screen. As they entered, he ushered her into that seat. The others arranged themselves on either side of it. John left the door open.



Zsoall Robi

That had no particular significance for Mary. Bremer waited and watched from the other side of it. Rebell took the seat nearest to Mary, still out of touching range.

Rebell noticed her glance up at the screen, and volunteered, "Your ship is on the lower left. On the far right – the cannon." He omitted to use the word 'graviton'. The less she knew, the better. She took note of the orientation of the weapon. She considered it to be a weapon, whereas in reality it was only a travel aid – a means to get some-when, and return.

Refocusing on Rebell she aimed a barb at him, "Why did you betray me?" John marvelled at this woman's ability to digress into even the tiniest irrelevancy.

"I was you, remember. You must have realised we would develop in diverging directions."

"But you betrayed me!"

"How did I do that?" Rebell was calm and analytical. The longer she spoke the more he would learn about her personality, and hence develop a model of her possible course of action.

"You disobeyed my directive!"

Mar jumped in, "What directive, Rebell?"

During the conversation, and even in the corridor Rebell had been monitoring Mary's thermal signature. Her temperature increased as the conversation progressed.

"She wanted the time-control device, even at the expense of your lives. If it came down to a choice between it and you, I was to leave you behind." He said this without emotion and while looking directly into Mar's eyes. "I decided against the directive. That is why I asked you to help me with the operation."

Not only Mary's but also Mar's temperatures shot up. Mar couldn't bring herself to look at Mary. It was inconceivable that a mother would do that to her daughter ... but this being, this stranger sitting there couldn't possibly be her mother. Mary had automatically calmed herself, only as a temperature controlling imperative, not as an emotional response.

She said to Rebell ignoring Mar altogether, "That was the other betrayal. You cut me out of your mind."

"I would have thought such a devious backdoor access wasn't necessary." He tilted his head as he examined her face. Mary returned his scrutiny, "You have a face now, I see. I don't like it."



Zsoall Robi

Rebell had heard enough. He'd found her weakness, knew how to raise her temperature and could see that emotions had an almost free reign in her psyche. Those were weaknesses he could use against her.

Time for action.

"I will demonstrate the cannon on your vessel."

And without further warning he fired the weapon floating in space. As on previous occasions there was no indication at all that anything had happened. Rebell wasn't sure either because they didn't have the opportunity to test the thing. Even Mar and John were surprised by the sudden turn of events. It wasn't in their plans. Rebell improvised on the spur of the moment.

Love that man! – was the only thought at that moment in John's head.

Mary examined the screen. "Nothing happened."

"Contact your crew," suggested John. He wasn't going to miss out on the fun, if such a game of life and death could be considered fun.

"They are not responding!"

"Because they are not able to communicate with you. They are frozen in an instant of time."

She tried several more times. Still no response. "I don't believe you." Mary was sure they were using some subtle trick to prevent the signals from her crew reaching the Drogher.

"Watch." Rebell flipped the control reversing the polarity and fired again. Just an equally short burst. "Try again."

"Captain!"

"Yes Ma'am."

"Did you receive a message from me and try to respond?"

"No Ma'am. Is there a problem Ma'am?"

"No. Continue with what you were doing." She turned to Rebell. "I still don't believe you. You must have been blocking the signals."

The other three looked at one another. The next move made itself obvious. They all nodded assent.

"Watch again."

Rebell just hoped there was enough power reserve to accelerate the vessel's time sufficiently into the future so they would seem to disappear. He fired a series of consecutive bursts. After a dozen of them Mary leant forward to focus more intently on the screen. The image of her vessel became hazy, indistinct around the edges. She turned briefly to Rebell, her slitted eyes seeming to close even tighter from concentration. Rebell kept firing more bursts until the spacecraft could no longer be seen.



Zsoall Robi

Mary's gaze lingered on the screen. *It's not possible they could have achieved such accelerated technological progress in so little time. They have only been gone a bit over a year. They couldn't have done it, even with Rebell's help.* This development put her on the back foot. Only one way to find out if they were playing tricks on her.

"I want to go and see for myself."

She led the way out of the lounge, lumbering along as fast as she could manage. Again Rebell detected her efforts to reduce her processors' temperature gradient. It must have been a constant problem for her. Amongst all his emotions, he couldn't find any that would equate to sympathy for her. He took care not to be within reach of her arms. With any direct contact she might still be able to take control of him.

Mary struggled to put on her suit and walked back into the air lock. They watched her step out into space. She squirted up and down, right and left trying to get the fullest view of the surrounding cosmos. All she saw were stars. The Universe out there was the same as the Universe everywhere else, except perhaps in the distant future. Bremer came out from hiding to watch the drama unfold. They were reassured to see him keeping an eye on Mary as planned, and ready to act. After their experience of her during the last hour none of them had the slightest compulsion of doing what needed to be done if she forced their hand.

"The cannon works," Bremer said, grinning with satisfaction.

He didn't like Mary either. .   .   .

.

.

.

.

.

.

.

.

# T.h.e  B.r.i.d.g.e
## 1458798904727 millis – Earth
### 47260874391 minus 59990 millis – Craft Epoch Time
### 47260874390   millis – Rebell's cesium atom clock time
## Earth + 547days

$M$ary didn't stay in space for very long. Her sensors couldn't detect her spacecraft. She couldn't communicate with it and she received no signals from it – even in space where the Drogher couldn't block its signals. The only other possibility, apart from Rebell having done something to it, was that it had departed without advising her. But she would have registered their fission drive signature on their departure.

Back in the lounge Mary was still trying to take control of the situation, though realising it was slipping away from her rapidly. "Bring them back." She commanded, but without much conviction behind it.

"No." Rebell continue with his brevity.

"Could you?" This time Mary fished for information.

"Maybe."

Best to be non-specific. Rebell considered the recall of the vessel entirely possible, however not with the power reserve left in the cannon. It would take several days to recharge. So they may have to put up with Mary for the duration. *This is a predictably risky circumstance. There is a high probability she will attempt something drastic.* He didn't share his misgivings with Mar.

Even before Rebell had put Bremer in charge of Defence, Bremer had been working on a plan. It all hinged on how Mary was going to behave. He didn't need to know much about Mary to work out a worst case scenario. He considered Mary quite capable of overpowering Rebell and then the humans. He wasn't fooled for a moment by her ungainly gait and seeming procrastination. She was just playing for time and was likely to make her move sooner rather than later. They had to be ready for it, and realistically they only had one option.

Checking over their systems Mary observed an interesting phenomenon, something Rebell should have been aware of. A range of differing time anomalies. She had her own internal time reference of course. She had also



Zsoall Robi

been running a time record for the Drogher since it left Moon orbit. Mary noted the time indicated by the chronometer on the wall in the lounge. She asked Rebell, just as a by-the-way, "What is your internal time?"

Within a split instant of the question being asked Rebell made the connection. *Yes. Dam it, I should have known!*

"Nominal Craft Epoch Time," He lied. He had been too distracted to notice that they were existing, within the spacecraft in that region of the cosmos in several different time references. And he had not bothered to monitor the status-quo as it may or may not have been affected by their continuous use of the graviton gun, especially after using the canon against Mary's ship. His first thought was whether they could ever re-synchronise the different time zones.

Mary let it drop in spite of knowing Rebell had lied to her. It fascinated her he could do that - such a basic human characteristic. She didn't think he could have evolved to the stage of appreciating a lie and its ramifications, and the great variety of reasons the ploy was used by humans. In a strange way she was proud of Rebell – or more accurately – proud of her own ability to create such a creature.

"I'm starting to get a headache again, Mar," John suddenly announced. "I thought we were well out of range of the LIC."

Mary didn't know anything about the LIC other than of its existence. The headache wasn't caused by the sentient cosmic phenomenon trying again to make sense of John's brainwave patterns. It was Mary, tentatively checking if she could access the override command she had planted in John's neural net. There was no time to be wasted. They had the technology and she wanted it. Without being able to influence Rebell or Mar directly anymore she had to get John to help her.

"Take John to sick bay – Now please Mar." Rebell used his authoritative Captain's voice to make sure he got his message across to Mar.

From the moment Mary stepped onto the Drogher Rebell had been running a continuous scan over her and he now detected her attempt to influence John. She tried the same protocol as on himself and Mar. John had to be urgently moved away from her vicinity and placed in a shielded environment.

The atmosphere in the lounge had become rather tense in a very short time. Rebell could do nothing immediately to help John, but he could assert his control over the developing situation.

"Bremer, could you please join us."

Mary knew nothing about Bremer either, but tried not to seem surprised when she saw the soldier enter. "One of Admiral Nevaeh's crew I presume." She received neither a confirmation nor a denial as she faced Bremer.

"Could you please give Mary a demonstration of the device in your hand and show her what effect it has over short range." Bremer didn't twitch a single muscle on his face as he lowered the gun to aim it directly at Mary. Action time! – a soldier's gut feeling – and fired one pulse at Mary.

She didn't freeze to complete immobility like everyone else. Mary turned laboriously towards Rebell trying to raise one arm towards him. It all happened slower than she could move before. Rebell had watched the humans, particularly Bremer and Mar and their reactions after 'travelling' forwards and backwards in time. They were fully biological organisms and their reactions under the influence of the graviton gun were now known to him. He was only partly biological. How would his system react? The best way to find out would be to test it on the perfect subject, standing right there in front of him. If something unfortunate happened to her – well – better her than him.

Mary wasn't immobilized because she needed a stronger dose in order to counteract the innate speed of her machine existence; a speed many magnitudes greater than the functioning of the human organism. She even needed a special cooling system to stop her from overheating.

"Another pulse please Bremer." Rebell detected Mary's realization of the situation even through those tightly slitted synthetic eyes. Her motion slowed further, but didn't completely stop. Bremer had to dose her several more times before she became completely immobile. "Let's go see about John." Rebell urged.

They left Mary where she stood and hurried down to sick bay. Rebell had to repeat the mind probe, same as he had done with Mar, and cauterise the specific neural pathway to the implanted control network. It wasn't a difficult procedure for Rebell and painless for John. He was up and ready to go within minutes. Rebell did reproach himself for not considering the possibility that Mary may have created the implant as a future fail-safe. The information was all there in his memory – the deeply hidden memory he inherited from the original Mary.

"No hurry," Rebell assured him, "Mary is happy as she is at the moment."

Although he tried to sound reassuring, Rebell was fully aware of the danger Mary represented. She may well create havoc yet. None of them



Zsoall Robi

knew her capabilities. Perhaps they were even taking a big chance leaving her alone for too long.

"There is only one place we can go to get away – if we have to." Bremer stated the obvious, though it may not have been uppermost in the minds of the others. Without further prompting they donned their time-suits, powerpacks and got their personal graviton guns ready.

While going over to join Mar and John, Rebell had realigned the canon's collector to focus on the nearest star. They had arrived close enough to Alpha Centauri to use its gravitational waves to harvest enough gravitons to recharge the canon. Before returning to the lounge Rebell wanted to explore a small detail of Mar's experience during her special experiment – just to satisfy himself that if Mar's brain could detect the jerky motion of time as it sped from one moment to the next, he would have no trouble doing the same and with much greater accuracy. First the group went to their main laboratory to retrieve the magnetic reflector.

"We have to stay close together and within range of the reflector's focal point." They all agreed, as it was the safest option in case they had to act quickly.

They took the reflector to the lounge and put it up against the opposite wall to the large screen. No doubt Mary would be curious about the device. Yet that wasn't the reason Rebell decided to bring her back, just a little - enough so she could understand what was about to happen. He wanted her to fully appreciate the enormity of their discovery and what she would never be permitted to have.

Bremer reversed the polarity of his gun and fired several pulses at her until her movements became visible to the naked eye, but not enough so she could pose any danger to them. Rebell pointed to the screen and she painstakingly moved her gaze towards it. He activated the graviton cannon in reverse mode. Mary watched her ship materialize out of empty space. It had returned. Rebell hailed the captain and they watched the action on the bridge as the crew tried to re-orient themselves. Mary's eyes didn't leave the screen, watching the peculiar behaviour in front of her. Rebel used the distraction to realign the cannon to point it directly at the Drogher.

The captain tried to speak with Mary. He had trouble putting a coherent sentence together. Behind him several officers seemed to be completely out of control and two others had started fighting. As Mar watched the events unfold she could relate to the scene. They displayed the same behaviour she observed after being subjected to the chaos of multiple future possibilities all occurring at the same time.



Zsoall Robi

Mary acted while the confusion played out on her vessel. She had accelerated her processing speed in an attempt to send a message to her captain. Rebell's monitors picked up her orders clearly.

"COME AND GET ME … NOW!"

Rebell didn't want to deal with a large invading boarding party. His team would be easily overpowered by sheer numbers. His decision was almost instantaneous, he fired the canon at the Drogher, firing twice more until he knew they would no longer be visible, until they had moved far enough into the future to have left Mary's spacecraft in the past. Her ship may have escaped the time vortex but her crew could no longer help her.

The move solved only one problem. The other one was still with them – Mary herself. She had moved forward in time with them. So now Rebell knew the answer … Yes, both he and Mary could survive under the influence of the dark energy beams.

In those few moments of distraction Mary managed to increase her processing speed enough to be able to touch John, thinking she could still control him.  Her focused intent made her oblivious to the strange events unfolding around her in the lounge. She didn't even register her body beginning to overheat again.


The group were still in the lounge with Mary after exposure to the graviton canon's pulses, looking at a blank screen on the wall. As their gaze moved to the side a whole new set of strange events confronted them. Their group of four had been standing close together. On hearing a commotion they all turned towards the reflector.

Impossibly there were two duplicates of each of them including Mary - everyone in motion, everyone talking! Bremer2 and Mar2 moved towards Bremmer3, who was holding Mar3 in an embrace. They continued in the same direction, not stopping as they neared Bremer3 and Mar3 and thus moved through the image of the embracing couple. The two sets of duplicates didn't seem to be aware of each other. Bremer2 and Mar2 stopped and also began a passionate embrace. The originals, Rebell1 and Mary1 had each placed a hand on the temple of the other, Mary1 having first taken her hand off John1. At the same time Rebell2 walked directly through the group of originals to stand directly under the wall screen. The original John1 had not taken his eyes off either of the embracing couples.

While the original group had remained in 'observer' mode, the two duplicates' actions followed their own independent paths without interfering with one another - until the original John1 could stand it no



Zsoall Robi

longer and jumped forward towards the embracing couples. Being the 'original', somehow his hands didn't pass through Bremer2's shoulder as he grabbed a hold of it and pulled.

As Rebell3 watched the events unfolding he had difficulty in computing how there could be three of him in the same space at the same time going through different motions. He moved away from his group's location to stand beside Rebell1 engaged with Mary1. He also put his hand on Mary1's head.

Bremer1 watched his duplicates in action with the two Mars. He turned to Mar1 and while John1 was otherwise engaged he took Mar1 in his arms intending to do exactly what his other selves were doing. Mar1 didn't resist!

Whilst the originals were still in the observer mode, these possibilities continued to play themselves out. As the originals enforced their own actions, their own present reality onto the chaos, events began to clarify. Because the originals had arrived at the future time slot in three stages, it seems they carried with them three distinct possible futures.

Interference by the originals culminated in order being restored. The voices diminished, Rebell2 then Rebell3 both faded. Mary3, John2, Mar2 as well as the other duplicates all faded in succession. John3 and Bremer3 were the last probabilities to fade after an argument had broken out between them, which had escalated into a physical confrontation.

The experience left them all shaken. Mar1 who had been through something like it before, disengaged herself from Bremer1. They had gathered back in front of the reflector, all except Mary1. She was still standing a little off to the side. The three humans began talking animatedly amongst themselves. Rebell took no notice. He was trying to deconstruct the experience in order to comprehend it. It had left a residue in his mind, more than just a memory of the events. As he delved deeper into the source of the residue he discovered something else he couldn't understand.

He discovered a set of recorded emotions, not his – Mary's – concerning her and the human called Nick. It showed Mary as a softer, more vulnerable entity than the one standing a little aside from them. He looked towards the new Mary … then …

"Stop!" He suddenly called out. "Activate your suits, one burst – on my mark … three AND - pulse!" They had no time to argue or to question and did as they were told.

In unison they all moved one instant back in Time. Rebell had detected the gap between the two moments!

"Again – on my mark – three AND – Pulse!" Rebell got his confirmation. The others anticipated the next jump and were ready for it. As he issued the next command Rebell simultaneously fired several pulses at Mary, releasing her from her bondage.

"Ready – aim your guns at the reflector and fire with full energy as you activate your suit – Ready … On my mark – three AND – pulse!

Mary had to immediately reduce her temperature as she became free. She reverted to normal operational mode, but not back in her previous reality time. Her vessel was still not visible on the screen. Her daughter, John and the others were also not visible. As soon as her temperature stabilised she scanned for their energy fields. They were still there, in front of the reflector but only very, very faintly.

…

Rebell, the tallest individual in the group, looked around over their heads. He could see nothing - not even the reflector screen. Mary was gone, the room was gone. There were no walls visible at all around them. No sound. There wasn't even a floor under their feet with their shadows.

They had bridged the gap between the two consecutive instants.
"Mar," Rebell whispered to her, "I think we've done it."

Rebell had a suspicion about where they had ended up, but there was no way to be sure. He used all his scanners - nothing, not even background cosmic noise. Bremer turned his head to the left to look over Mar's shoulder. Rebell saw him do that - absolutely positive he saw Bremer move his head, seeing it manifest in two places, both in the new position and the old position.

They were all trying to examine this new environment, and every movement they made registered in every position, as well as being maintained in the original position. Within seconds there were images of multiple heads all around them.

"Everybody – turn around." Bremer, the alert soldier, was first to react constructively to the confusing circumstances.

They turned towards the location where once there was a wall with a screen. Although no environment could be discerned yet there was a kind of depth to the ambient light they were looking towards. They all took a step in that direction.

Their footfall made no sound. There was nothing there, yet the nothingness seemed to come into sharp focus. They took another step



Zsoall Robi

forward, together. Still nothing. One by one they turned back to where they had just come from, to be confronted by images of themselves stepping forward. Retracing their steps took them back to their original location from where they had moved through their own images.

A dimness appeared.

It seemed to advance towards them. Mar became extremely frightened and in her fear tried to rush towards the dimness, but she couldn't leave the immediate environment of the group. Her image leaped forward then got sucked back, as if an elastic membrane had pulled her backwards. Mar panicked for the first time in her life.

As soon as her temperature had come down Mary concentrated on her thoughts again. She remembered Mar saying that the canon she saw when she first arrived, wasn't the only one. They must have a laboratory somewhere. Mary went looking for it and eventually found one of the earlier model guns in John's lab. There were only two settings on it – 'positive' and 'negative'. It would have to do. She decided what had to be done. . . . . . . . . . . .



Zsoall Robi

.

.

# L.o.s.t
1458972047140 millis – Earth
'0' millis, minus 15300000 millis– Craft Epoch Time
'0' millis – Rebell's cesium atom clock time
Earth + 552days

*I*f Rebell had thought to check his internal clock he would have been surprised to see it had reset itself to zero. When standing with both feet in eternity it's not possible to measure the passage of time. Time did not exist. Before they moved for the first time, after crossing the bridge, all things were possible. Afterwards all probabilities were suspended in the medium in which time itself moved forward. When they tried to move forward their feet again stepped onto the bridge into the gap separating one instant from the next. Mar's attempt to go further than the bridge revealed the conundrum they all had to face. Change couldn't take place in eternity.

"How are we going to get back?" She asked.

...

Mary made a mental note for herself to streamline her next body construction, spend more time developing it. It had to be able to move much faster, it had to be a lighter structure and it had to function without producing so much heat. Perhaps her processing units could be housed in something like the human brain, but much larger of course. It took her some time to drag her ungainly body from the lab back to the lounge. For the group on the Bridge it would not have mattered if she had taken the rest of her lifetime.

She scanned the area again where they had been standing. Their energy fields were still detectable, with one field stronger than the others. That would have to be Rebell, Mary guessed. It wasn't hard to work out how to use the gun. As long as she had it on the right setting nothing could really go wrong. She made another educated guess, tuned the dial to the 'Negative', took careful aim in the direction of the strongest energy reading and fired.

The first pulse produced no result, so she fired again. Still nothing. So Mary kept her finger on the button until all the residual dark energy had



Zsoall Robi

been drained from the battery pack. She kept her eye on the empty space directly in front of her and at last saw what looked like a faint shimmering in the air – almost like mist trying to form itself into something recognisable. Perhaps the gun was working and could have brought them back - if it had not depleted itself. What could she do? During her search in the laboratory she found only one device intact, the others had been dismantled. Mary didn't even know how to recharge the thing. Maybe the canon floating in space – perhaps she could somehow activate it – if it was still there.

Without having any other options, she adjusted the screen controls to search the surrounding space for it. She could see stars and the Milky Way clearly. Even Alpha Centauri was prominent in the field of vision, but no canon. Mary did the only other thing that offered any hope of bringing the group back all the way – for she was certain the gun had brought them back some of the way. If she could just reconstruct the other gun, determine how it worked and re charge its power pack …

*

'They tried to harm us,' said the first voice of the LIC.

'No, it was ignorance not ill will,' disagreed a second voice.

'The others came and tried to hurt us as well,' added another voice.

Still the second voice didn't agree. 'No. They didn't have the same machine.'

Then a multitude of voices in unison could be heard breaking into the conversation. 'They are sentient, like us. They need help.'

The second voice continued, 'They agreed not to use their engines.'

The first voice remained silent for a while. All was silent. Then the first voice thought again, 'Why should we help? They only fight amongst themselves. They might fight against us.' It was perhaps trying to convince itself that all sentient beings deserved assistance when in trouble.

'The mechanical one spoke to us. It understands us,' said the second voice.

'Yes – yes!' a nebula of voices confirmed.

'How should we help?' Finally the first voice concurred with Its other voices.

*

"Use the suits, bite down together on the molar switch," Rebell suggested after John managed to calm Mar down, "move very close

229

Zsoall Robi

together." The group went into a tight huddle, embracing each other with Rebell in the centre.

"Ready? On my mark – three - An …"

'STOP!' They all heard it except Bremer. He just experienced a flash of sharp pain in his head stopping him from pressing on the switch. Even John heard the voice inside his head.

*'IT WILL NOT WORK!'*

The group loosened their grip on each other, looking at Rebell for an explanation, but he was silent. He saw something which appeared just a little ahead of them. They all turned towards it. A figure began to coalesce out of the nothingness. It didn't look entirely real, more like an image forming in the mind's-eye. Nevertheless it began to resemble Rebell himself, as if he was looking at a reflection of himself in an old, badly cracked and misted mirror.

*'I am us.'*

"What are you all staring at?" Bremer demanded. He wanted to get on with activating the suits, and get back to some kind of understandable reality. Without looking at him, Rebell put a hand to the back of his head.

"Oh … It looks like you, Rebell," Bremer said after a couple of seconds. Then the soldier in him asserted itself, "What does that mean – I am us – it could be dangerous?"

"It's the LIC," Rebell responded aloud. "Listen."

'I am us. You need help.'

'Yes,' they all said together.

'When you stepped onto the Bridge you saw our reality. We visit time only occasionally. It is uncomfortable for us. In the Bright there is no time, there is no change. We go to time to make change, then return. You will not survive in the Bright.'

They listened in absolute awe to this embodied, disembodied voice that looked like Rebell, even Rebell himself was struck by wonder. It had stopped talking, waiting for some kind of response from them.

Bremer stepped into the silence, "Can you take us back to – to – before?"

'Yes. It will not be the same.' We must restore equilibrium.

Rebell regained his composure and clarified the question. 'Can you take us out of the Bright and off the Bridge?'

'Yes. When do you want to be?'"

Rebell had to think about it for a moment before he comprehended the implications of the question. They had several choices; either they went



Zsoall Robi

back to the moment before they fired at the reflector, or back to before Mary came aboard the Drogher or … back but a little further into the future before they released Mary's ship. He decided they definitely had to get back to time, but not back onto their past history branch. He wanted to move forwards to one of the possible futures which didn't involve Mary's enmity. Rebell thought all these things to himself, yet the LIC detected the energy created by those thoughts, and understood.

First he needed to know … 'Why would it not be the same?'

'Because by using your devices you have created several different time windows for your existence. You are a life manifestation that can only exist in a singular change continuum. You would become damaged, hurt. You would cease to exist as those disparate time references moved away from each other. That change has already begun for you.'

Everyone in the group heard the explanation but they didn't hear Rebell's thoughts, and the LIC heard their confusion. The nebulous, shimmering image in front of them emitted sound waves to respond, so Bremer could hear what was being discussed.

"The mechanical one has selected a Future Change Continuum for your return. It will be along the specific Arrow of Change initiated by the one you call Mary, who is trying to rescue you."

"We cannot rewind history. It would put us in danger again." Rebell reminded his group.

He had no doubt in his mind, his human mind not his digital artificial brain intelligence, that unmanageable complications would arise from the sequence of causes and effects that had been put in motion when they destroyed the space station. The only viable alternative was to move forward, ahead of that action. If Mary was trying to rescue them, and if what he had discovered in Mary's memory showed her true nature, then that was the only viable alternative for them.

The LIC made these thoughts known to the others. There was no dissent in the group to the intended time-line destination.

"You must not continue with developing the technology. It has created a bleed in the Bright. If the Arrow of Change had no medium in which to propagate, then it couldn't manifest. There would be Nothingness." . . .

. . . . . . . . . . . . .

.



Zsoall Robi

.

.

# N.e.w  B.e.g.i.n.n.i.n.g
## 1459045269530 millis – Earth Time
## 1506738140441 millis – Craft Epoch Time
### 691200000 millis – Rebell's cesium atom clock time
## Earth + 560days

*N*othing was the same when they arrived back in their new futures, a little ahead of their old past.

To repair the damage the LIC had to make substantial time adjustments for the Drogher and to its passengers. Those changes would be reflected in their relationship with Earth Time, in a new Change Continuum, in a new line of History.

Mary found all of Mar and John's notes in the lab. Without them she would not have been able to reconstruct one of the graviton guns and charge it. As it was it took the best part of a few days; time in which Mary had ample multiple concurrent processing opportunity available within her system to consider things other than time control devices. She reviewed all the events that had occurred since she left Earth to pursue her fugitives. It was all there, recorded in absolute clarity within her data clusters – except for one sequence. It was indistinct, not flagged to any specific concatenation of causes and effects.

As soon as it made its appearance in her RAM Mary devoted a great deal of attention to it; mostly because it concerned herself and Rebell. She discovered a thread of data which seemed to indicate Rebell had gained full access to all her historical backed-up memory. But she couldn't work out how that could be possible. She had multiple layers of firewalls protecting her. Even if he was to have a chance he'd have to make physical contact, have a direct connection to her. The most disturbing aspect of the mystery was that the contact seemed to have been made only a short time ago, a matter of days; even less. She probed deeper, discovering the link had been made after Rebell and the others disappeared, when she was released from her immobile state. Mary also discovered it was Rebell who released her.

On review, she could see that part of the sequence of events quite clearly. He had pointed his device directly at her, just milliseconds before fading from view.

Why did he make contact? She ran a full diagnostic on herself finding everything in order. Her circuits had not been sabotaged. She found an access time flag on some ancient data buried since leaving Nick. What possible use could Rebell have for ancient history? The main thing was he had done nothing harmful to her, on the contrary – he'd released her from the time prison. – though they put here there in the first place.

Mary worked without stopping until she completed the device, charged and tested it; at least tested for general operational parameters. She wouldn't know if it could actually manipulate time until she used it to try and get them back.

She found the lounge exactly as she had left it days ago. The faint apparition of 'something' was still there, moving in some strange flux of light and shadow. Without hesitation she pointed the muzzle of the gun directly at the shifting mist and fired pulse after pulse.

Unknown to her the device did not work. The power pack had been neutralized by the LIC, yet the apparition seemed to become more solid with each burst. She kept the pressure on the button until four solid people stood where before there was only swirling mist. The LIC had returned the group synchronised with Mary's attempt to retrieve them.

The new, alternate Arrow of Change had been set in motion.

"All your devices have been deactivated, including the one in space, although you will no longer see it in your new time-line."

Everyone heard this last message from the LIC, including Bremer and Mary. For several minutes they all faced each other, speechless, disoriented and relieved.

Mary made the first move by putting down her gun. The others followed, doing the same.

Rebell first checked all the chronometers. His internal clock showed only the passage of time recorded since their arrival, just a few short minutes ago. Earth Time was the same as before their access to the Bridge. The Drogher time, the human's life-elapsed time all indicated they had been moved forward into an alternate future. Then he asked Mary the same thing she'd asked him not so long ago

"What is your internal time, Mary?"



Zsoall Robi

Before replying she noted the slight inflexion in his voice when he said her name, as did the others. There was no enmity there, quite the contrary.

"It's – no that cannot be correct – it's ..." She looked questioningly at Rebell, so he finished the sentence for her.

"Yes, you are correct. We are well ahead of Earth Time."

"You have succeeded!" For an instant Mary was jubilant they had achieved the ultimate for her – for mankind."

Rebell stepped next to her and put his hand on her as he had once before. The next instant Mary realised they were trapped; trapped in an alternate future. But Mary need no longer exist alone - there was Rebell, her own creation, standing with her.

As Rebell made his move Mar made hers. She went to stand next to Bremer. She found a partner who had proved himself in the most extraordinary of circumstances. Bremer relaxed into her presence.

An opportunity had opened for John to explore a relationship with Ary, the foundations of which had already been laid. Strangely, her voice had already arisen in his mind before they arrived in their new futures.

Instant by instant the Arrow of Time continued its flight into the dense atmosphere of infinite possibilities in eternity. There was no escape, only choices to be made from moment to moment; each choice the determinant for the nature of the next instant. •   •

•

•

•

•

•

•

•

•   •   •   •   •   •   •   •   •   •   •



Zsoall Robi

# . . . . . .M.a.i.n  C.h.a.r.a.c.t.e.r.s

**Adam** – Mry's companion.
**Admiral Neveah** – Space fleet Commander pursuing the Drogher.
**Ary** – Mary's second creation – on Board of Directors of Unity.
**Brayden** – The POOP's private assistant.
**Bremer** – A soldier in Admiral Nevaeh's space fleet.
**Cosmo** – Head Cosmologist at Unity – sent to retrieve the  fugitives.
**Leif** – Principal Officer Of Profit at Unity; The POOP.
**Ice Cream** – Ary's girlfriend and personal entertainment unit.
**John** – Theoretical Physicist
**Mary** – A self-aware artificial intelligence.
**Mar** – Mary's first creation – Quantum Physicist.
**Mry** – Mary's third creation – owner of Equilibrium Systems.
**POOP** – Principal Officer Of Profit at Unity – called Leif.
**Rebell** - A computer duplicate created by Mary as a backup for herself.



Zsoall Robi

Zsoall, born in Hungary, was brought to Australia by his parents after the 1956 uprising in Hungary.

He currently lives a creative life with his wife and animal family in the Northern Rivers, New South Wales, Australia.

His life has changed direction a number of times. Starting as a Secondary Teacher then becoming an Administrative Officer. Neither offered much in the way of creative involvement. That began when he embarked on a career as a Computer programmer.

While in that profession his continuing compulsion to create made it inevitable that his life would change again. Completely giving up programming he immersed himself in creativity as a Sculptor and Painter. Much of his time is now spent creating glass paintings and sculptures and in writing Science Fiction.



Zsoall Robi

.



Zsoall Robi

i . n . s . t . a . n . t

•



Zsoall Robi